# Praise for Bianca Sloane and *Killing Me Softly*
## (Previously published as *Live and Let Die*)

Thriller of the Month by www.e-thriller.com (May 2013)

"2013 Top Read" by OOSA Online Book Club

"[A] cross between 'Sleeping with the Enemy' and a superb murder mystery."

—a CrimeReadersBlog.Wordpress.com

"[*Killing Me Softly*] is a book that will leave the reader scratching their head trying to figure out the villain. And, just when the reader thinks they have it all figured out–think again–AND AGAIN!"

—Examiner.com (New Orleans)

"If you love puzzles and you like it when the author fools you all the way to the last page, you can't go wrong with [*Killing Me Softly*]."

—Ionia Martin, Readful Things Blog

"For a debut novel, [*Killing Me Softly*] flows very smoothly–or perhaps I should say "gallops," because I was reading at a frantic pace to discover what happens next."

—SheTreadsSoftly.Blogspot.com

"This is one of those novels that will keep you turning the pages wondering what kind of secrets are going to be unearthed."

—OOSA Online Book Club

"A gripping suspense read."

"It's been a really long time since I've read a thriller book that just completely wowed me as much as this one did. Considering that I am a huge suspense and thriller fan of many authors that have books that have just blown my mind, for a debut novel I think [Bianca Sloane] did outstanding!"

"This is American author Bianca Sloane's first novel. You wouldn't know it. This is a great story that carries you along with it from the first page… enjoy the ride!"

# KILLING
# ME
# SOFTLY

(Previously published as *Live and Let Die*)

# Also By Bianca Sloane

*Sweet Little Lies*

## Coming Soon

*Every Breath You Take*

*To my 94-year-old grandmother,*
*who's probably going to outlive all of us*

# AUTHOR'S NOTE TO THE READER

In 2012, amid a flurry of nerves, I released *Live and Let Die,* my first suspense novel, out into the world. Truth be told, I wasn't crazy about the title, but at the time, I felt like it was the best moniker for the story, so that's what I went with.

As time went on, I grew more dissatisfied with the title and decided to do something about it. One of the great things about being an "indie" is you can change course anytime you want. So, I made the decision to rechristen the book and chose *Killing Me Softly,* a title I am *much* happier with.

I decided to go one step further and do a "refresh" on the cover. It just made sense to give my book a new cover to go along with its new title. Out with the old, in with the new and all that. As with my original cover, I am in love with this one and as always, my eternal gratitude goes out to my ace cover designer, Torrie Cooney.

I've also made a few minor edits—little nits I missed the first time that I decided to fix. There are no editorial or structural changes to the original story; there are no new characters, no new scenes, no new plot twists or new chapters. It is the exact same story I released in 2012.

Thank you for giving *Killing Me Softly* a try; I hope you enjoy it.

Bianca Sloane

# KILLING ME SOFTLY

BIANCA SLOANE

# PROLOGUE

He drove through the night, stopping twice for gas and once to take a piss off the side of the expressway.

During one of the gas station stops, he'd made a phone call, then got back in the car to head toward his destination. He pulled up to the back entrance of the building, feeling good about what he had planned. He just needed to refine it.

He was mildly surprised to see Keegan's gleaming black Mercedes waiting for him. He parked and got out, while Keegan did the same, leaving his motor running. Keegan looked older than he remembered, worn out. Of course, it could have been because he had rousted the man from bed in the middle of the night.

Or it could have been that he was just old.

He extended his hand toward Keegan, who kept his hands shoved into the pockets of his long, belted black wool coat. Wisps of salt and pepper hair escaped from beneath the brim of his gray fedora. He looked around, annoyed.

"All right, you got me out here in the middle of the fucking night, so what do you want me to do?"

"Like I told you on the phone, I need you to admit a patient. She's a special case and requires your personal supervision."

"Who is she?"

He sniffed. "That's not important. What is important is that you keep her in solitary away from everyone else."

Keegan scoffed. "That's impossible. I can't be here twenty-four hours a day."

"All right, all right, draft a nurse to help you. But I don't want a parade of orderlies and other people in and out to see her. You're the only one I want handling the case."

Keegan started to shiver. "What is it you want me to do with her?"

"First, there's a drug protocol I'm gonna want you to administer. Second, there's some very specific therapy she'll need, but I'll fill you in on all that later. For now, just keep her sedated, keep her clean, keep her fed. And keep her away from people. That's the most important thing. She'll get hysterical."

"How long am I supposed to keep this up?"

"Until I tell you not to. And you better follow my instructions to the letter.

Otherwise—" He made a slicing motion across his neck.

Keegan clicked his tongue and shook his head. "Goddamn, I wish I'd never met you."

He chuckled. "Yeah, well, we can talk about that later. Right now, we need to get her inside." He glanced back at the car. "She's going to be waking up soon and I'll need to explain to her what's going on so she won't be scared."

Keegan turned off his car. He slid into the backseat of his own car and shook her gently. She stirred a little and he smiled.

"Hey, there. How are you?"

She looked around, her eyes drowsy slits in her face. He cradled her and ran a finger across her cheek. "I'm going to take care of everything. I promise. I'll always take care of you."

She moaned softly and her head lolled back against the crook of his arm. He maneuvered her out of the car before he hoisted her up and started to walk toward Keegan, who held the back door open. He ducked into the building, grunting as he adjusted her weight. Happy to be out of the cold, he followed Keegan through the maze of hallways and doors, warmth seeping back into his body. His sneakers squeaked against the shiny tiles, while Keegan's black Crocs made silent thuds. Finally, they arrived at the padded rooms and Keegan instructed Phillip to place her on the bench outside of one.

"I'll have to get a key, so wait here. I'll also need to check her in."

"Don't do that."

"Jesus Christ, I have to account, some way, somehow, for some woman springing up overnight in a padded room. She didn't just wander in off the street."

"All right, all right. Just keep everything close to the vest."

Keegan rolled his eyes. "Yeah, I got it. Can I at least get a name to put on the paperwork?"

He looked down at her and brushed a stray lock of hair from her face. "Paula. Her name is Paula."

# ONE

Sondra stalked across the plush sage green carpet, her bare feet squishing deep into the soft fibers. She went to rake her fingers through her long and tangled black waves, forgetting they had been swept back into a sleek ponytail for the occasion. She let out an irritated sigh and looked for the millionth time at the closed bathroom door.

"Tracy," she called out. "Come on, I need to smoke before all this."

"Just a sec," came her sister's muffled reply from the other side of the door.

Sondra rolled her eyes and began to gnaw on the raw and bloody cuticle of the ring finger of her right hand. Finally, she heard the click of the door and saw a sliver of light slash the carpet. Tracy Ellis stepped into the bedroom and stood with pride in front of her older sister.

"So...?" she asked.

Sondra stopped her pacing and looked at her sister. Tracy's olive skin, hazel eyes and lush chestnut brown hair had always meant she never wanted for attention—even female at times—but that old cliché about a woman never being more beautiful than on her wedding day was an apt description at that moment.

"Well, you sure clean up nice," Sondra said with a lump in her throat.

Tracy smiled and looked down at her elegant white silk halter dress, smoothing it down the length of her size four waist.

"I can't believe I'm getting married," she murmured, her smile never disappearing. Tracy looked up at Sondra, her face beaming.

"Do you think Phillip will like it?"

"Oh, jeez, Tracy, that's a stupid question."

"Humor me."

"All right, I'll play along. He won't be able to keep his eyes off you. Probably not his hands either."

"Well, that should make for an interesting ceremony."

Tracy turned to look at herself in the bedroom's full-length mirror, examining herself from every angle. "You know why I wanted you to wait, right?"

Sondra chuckled. "I knew something had to be up. All right, spill it."

"My something new. Mommy gave me something blue and borrowed, Cicely gave me the old, so… that leaves you as something new." Tracy started examining her eye makeup in the mirror. "God knows I don't want anything old or borrowed from you. No telling what trashcan you might have pulled it out of."

"Jeez, you drag one table home from a curb in the eighties and you're branded for life."

"Keep playing innocent. Now, come on, let's go. Cough it up."

Sondra tried for all of thirty seconds to look clueless, before she started laughing. "All right, all right. Yes, I was responsible for the something new." Sondra walked over to pick up her oversized bag from the bed and withdrew a small blue Tiffany box.

"All right, Blackie O, get over here."

"Shut up."

Sondra laughed and held the box out to Tracy, who took it gently from her sister's hand. She looked at Sondra for a moment before she sat on the edge of the bed and began to unravel the signature white bow. Slowly, Tracy lifted the lid off the box and pulled out a small blue cloth pouch. Because her fingers were trembling, it took her a few tries to unsnap it, but when she did, she found a delicate sterling silver necklace inside.

"Oh," she said softly as she let it dangle from her fingers. She ran the tip of her French manicured nail across the lone charm to see what it was. "T," she whispered, her eyes welling with tears at the realization the looped and swirling letter was her initial.

Sondra took the necklace from Tracy's shaking fingers and began to undo the clasp. "We all know you're the pretty little poodle to my mangy, slobbery Saint Bernard," she said as she fastened the necklace around Tracy's slender neck. "So, I thought you should have something princess-y." Sondra stood back to admire her sister and smiled.

"Like I said, you clean up nice."

Tracy turned and grabbed her sister by the elbows, tears sliding down her face, streaking her foundation.

"I love you, Sonny," Tracy said.

The two women hugged each other when suddenly Sondra pulled back and looked at her sister.

"Are you happy?"

Tracy nodded and dabbed at her eyes with the blue handkerchief from her mother. "Happier than I can say."

Sondra gave a quick nod and released Tracy from her grasp. "Okay," she said, fumbling for her cigarettes in her bag, trying to keep her own tears from spilling over. "Okay." She found the box and pulled them out. "That's all I wanted to know. Now. I'm gonna have my smoke and when I get back, we're gonna get you married."

• • •

It was, as days go, a perfect day for a wedding. Though it was early August, it was a balmy eighty-five degrees and there was a slight breeze that just kissed the bare arms and legs of the thirty-some odd guests gathered to witness the union of Tracy Ellis and Phillip Pearson. Tracy's best friend, Cicely, had offered up her spacious Winnetka home for the ceremony, and the attendees were all gathered in her backyard surrounded by fragrant rose bushes and sweet honeysuckle.

Sondra stood at the edge of the white runner waiting for her cue to make her way down the aisle. Though Tracy knew a ton of people, she and Phillip had decided to keep the whole affair small and low-key, inviting only their families and closest friends. Sondra was the lone bridesmaid and a co-worker Phillip was relatively close with, served as best man.

Sondra cocked her head slightly as she looked at her brother-in-law-to-be standing uncomfortably at the altar. He stood stiff as a board in his navy suit, his hands clenched together in front of him. The glare of the sun turned his coke-bottle glasses white, making him look like a character from the old "Annie" comic strip. He licked his lips as he swayed from side-to-side.

Sondra thought Phillip was an odd choice for Tracy. The couple had a whirlwind courtship, becoming engaged four months after meeting and now, six months later, getting hitched. While she got hit on just walking out her front door, time and again, she went for tall, dark and handsome.

Phillip was anything but. Phillip reminded Sondra of Urkel, with his small build, high-pitched voice and dated box-top haircut. It wouldn't have surprised her if he had a pair of suspenders stashed in his closet. However, unlike the madcap and boisterous Urkel, Phillip was painfully shy, introverted and far from a breezy conversationalist. He was a mild-mannered pharmacist, which was in fact how they'd met; he'd filled a prescription for Tracy. Although Sondra had reservations, as far as she could tell, he treated Tracy like gold, which was all that mattered to her; she just wanted her sister to be happy.

The harpist began to play "Ave Maria," giving Sondra her signal. She wobbled a bit in her rhinestone-laden high-heeled sandals, her feet unaccustomed to wearing anything that wasn't a flip-flop or Doc Marten. Her knee-length, size six pink taffeta tank dress made a soft swish as she proceeded down the aisle. She caught her mother's eye and winked as Mimi Ellis gave her a broad smile. Sondra reached the altar and looked down the aisle, waiting for her sister to make her entrance.

As their father gripped his youngest daughter's arm, the guests stood to watch Tracy make her way toward her groom. She couldn't keep the smile or tears off her face as she looked into the eyes of the man who was to be her husband. Phillip let out a breath as Tracy got closer and shook his head a little and Sondra could see him mouth, "so beautiful," to himself as he continued to watch her, wiping his own tears away.

Gordon Ellis kissed Tracy on the cheek, gave Phillip a firm handshake before he placed Tracy's hand inside his future son-in-law's, and joined his wife in the front row. Sondra took a deep breath and watched in silent awe as her sister got married.

• • •

The balmy breezes continued to waft through the air as Sondra stood at the end of the driveway enjoying the first cigarette she'd had since the ceremony ended. She had to admit, it had been beautiful. The couple had written their own vows and everyone cried, Sondra included. The first dance had been to "Let's Stay Together," the father-daughter dance to "My Girl." Sondra gave a touching toast honoring her sister and Phillip that brought out everyone's hankies. Tracy's own speech about what a difficult road it had been to get here, but how she would take the trip again if it would lead her to Phillip, made couples snuggle closer and singles hopeful that one day they too would find their true love.

Sondra stubbed out her cigarette and as she made her way to the backyard, she caught sight of her parents and Tracy and Phillip talking, each couple with linked hands. She watched them, taking mental pictures: their statuesque, blonde, blue-eyed German mother, a former Olympic medalist swimmer and now a sought-after swimming coach; their black father, a renowned professor of cultural studies at Stanford and best-selling author of several books examining the influence of blacks on popular culture; and Tracy, a slightly darker version of Mimi, was a TV news producer here in Chicago.

Sondra crossed her arms and let her finger trail up and down along the curve of her own rich, buttery caramel neck, her sable brown eyes misting over. She wanted to hold this moment in her heart and mind for as long as she could, knowing it would be a long time before they were all together again.

Out of the corner of her eye, she saw the cake table and realized she hadn't had any yet. She wiped away the tears and began to walk in that direction when Phillip caught up to her.

"Hey," he said as he touched Sondra's elbow.

"Hi," she replied as she picked up a plastic fork and white Styrofoam plate supporting a small piece of lemon chiffon cake with buttercream frosting and began to nibble.

Phillip shoved his hands into the pockets of his tuxedo pants and smiled. "I just wanted to tell you how much it meant to Tracy that you could be here today."

Sondra swallowed and shrugged. "Where else would I be?"

"Well, I mean, I know you have a lot to do and all with your trip coming up. When are you leaving?"

"Next Friday, so I've got almost a week to get everything together."

"What's your documentary going to be on?"

"Images of beauty around the world. Plastic surgery, rituals, that kind of thing."

"Sounds cool. How long will you be gone?"

"About a year and some change. Then I'll come back and do the editing. It's going to be an intense time."

"Tracy is really going to miss you."

Sondra looked over Phillip's shoulder and saw Tracy bouncing a friend's little girl on her hip while she talked animatedly to another guest. "I'm gonna miss her too. But, you know my cell phone is one of those global things and I'll have access to email, though it may not be the greatest." Sondra put the plate down on the table, only half of the cake eaten. "We'll still be in touch."

Phillip nodded absentmindedly then opened and closed his mouth, seeming to struggle with what to say.

"Listen, I know you think we rushed into this—"

Sondra held up her hand. "Do you love my sister?"

Phillip nodded. "More than I can say."

"Then that's it. As long as you love and take care of her, that's it."

Phillip pursed his lips together into a grateful smile. "Don't worry. I'll always take care of your sister."

• • •

The reception had run well into the night and Sondra was exhausted. She had a seven A.M. flight back to New York, and Tracy and Phillip would be leaving for their honeymoon in Jamaica on Sunday afternoon, so Sondra wanted to make sure she said goodbye to Tracy before the limo took her back to her hotel in the city. She leaned against the jamb of the front door watching Tracy hug the last guest, the straps of her rhinestone sandals slung around her wrist. She waved brightly to them until they climbed into their car and drove away. Tracy's shoulders slumped a little and she looked over at Sondra.

"So, a year, huh?" she said as she walked over to join Sondra in the entryway.

Sondra nodded. "Yup. Will I be an aunt by the time I get back?"

Tracy winked. "I have a pretty good feeling you will."

Sondra's head flipped up. "You're not—"

Tracy giggled. "Oh God no. No, no, but we've talked about starting a family in the next year or so." Tracy hugged herself and closed her eyes. "I can't wait."

Sondra looked down at the front walk in front of her, tracing a pattern with her toe.

"You'll be a great mom." She looked up and smiled. "I can't wait for you either."

Tracy's face grew somber as she looked at Sondra. "You just make sure you come back."

Sondra held up two fingers. "Scout's honor."

"Didn't you get kicked out of Girl Scouts?"

"Yeah, because I flashed my party pants at a Cub Scout."

Tracy playfully pinched Sondra's arm, who went to put her sister in a headlock. The two women stopped laughing long enough to give each other a lingering hug.

"I love you, baby girl," Sondra said.

"Back at ya, Sonny." Tracy smiled. "I'll see you soon."

# TWO

All ten of Sondra's fingers were red, ragged messes. She'd been flying all day and night and, unable to smoke, had nearly chewed each digit to the bone. The pilot announced their initial descent into Chicago and if she could have parachuted in, she would have.

As the plane descended, Sondra flattened her forehead against the window of the plane, searching for the landscape of the city hidden beneath the white swell of clouds, frantic to land, to know…

Finally, the plane taxied to the gate and Sondra ripped her seatbelt from across her slender waist, waiting for the doors to open. The aisles filled with passengers hauling down luggage, turning on cell phones to check messages and chatting away about emails, business meetings and what restaurants they would dine at while visiting Chicago. Going on with their lives as normal.

Sondra went to turn her own phone back on, before remembering the battery died just as she boarded. She balled her hand into a fist and bit her knuckle in a futile attempt to give her decimated fingers a rest. She wondered how long it would take the air marshal to catch her if she tried to shove past all these people.

The traffic began to inch forward. The tip of Sondra's tongue caught the saltiness from the perspiration on her upper lip as she folded her lanky frame over the seat in front of her, waiting for her turn in line. Clutching her one carry-on bag, she shuffled her way into the aisle before finally reaching the door.

She tried to keep her cool as she went through customs. She kept a level gaze on the gate agent as he queried her about her time overseas and what she would be doing while in the U.S.

She had to force the tears to stay inside while answering him.

As soon as she was free of customs, she broke into a run, her smoker's lungs protesting the whole time. The soles of her flip-flops slapped against the shiny tile like lit firecrackers as the crowds of arrivals and departures parted once they heard her pound towards them. She knew her feet would freeze, but she didn't care. Tears stung Sondra's eyes and she swatted at them as if they were errant gnats buzzing around her face as she scanned the boards overhead for directions to ground transportation.

Panting, sweating, and nearly hacking up a lung, Sondra found the door leading to the taxis. The doors slid open and the blast of arctic air almost knocked her to the salt-stained sidewalk. Shivering in her thin sweatshirt, Sondra ran her trembling, blood-crusted fingers through her wavy, black tresses as she darted to the taxi stand. She hopped from one foot to the other to keep warm while she waited for yet another slow line to move forward. The fat black dispatcher, dwarfed beneath a dusty black down coat and furry earmuffs, gave her the once over.

"What happened to your coat, young lady? You know this is Chicago in January," he laughed, his breath billowing out from beneath jagged, yellow buckteeth to mock her.

Sondra ignored him and ran to the orange Wolley cab he indicated. She jumped in and gave the driver the address, blowing breath into her hands to revive them. She was about to fish out her cigarettes when she noticed the 'No Smoking' sign taped to the back of the seat. She groaned to herself and sat on her hands, rocking back and forth in a feeble attempt to keep herself calm.

The gray and grit of the city looked repulsive to her on this frigid afternoon. She didn't hear the low murmur of NPR—the universal radio station of cab drivers—as she stared unseeing out the window while smiling billboards sheathed under the sludge of winter, decaying buildings and grimy El trains hissed past her in a haze. After an eternity, the cab turned down her sister's North side street and came to a stop in front of her house. Sondra threw a wad of crumpled twenties at the driver and flung the door open, not bothering to close it. She didn't hear the cabbie yelling after her as she bounded up the front steps of the house and slammed herself against the door to make it open.

The first thing she heard was her mother's pained cries. The first thing she saw was her father's face, and the shake of his head.

Sondra's knees buckled and she crumpled into a pile on the gleaming hardwood floor.

# THREE

The ensuing days were draped in heavy fog. Before Tracy had gone jogging she talked to Phillip, out of town for a pharmacy convention, mentioning that if the promised snowstorm didn't materialize, she was going to stop at the store on the way home for a few things and would call him when she returned.

He never heard from her.

Her body had been discovered along the lakefront, her face bashed in. Her empty wallet was found a few feet away and the police ruled it a mugging gone wrong, but had no leads. Phillip took on the gruesome task of IDing the body. Tracy had requested cremation and Sondra was thrust into the role of trying to comfort her parents and be strong for Phillip. Her mother, Mimi, never stopped crying, while Phillip and her father, Gordon, cycled between stoic strength and jagged sobs.

Tracy's memorial service brimmed with people from all corners of the country. Sondra, unable to read the poem her mother had requested, broke down mid-stanza. Phillip rushed to her side and with one reedy arm planted around Sondra's shoulders, finished reading it for her, his own voice quivering with corked tears.

In the end, it had all been too much for Mimi who, after the service, fled in a taxi back to her hotel downtown, leaving Gordon, Sondra, and Phillip to accept the well-meaning platitudes and stifle their own tears. Sondra wished she could have hopped a ride with her mother, because, truth be told, all she wanted to do was lie down on the floor, curl up in a ball and cry herself tearless. When people didn't think she could hear them, they would tut-tut about how terrible it was to outlive your children.

Sondra was starting to think it was pretty shitty to outlive your younger sister.

It took the better part of five hours to clear the house of mourners—people reluctant, it seemed, to leave, as if the simple act of departing Tracy's house would mean they really would have to say goodbye. They lingered long into the night until Sondra had finally started to hint it had been a long day.

Exhausted, Sondra flopped onto the couch in the living room, watching the promised flurries float across the night sky. She heard a noise and tilted her head to see Phillip come in. He too seemed mesmerized by the fat, juicy flakes drifting to the frozen ground. She noticed he was clutching Tracy's burgundy cardigan sweater.

"When it finally hit me that she was missing, I found myself carrying this sweater around, wondering if she was cold and just wishing I could wrap her up in it." He sighed. "And it smells like her."

Sondra sniffed and turned her attention back to the snow. "I wondered the same thing. If she was cold, I mean."

Phillip sat down on the couch next to Sondra. For several minutes, neither of them spoke.

"You know she called me a few days before... I was right in the middle of something and I told her I'd call her back and then I forgot..." Sondra said, her voice trailing off.

"Don't blame yourself, Sondra. It's not worth it."

Sondra sighed, shaking her head and they both fell silent again.

"Was she happy?" Sondra asked to break the silence.

"What?"

"I mean... was she happy? The last few months..." Sondra was unable to keep her eyes dry.

Phillip sighed. "Yeah, I mean... she loved her job, her friends, we were talking about starting a family in a year or so... she... God... that last time we talked, she told me how much she loved me..."

Phillip cried as he remembered his last conversation with his wife. "We just didn't have enough time. We were supposed to have our whole lives together." Phillip stopped and looked down at his hands, rolled together like balls of yarn.

"At least she was happy," Sondra murmured, the tears streaming down her cheeks. "That's something at least…"

"Without her, I just…" Phillip's voice cracked as another tidal wave of tears washed over him. Sondra reached out her arms and drew him into them and they sobbed together.

# FOUR

Phillip closed the door and walked over to the picture window to watch the cab that would ferry Sondra to the airport so she could go back to India to finish work on her documentary. He stood rooted in this spot for at least five minutes, wanting to be sure she didn't come back for some forgotten book or blow dryer. It had been brutal to have them there, fawning all over him, offering their condolences and memories. He'd wanted to run screaming from the house and counted the minutes until he was free of all well-wishers, grieving friends, and in-laws.

Satisfied, he turned and went in search of his phone, dialing the number from memory.

"I'm on my way. Be ready for me when I get there."

He clicked the phone off and walked over to a picture of Tracy and him on their wedding day. He let his finger trail down her cheek before he picked it up and kissed the image.

"Sometimes, we do what we have to do."

He lingered over the picture for a few more minutes before he grabbed his coat and keys and left.

# FIVE

Sondra stood in front of the bakery window, captivated by the display of enormous yellow cupcakes obscured beneath fluffy white frosting, rainbow sprinkles nestled in the crevices. Sondra stubbed out her cigarette, went into the bakery and bought one of the cupcakes along with a cup of coffee.

They even gave her a candle.

She found an empty table along the back wall and gingerly set the cupcake down in front of her, swirling her finger along the edge, catching a glob of frosting on the tip. She licked it and groaned, savoring the gritty sweetness. She lit the candle and closed her eyes for a moment before blowing it out. Sighing, she leaned back in her chair, watching passersby outside as she ran a hand through her wavy black hair.

About a year and a half had passed since Tracy's brutal death and today was her sister's birthday. Sondra continued to pick at the cupcake and after eating barely half of it, tossed it and her empty coffee cup into the trash. As she headed back to her hotel, she fumbled around the bottom of her large bag for her cigarettes. Locating them, she rapped the box in the palm of her hand, making several definitive *thwack, thwack, thwacks*. As she went to light up, her phone jangled from somewhere in her bag.

"Damn," she muttered when she saw who it was and dropped the cigarettes back in her bag. Sondra knew even through the phone, Mimi would be able to tell she was puffing away.

"Hi, Mommy."

"I'm sorry I missed you earlier. I was coming back from Sacramento. You're okay?"

"Yeah, I'm good," Sondra said as she navigated the throngs of people on Broadway. "I'm on my way back from the doctor now. He ran every test known to man, and he expects I'll have a clean bill of health."

"Well, you know I worry. I just don't want…"

Sondra looked up to see the Times Square Jumbotron telling her to watch ABC Thursday nights at nine, and mentally completed her mother's unspoken words.

*I just don't want to lose another daughter.*

"Mommy, I promise, I'm fine. I would tell you if I weren't."

From California, Sondra swore she could hear her mother close her eyes and send a silent thank you to God.

"I know; I'm just overreacting…" Mimi's faint German accent halted a bit before trailing off. There was a quiet moment between mother and daughter.

"I stopped at a bakery a few minutes ago and had a cupcake. You know the yellow ones with all the frosting? They even gave me a candle."

Sondra could hear Mimi sniffle. "She always loved white frosting on her cupcakes. She never wanted anything on her birthday but yellow cupcakes with white frosting, even when she was little."

"I still can't believe she's gone."

"She would have been thirty-five. So young."

"I know, Mommy."

"I catch myself thinking about her at the strangest times. Like yesterday, I was getting in the car and was remembering when I was teaching her how to drive. I sat in the driveway crying for twenty minutes."

"I know, Mommy. It's hard."

"Then Mrs. Pinkus came over knocking on the window, yammering on about her dog being hit by a car last year. Like you can compare the two."

"In her mind, you can."

"Sonny, I don't think it'll ever stop hurting."

Sondra shook her head, tears now welling in her eyes. "I know," she said. "I know."

"I sent a box of her things over to your apartment. Mindy said she would keep it for you until you got back. I thought you would want them. I just… I tried to go through it, but… I just couldn't…"

"Yeah, Mindy told me. I won't be back in the apartment for a few weeks, so I'll go through everything... at some point." She paused. "How's Daddy?"

"He's good, good. Working on a new book, so he's down in L.A. for a few days doing some research."

"Oh yeah? What's this one about?"

"He mumbled something about the movies. You know how he gets when he's in the zone."

Sondra chuckled and wiped the back of her hand across her nose. "That I do."

"Oh, oh, speaking of, that's daddy on the other line. I've got to go."

"Tell him I said hey."

"Okay, sweetie." Mimi paused. "I'm so glad you're home. Safe and sound."

Sondra closed her eyes and sighed at the sadness in her mother's voice. "I know. Bye, Mommy."

Sondra hung up and continued down Broadway towards The W where she was staying for a few weeks. She retrieved her cigarettes once more and lit up, sighing with satisfaction as the nicotine flooded through her. As Sondra took drags off her cigarette, she found herself lost in thoughts about Tracy.

It was a warm April day in Manhattan, but the image of her sister lying alone and bloody beneath the blowing and drifting snow of a vicious Chicago winter made Sondra shiver, just as she had that day in India when her mother had called to tell her Tracy was missing. She stopped in the middle of the sidewalk, much to the ire of New Yorkers trying to steer around her. Sondra trembled again and wrapped her arms around her waist.

Her cigarette had burned down to a nub and she jumped as the ash stung her finger. She dropped the cigarette on the sidewalk and resumed walking, Tracy's face spinning in her head.

# SIX

Sondra put on her sunglasses as she glided through the lobby of her apartment building on her way outside. The burly new doorman swung the revolving door for her.

"Good morning, Ms. Ellis. Need a cab?"

Sondra smiled. "Please, call me Sondra and no, it's such a nice day out, I'm going to walk. Besides, I need the fresh air," she said, winking at him as she waved her newly extracted cigarette in his direction.

"Have a good day," he laughed.

After a year and a half of criss-crossing the globe for her latest documentary on women's beauty rituals, Sondra had moved back into her apartment a few weeks earlier and had been working nonstop on post-production ever since. Yesterday had been a seventeen-hour day and today promised to be yet another marathon session. She lit up and had just taken her first inhale when she saw a tall, handsome black guy in an obviously expensive suit walking towards her, talking on his cell phone. She stopped dead in her tracks, not believing it was him. He saw her and did a double-take as well.

"Hey, I gotta go," he said just before he hung up. He smiled and swallowed her into a bear hug.

"What are you doing here?" she gasped and laughed as she returned Jack's fierce embrace.

"I'm in town for a few days on business. How are you?"

"I'm okay, I'm okay." She put her hand on her forehead. "Man, how long's it been?"

"I think the last time I saw you was when we came out for the premiere of *The Deepest Cut* about four years ago."

"Wow, that's right, that's right." Sondra stepped back to take a good look at her sister's ex-boyfriend.

Tracy had met Jack Turner about a month after she moved to Chicago. He owned two popular restaurant/bars in Chicago called Dive and Flow, respectively. Tracy was having drinks at Dive with one of the producers from her station when Jack spotted her and introduced himself. They became inseparable within a matter of days. Jack was rich, successful, good-looking, and easygoing, possessing the same energy and wit as Tracy. Everyone had loved Jack, and all signs pointed to a walk down the aisle. However, after four years together, they'd suddenly broken up, much to everyone's surprise and, as Sondra joked, devastation.

"You look great," she said in all sincerity. "What are you up to these days?"

"Still in the restaurant business. I'm looking to open up a spot in Harlem."

"Wow. Will this be anything like the other two?"

"Naw, this is going to be more of a fusion thing."

Sondra nodded her head in appreciation. "That's great news. Does that mean you're moving up here?"

"Come on now. You know better than that. I hate New York."

"Watch it," Sondra said with the practiced growl of a New Yorker who despised anyone ragging on her city.

Jack laughed. "I've got a partner I'm going in with. He'll be the man on the street here."

"Ah, okay. Very cool."

"How are you? Really?"

Sondra let out a long, anguished breath. "Do you want the polite answer or the truth?"

Jack stole a quick glance around. "Hey, let's grab a quick cup of coffee. I mean if you have time."

Sondra looked at her watch and nodded. "Yeah, yeah, let me just make a phone call."

Sondra let her production team know she'd be in a little late and she and Jack ducked into a small diner a few feet away where he got them cups of black coffee.

"Thanks," she said as she dumped six packets of sugar and two vials of cream into her mug and stirred.

Jack looked down into his cup. "How are your parents?"

"Um, okay. Mimi's still teaching swimming a few days a week and Daddy's working on a new book."

"That's not what I meant."

"I know."

Sondra looked at the mother and little girl at the next table engaged in a game of pattycake. Her heart skipped as she thought about the children Tracy had longed for and would never have.

Sondra took a deep breath. "Taking each day as it comes. I've actually been hopping all over the world for the past year working on my next documentary. I did come back for a little while, after..." Sondra's voice went whisper soft and she took a sip of her coffee.

Jack hunched over his cup, lost in thought. "Yeah..."

"So, you married, kids, what?"

Jack shook his head and ran his hands across the green Formica tabletop. "Nope. I mean I'm dating a couple of people, but not getting married anytime soon or anything."

Sondra frowned, turning over in her mind the words she wanted to say. "So what's your side of the story?" Sondra cocked one eyebrow and waited for Jack to pick up the thread of her inquiry.

Jack slurped on his coffee. "I was stupid."

Sondra took another sip of coffee, watching him.

He ran his lean, massive hands across his face several times before he gave her a wry smile. "Tracy was the love of my life. I'll never love another woman the way I loved her. She wanted to get married, start a family and I was too scared. Typical stupid bullshit. She basically said propose or she was leaving. I didn't, so she did."

Sondra drummed her index finger on the table and pinched her lips together. "Do you regret it?"

Jack gave Sondra a sad smile. "Every day. Honestly, I thought we'd work it out, you know, like she needed time to cool down. I realized too late she wasn't coming back."

"What were you afraid of?"

"Losing my so-called independence. Stupidest thing I ever did was let that woman get away. Next thing I know, she's married to someone else."

Sondra sighed and looked out the window. "Regret is a terrible thing to have to live with."

"If I had it to do over again, I would do it so differently."

"Can't un-ring a bell."

"Did you get to see her before...?"

Sondra sipped her coffee. "I was her maid of honor. I left for India two days later, so that was the last time I saw her."

"Ah. Right. Of course. What was that, about six months or so before she died?"

Sondra nodded. "Yeah. They didn't have much time."

"I saw her before she... disappeared," he said.

Sondra's head jerked back to face Jack. "What? When?"

"That Friday."

Sondra straightened up, confused. "Did you tell the police?"

"No. I mean, I didn't know what good it would have done. It wasn't like I was the last person to see her. And it wasn't for long. Besides, I didn't want her husband to hear about it, you know, get the wrong idea..."

"How, where?"

Jack ran his tongue across his teeth. "Downtown. She was out running some errands, and kind of like you and me today, we just ran into each other."

"How was she? I mean how did she seem?"

Jack hesitated for a moment. "Unhappy."

"What, like she was having a bad day?"

Jack shook his head and slumped back against the peeling vinyl seat, the material crackling under his movements. "No, that wasn't it." Jack took a deep breath. "Man, I've never told anyone about this." He looked at Sondra.

"Like I said, we ran into each other and I asked if I could buy her a drink for old time's sake. We went to Ian's, one of our old spots. She was real fidgety. Distracted."

"Okay, Jack, to be fair, she was probably nervous because that was the first time you guys were seeing each other in a while."

Jack leaned closer. "Sondra, I lived with Tracy for three and a half years. I knew her inside and out. Every mood, every expression. Every little quirk. Something was definitely off."

Sondra pursed her lips. "All right. Go on."

"I asked her how she was. And she just looked at me, those big, beautiful eyes full of tears and said she was unhappy."

"What did she mean by that? Unhappy about what?"

"That was all she said and as soon as it came out of her mouth, she said she was sorry, and that she had to go. She picked up her stuff and ran out." Jack took a sip of coffee. "And that was the last time I saw her."

Sondra sagged against her seat, shaking her head. "I wonder what it was."

"I wanted to call her over the weekend, but, well... I felt like it wasn't my place, you know since she was married and our history. And then... she was gone."

Jack's cell phone rang and he excused himself to take the call. Sondra remained seated at the table, still reeling from this bit of information.

"Sondra, I'm sorry, but I've gotta run. I'm in town until tomorrow if you want to try and have lunch or something."

Sondra snapped back to what Jack was saying and stared at him for a moment before she shook her head. "Uh, no, I can't tomorrow, but send me an invitation to the opening of your new place."

Jack nodded and looked down at the floor, his hands in his pockets. "Sometimes, I've felt responsible. You know, if I had married her instead, she might not have been out on the lakefront that night. Or even if I had called her that weekend, maybe she would have been on the phone with me instead of out jogging." He shook his head. "Too many 'if-only's'."

"I know," Sondra whispered.

# SEVEN

New York had been under a gentle, misty rain for five days straight. The pitter-patter of raindrops against the window of her thirty-fifth floor apartment on Manhattan's Upper East Side was comforting to Sondra on this Saturday morning. The drab weather outside matched the melancholy she felt inside; she even had on gray sweatpants and tank top.

Sondra sat at her kitchen table, one hand wrapped around her favorite chipped blue coffee mug, the other balancing a cigarette between two slender fingers. One foot rested on the chair underneath her. She hadn't been able to stop thinking about what Jack had said a few days ago. What could her sister have been unhappy about? From everything she'd seen and heard, Tracy's life had been close to perfect.

The box was sitting in the living room, in plain sight, but Sondra wanted to ignore it for as long as she could. She had decreed today would be the day she went through everything, but now that today was here, she was afraid. Part of her sister's life was in that box. Maybe even some clue as to what she was unhappy about. Sondra kneaded her forehead and looked out her picture windows at Central Park sliding down like a child's messy watercolor. Sondra and Tracy had loved the rain as kids, doing what most do by running around trying to catch the drops on their tongues. It always tickled them to feel the cold little splashes against the warmth of their tongues. They would always try to one-up each other with each claiming she had caught more.

Sondra took long, slow drags and held them for a few extra moments, enjoying the acrid taste rolling around her mouth.

Okay. It was now or never. Sondra stubbed out her cigarette and picked up her coffee mug. She padded into her living room and set the mug down on the faded Oriental rug on the floor before she joined it. She pulled her long black hair up into a messy knot and took a few deep breaths. Sondra placed her hands on top of the box and held them there for a few moments.

With timid yet deliberate motions, she opened the flaps, as though something might jump out at her. She went through the contents, taking inventory. Photo albums, Tracy's last two date books, greeting cards. Sondra picked up a small purple photo album and opened it. The first picture was of all of them at Christmas one year, a few years before Tracy got married. Tracy wore an elf hat, silky red pajamas, and a dazzling smile. Sondra had her usual sullen expression, her messy topknot hidden beneath the red Santa cap Tracy had slapped on her head at the last minute. Their parents beaming as usual.

Sondra continued to thumb through the album. More family photos, friends, some solo shots of Tracy at various parties or functions, a few of the two sisters together, including the night Sondra won her Oscar. Sondra didn't spend nearly the amount of time on her appearance Tracy did; if her clothes were clean, that was good enough for her. Tracy on the other hand, was all about the looks: perfect nails, perfect hair and a designer wardrobe. Tracy spent months getting Sondra ready for the Oscars, calling stylists, looking for gowns, and scheduling all kinds of beauty treatments. Sondra had grumbled, but secretly, she kind of enjoyed it. No one was more surprised than Sondra at how incredible she looked that night. Tracy had laughed and said she cleaned up real good. In the end, she was glad for all the primping and preening; she would have hated to have accepted the Oscar in the kind of unholy mess she was likely to have worn without Tracy's intervention.

There were three years between the sisters and they'd been exceptionally close their whole lives, managing to sidestep most of the bickering and sniping that plagued most siblings, a major feat, considering how different they were. Of the two sisters, Tracy was the social butterfly, while Sondra had many acquaintances, but only a few close friends; Sondra was goth before anyone knew what the hell goth was. Her father used to tease her by calling her his little ray of sunshine because she'd been in a perpetual bad mood since the age of four. Sunshine became Sonny and the name stuck. Tracy was the bubbly cheerleader and top-notch swimmer, pretty and popular with a non-stop stream of giggly girlfriends, hunky boyfriends, parties and fun. Sondra usually had her nose stuck in a book and a scowl on her face.

Sondra thumbed through Tracy's last two datebooks, which were crammed full of lunches, dinners and parties. Sondra shook her head at her sister's ability to hold down a job with the hurricane that was her life. Of course, Tracy moved a million miles a minute, so really, it shouldn't have been a surprise.

Even though she'd gone missing in late January, her new datebook still teemed with appointments and events well into the New Year.

Sondra picked up a larger white satin photo album and realized it was from Tracy's wedding. With shaky hands, Sondra flipped through the pages. She stopped at a picture of Tracy and Phillip.

Sondra had only met Phillip once before the wedding, when she'd come to town for the Chicago Film Festival. Tracy had managed to snag a reservation for the three of them at Frontera Grill and Sondra would later describe the evening to Mimi as awkward. Sondra could barely pull any personal information out of Phillip, much less have an enjoyable dinner conversation with him. Tracy was so outgoing and vibrant, and this guy was just so quiet and withdrawn. Tracy said once you got to know him, he was sweet and funny. Sondra wasn't convinced, but kept her opinions to herself.

Sondra kept flipping through the pages, watching the story of the day unfold, feeling the flood of memories. Tracy had been giddy and Phillip's eyes stayed glued to her the whole day and long into the night. The black and white photos revealed a blissful couple, deeply in love and eager to begin their new life together. Their first dance, the champagne toast, and many, many photos of them kissing. Sondra felt a small twinge at the love and affection that spilled from the pages.

Sondra set the album aside and reached into the box. She smiled when she spotted a small Tiffany's box, already knowing what was in it. Sondra grinned as she held up the necklace, the small charm twisting and turning as she examined it. At the bottom of the box, Sondra found her sister's diaries and started to flip through them. Sometimes the entries were daily and weekly; at other times she'd go months without writing anything, then either fill in the updates with blow-by-blow accounts or just jot down brief bullet points of what had been going on.

No matter the form, Tracy had recorded the details of her life from the time she was eight. Travis Collins, their twelve-year-old neighbor and first major crush. Her first period; the silly dramas she and her immature girlfriends played out over boys, clothes and each other; Jimmy Byrd, her high school boyfriend and first lover; meeting Jack and later Phillip. Sondra skimmed much of the early books, but took no such liberties with the last few, hoping for a clue as to what may have been upsetting Tracy.

While Sondra had to laugh at Tracy's Valley-girl vernacular, even as a grown woman, she was still enthralled by the descriptions of her relationship with Jack. There was no doubt they were in love, though Tracy's growing disillusionment with his refusal to "shit or get off the fucking pot" leapt off the pages with stunning ferocity. Jack had shattered Tracy when he wouldn't take that next step. She packed endless pages with her despair about never being able to get over Jack, calling him "the love of my life."

And then there was Phillip, who came along to chase the hurt away with his kindness and patience. Tracy found herself charmed by this quiet and humble man.

*"Had an amazing date last night with an incredible guy. His name is Phillip and he's a pharmacist. Well, I guess I should back up. So after three years of ignoring my oral hygiene, I went to the dentist and turned out I had three cavities. Yikes. So they gave me a prescription for Vicodin, which, hello, should be every dental patient's best friend. Anyway, so I go get the prescription filled and the pharmacist, cute in a nerdy kind of way, very sincere, very earnest, takes a really long time explaining the ins and outs of Vicodin to me. Didn't think anything of it until he called me two days later to see how I was doing and if he could take me out for an omelet. I have to say, I was both really surprised and charmed all at the same time. I hesitated, but decided what the hell; I hadn't had a date since the big*

*meltdown with Jack. So we met at this little diner over on Clark. He actually lives in Uptown, but said he would come to my hood. He's from Detroit and came here as a psychology major at the University of Chicago, but decided he didn't want to go into that field after all and switched to pharmacy at UIC. Anyway, I had the best time; the best I'd had in a while. He was funny, charming, as I said, sweet and just NICE. I mean, he is a really nice guy and I mean that in a good way. A true gentleman. Afterwards, we went down to Diversey Harbor and talked about everything and nothing. I really like this guy. Different. We're supposed to have dinner tonight, so we'll see how things go. More to come!*

The ensuing pages described Tracy and Phillip's somewhat rapid relationship; their first kiss, meeting each other's family, weekend trips they took, endearing and thoughtful gestures from Phillip to show Tracy how much she meant to him. She described mundane details such as Phillip bringing her breakfast in bed, warming up her car on cold mornings, sending her flowers for no reason and writing her romantic letters. The star attractions of this book were the endless blissful if boring ruminations on holy matrimony and how she couldn't wait to start a family with Phillip.

Sondra finished the last entry, made about three months before Tracy died. The rest of the book was empty. Sondra dropped the book in her lap, frustrated. Nothing in here at all that would point to her being unhappy about anything. Unless she was too upset to write about it. Sondra shook her head and rubbed at the fatigue in her eyes. No, if something was wrong, it would have been here. Maybe Jack just heard what he wanted to hear because he was still in love with Tracy.

She plopped her face into her hands, exhausted. She went in search of her cigarettes and as she lit up, she stood in front of her picture windows. It was late afternoon and New York was still awash in rain. Sondra took long, slow inhalations, sadness filling her up with each breath.

# EIGHT

"I wondered how long you would hibernate in Gotham before you called me."

"I've been busy."

"I thought perhaps you got lost on the way back from your globe-trotting adventures. Your sense of direction is absurd."

"Ha, ha."

"Precisely."

"Glad to see that after all these years, your biting wit is still intact."

"So, will I be thanked in your next acceptance speech? I think it should become a tradition."

"Maybe. If you're nice to me."

"Wasn't I always?"

"Most of the time."

It was Saturday night and unable to face being alone in her apartment with depressing memories of Tracy tugging at her brain, Sondra had called her ex-husband, Gary and asked him to take her to dinner. The pot had been sweetened when she said they could go to Sardi's, his favorite, helped in no small part by his longtime friendship with the owner. After a hearty dinner of a Cobb salad for Sondra and the sirloin for Gary, they were now lingering over her coffee and his single malt Scotch.

"Feeling better, love?"

Sondra pushed the empty sugar packets around on the linen tablecloth, the small white crystals creeping out to leave a grainy trail.

"Yes. Thank you."

"I must say, you could have fooled me. You still seem rather morose."

Sondra laughed. "Gary, you're the only person I know who drops 'morose' into casual conversation."

"I refuse to capitulate to the incessant butchering of the English language to which our present society is so prone. I do have a reputation to maintain."

Sondra chuckled. "Wow. 'Capitulate'."

Sophisticated, witty, urbane, Sondra always thought Gary was Frasier Crane's long-lost black twin. His designer suits were impeccable and he kept his handsome, unlined toffee-toned face free of facial hair, moving through life with a charming, somewhat pretentious swagger. Their affair and subsequent marriage had been passionate, volatile and electrifying. At first, those vodka-soaked days and nights had held an irresistible allure; hobnobbing with his intellectual circle, holding court from his table at the Plaza or Le Cirque, summering at his house in the Hamptons, her astonishment at his ability to finish the Saturday Times crossword—in ink—every Saturday. It was surreal.

Until one day Sondra woke up and realized she wanted more, wanted to get her documentaries made. She needed to figure out who Sondra Ellis was, because Sondra Tate spent way too much time bobbing at the bottom of a Scotch bottle.

The inevitable split came and they put the marriage out of its misery. They remained close, justifying their break-up by saying they were better halves apart than together. However, in her quieter moments, Sondra missed Gary more than she could say. She'd dated a little, though none of her subsequent relationships came close to what she'd had with her ex-husband. She always shrugged off questions about whether or not she'd marry again by saying she was too busy globetrotting for work. The truth was she knew her heart and soul belonged to him. If Gary ever stopped boozing, Sondra had no doubt she would be knocking at his door suggesting they give it another try. That didn't seem likely, so Sondra was content to remain friends.

"So, will I get a private screening?"

Sondra snapped back to the present. "About what?"

Gary adjusted the collar of his navy blazer. "The film."

"Oh, yeah, sure. I'll even spring for the popcorn."

"Try again."

"All right, a bottle of Courvoisier."

"So good you are to me, love."

Sondra leaned back against the booth. "Oh, but I try."

"Love," Gary said as he leaned toward her. "I know you were lying before when you said you were feeling better. Yes, what happened to your sister was a cold and cruel tragedy. But truly it would be best for you—and for her—if you just let her rest in peace."

Sondra winced, knowing that Gary was right. Tracy was gone and she wasn't coming back.

"I hate it when you're right."

Gary gave her a smug smile as he lifted his glass to his lips. "Always am."

# NINE

Sondra looked at the meter and handed the driver a twenty before she got out in front of her building. She waved to the doorman, and as she rode upstairs in the elevator, she was alternately preoccupied by thoughts of Tracy and of her documentary.

She had been working on the narration and it wasn't gelling the way she wanted it to. It was Friday night and she'd spent the day enveloped in the solitude of the New York Public Library, clacking away at her laptop, creating and discarding draft after draft of the script. She decided to take the weekend off from working and let her mental battery recharge.

Sondra opened her door, her rubbery legs threatening to drop her in a bundle in the doorway. She had just lain down on the cranberry colored couch, when her cell phone rang from across the room. She groaned, peeling herself off the couch to go in search of her purse.

"Hi, daddy."

"Hey, honey. I was just thinking about you, thought I'd call." Gordon Ellis paused. "What's wrong?"

"Working non-stop and I'm just fried."

"How's it coming?"

"I'm taking a few days away from it so I can make it flow the way I want it to."

"How's everything else?"

"Okay. How are you?"

"Oh, you know, busy as always."

"You and mommy are way too active for me. Book clubs, golf outings, cooking classes. You guys give me a headache," Sondra said as she picked at the fuzz balls on her faded black sweatpants.

"What can I say? We're not ready for you to roll us into the old folks' home just yet."

"No chance of that, the way you two keep going. Did mommy tell you I went through Tracy's things?"

"Oh, yeah, she said there were a few things you were going to send us."

"Yeah." Sondra was quiet for a second. "Have you all talked to Phillip lately?" she blurted out.

"Once in a while. Actually, he called us not too long ago."

"How is he?"

"Well… he called to let us know he'd gotten remarried."

Sondra almost fell off the couch. "What? How could he do that?"

"Sonny, it's been over a year."

Maybe it was because she'd just finished reading her sister's passionate retelling of their courtship, but it bothered Sondra to know Phillip had moved on. "It's… it just seems so soon I guess," Sondra muttered, still stunned.

"She was his high school sweetheart and I guess they reconnected after he moved back to Michigan. In fact, he sent us a nice letter and picture of him and his new wife. They looked very happy."

"Where in Michigan is he?"

"Detroit, where he grew up. Moved back when his mother got sick, wound up staying."

Tracy remembered that Phillip's mother had been too sick to attend the wedding. In fact, he didn't have any family there. His father had died while he was in college, and like his parents Phillip was an only child. Therefore, he had no cousins, no aunts, and no uncles. Between the Ellis family and the Brauns, Sondra had relatives coming out of her ears.

"Well, what did the letter say?"

"Just a very nice note about how much he loved Tracy, but that he knew she'd want him to be happy. I'll have your mother send it to you. Maybe it will help."

"Help what?"

Gordon sighed. "Well, you haven't had the time to grieve like we have. I mean, being away from us, working on your film. I just think it might help with part of the process."

Sondra pursed her lips and closed her eyes. "Maybe."

"Sonny… I can get away for a few days, come and see you. It's been a while."

"Oh, Daddy, I'm going to be so busy trying to finish this film. I promise, as soon as I'm done, I'll come out for a long visit. At least a month."

"I'm holding you to that. We really want to see our girl."

"I know, I know and like I said, as soon as I'm done, I'll be on the next plane. Promise." She paused. "I love you."

"I love you too. We'll talk to you soon."

"Bye, Daddy. Oh, and don't forget to have mommy send me that letter."

"I won't. Bye."

# TEN

*Dear Mimi,*

*It was wonderful to talk to you the other day and catch up. I was glad to hear you're still teaching swimming and that Gordon continues to be as prolific as ever. Sounds like you're both really enjoying life. It's great to know that some things never change.*

*Thank you so much for your condolences on my mother. As hard as it was watching her in so much pain before she passed, ironically it helped me to have her to focus on while I got over Tracy's death. Still, I found myself asking how much one man can take in such a short time. I guess what they say is true, that God never gives you more than you can bear.*

*I don't know if I ever let you and Gordon know how much Tracy meant to me. She was a beautiful, loving, wonderful woman who I was very lucky to have found. I flatter myself to think she felt as lucky as I did. Although we didn't have nearly enough time together, we were so fortunate to have what we did. It took me a long time to get over what happened to her, and now it is only the good times I remember, not the horrible end.*

*As I told you on the phone, I recently remarried. Paula and I knew each other in high school and well... she's been just wonderful to me. With her patient and loving spirit as my guide I have been able to heal. I have to confess that at first, I felt guilty, like I was betraying Tracy somehow. But I also know she would want me to be happy and I am with Paula. We live a quiet (some might say dull!) life here, but we enjoy it and each other immensely. I'm working for another pharmacy here and Paula is a homemaker. I am fortunate to have been blessed with two wonderful marriages to two amazing women.*

*I will never forget Tracy or everything she meant to me. She taught me how to love and what it meant to have a good relationship. For that, I'm forever grateful.*

*Please give both Sondra and Gordon my best.*

*Phillip*

Sondra re-read the letter several times. She looked at the picture he'd enclosed of himself and his new wife. She was tiny, a good foot shorter than Phillip, with a wide, toothy smile that dominated her smooth ebony visage. She was clad in a pink sweater and black skirt and held one arm loosely around Phillip. Her brother-in-law still wore the same thick glasses and dated hair, and his propensity for plaid remained intact. The busy red, green, and blue pattern of his short-sleeved button-down shirt was tucked into blue slacks.

Sondra stared at the photo for the better part of an hour before putting it and the letter back into the envelope and placing it on her kitchen table.

After blowing through two cigarettes and a random late-night rerun of *Family Ties*, Sondra finally shuffled off to bed.

# ELEVEN

Drop off dry cleaning. Done. Stop at Target to return the teakettle that didn't whistle. Check. Get groceries for tonight's dinner and tomorrow's breakfast. Check, check. The only thing left to do was go home. Paula loaded the last of her packages into her folding shopping cart. Before she wheeled off in the direction of home, she took a tissue out of her purse and dabbed at the dots of sweat on her forehead. Her face was devoid of makeup, so the only thing that smeared the white tissue was a thin layer of dirt from the day. She smoothed back her crinkly black hair, tucking a stray piece into the tight knot at the nape of her neck. Satisfied, Paula began the short walk to her house. She hummed to herself as she walked, the mottled black wheels of the cart raking over the wide concrete sidewalk in a rhythmic clatter.

Paula lived in a master-planned community shrewdly labeled by developers as a suburban village known as The Crossings. The idea was that you never had to go far for either your essentials or your entertainment, because they were all conveniently located within The Pavilion in the center of the community.

While the Crossings had its fair share of strip malls and stand-alone big boxes, The Pavilion, a behemoth compound that housed just about everything one could possibly need, was the pulse of the community. The Pavilion hummed almost around-the-clock with a stream of activity. A sprawling Kroger offered a coffee shop, salad bar and specialty meat and cheese counter; a Cheesecake Factory always crammed with couples on dates, couples with two-point-five screaming kids and couples celebrating because their two-point-five kids were finally out of the house; the Super Target with its endless supply of plush towels, kitchen gadgets, artwork, and DVDs. Rounding out the Pavilion experience was a Barnes & Noble, a twenty screen multiplex, arcade, pottery painting studio, ice skating rink, a man-made lake with gondola rides and a dizzying array of Banana Republics, Eddie Bauers, Gaps and Forever 21s, all cascading into one another. Bright red trolleys ferried customers around the complex to designated pick-up and drop-off points, and the valet stands at The Pavilion's nicer restaurants were perpetual logjams.

Surrounding the perimeter of the Pavilion were several residential subdivisions named for trees: The Willows, The Elms, The Oaks, and so on. Many of the streets of these neighborhoods were named for flowers.

Paula's home, rather removed from the hustle and bustle of the Pavilion, was located in The Maples on Red Rose Lane. Typical of The Crossings, Red Rose Lane was a quiet tree-lined street adorned with a mix of bungalows, single-family and ranch-style houses. As its name suggested, many of the yards were festooned with lush rose bushes in a spectacular array of peach, yellow, white and, of course, red. In the neighborhood beautification contest held each summer, Red Rose Lane swept the Best Gardens competition every time. Red Rose Lane was one of the community's most diverse neighborhoods, boasting an Indian family, an Asian family, three Hispanic families, and four black families including Paula and Phillip, with the remaining five families white.

Paula turned her cart into her driveway as a gentle breeze whispered through the tree-lined street and the rose bushes of Red Rose Lane on this hot, sunny day. As Paula opened the door of her spacious yet quaint home, she was greeted with a whoosh of coolness from the air conditioner. She took the three bags of groceries out of her cart and set them on the gleaming white ceramic countertop in the kitchen before she folded up her cart and placed it in the laundry room.

Everything in Paula's house was sterile white. And immaculate. She spent hours every day vacuuming the plush white carpet, dusting the white bookshelves and scrubbing the white porcelain of her toilet. Not only was the house free of dirt, it was barren, lacking any personal touches or warmth. A few simple framed pictures of flowers were the extent of the decoration along with a small bookshelf topped with a green vase of fake begonias and a smattering of gardening books. All in all, it looked more like an unfinished model home than one a married couple actually lived in. And that's the way Paula liked it. It was a three-bedroom ranch with a tidy front lawn that Phillip paid a service to tend to on the third Tuesday of the month, though there were no roses, or any flowers for that matter, to decorate the yard. It was just a small patch of green for a lawn and a single row of bushes to the left of the front door. Inside was the master bedroom, Phillip's office and the guest bedroom that had never seen a guest as long as the couple had lived there.

Paula smoothed her hair back and began to put food into her color-coordinated pantry and cupboards. Paula prided herself on the order and cleanliness, with everything lined up in nice neat rows, labels facing out. Not a can or a box was out of place. It was Wednesday, which meant for dinner they would have baked chicken, salad, green beans, mashed potatoes, a glass of iced tea with three ice cubes, a half a pack of Sweet'N Low, no lemon, buttered rolls and for dessert, a cup of coffee to go with their apple pie with one scoop of vanilla ice cream. Paula unhooked her frilly white apron from its hook in the laundry room and worked in silence for the next hour and a half, keeping a careful eye on the clock.

Finally, Paula set the table for two, arranging each place setting symmetrically. Her last act was to drop a straw into Phillip's glass of iced tea with practiced flourish. She glanced at the oven clock and went down the hall to the master bathroom to get ready. She held a damp washcloth to her face then pulled her hairbrush from the drawer and ran the stiff bristles along the sides and top of her head. She smoothed her hands down the front of her short-sleeved gray housedress and adjusted the seams of her stockings, which ran into sensible white flats.

She heard Phillip's car pull into the driveway. Paula threw her shoulders back and greeted her husband when he opened the front door. With a wide smile, she held out her arms, beckoning him.

"Hello dear. How was your day?"

Phillip smiled and gave his wife a chaste hug. "It was fine. And how was your day?"

"Oh, fine. Let me take your jacket. Dinner is ready. Baked chicken, your favorite," she sing-songed.

"Mmmm, that sounds delicious. I'm starving."

As Phillip waited, Paula took her husband's blazer and hung it up in the bedroom closet, taking care not to let it press against any other clothing. Paula came back to escort Phillip to the small white wood dining room table and pulled out his chair. She smiled and picked up the white linen napkin next to his plate and tucked it over his blue striped tie and into the collar of his crisp blue shirt. With a small smile, she dished up dinner for them both. She picked up his glass of iced tea and brought the straw to his lips.

"Tell me when," she said as she held the straw. He took a few hearty sips then nodded his head, indicating he was through. With a contented smile, Paula put the glass down next to Phillip's plate before she took her place at the table across from him.

"Did you complete your errands today?" Phillip asked as he took a small bite of salad.

"Yes. I got the money back from the teakettle that didn't whistle. It's in my purse."

"Go ahead and keep it," Phillip said. "Add it to next week's grocery allowance."

Paula smiled, pleased. "Oh, thank you, dear."

Phillip gave his wife an adoring look. "I thought you would like that."

The two continued dinner in silence, each concentrating on their food and little else. When Phillip was done, he cleared his throat and Paula put down her fork, though her plate was half full. Paula stood and cleared both of their dishes, throwing all the food down the garbage disposal. Phillip didn't like leftovers—unless it was dessert—preferring a freshly prepared meal each day. She brought out two plates of homemade apple pie that she'd made that morning, one scoop of vanilla ice cream apiece.

She proudly placed her husband's apple pie in front of him and went to pick up his fork to feed him his first bite when he placed his hand over hers.

"Paula."

"Yes, dear?"

"Paula, what have you forgotten?"

Paula looked over the table, searching for the offense. Her face fell as she realized. "The coffee," she whispered. "I forgot the coffee."

Paula dropped to her knees, her breath coming in short bursts before the floodgates opened and she sobbed, unable to stop. She clutched the space between the tops of her husband's brown loafers and the hem of his blue slacks.

"Oh, please, please forgive me. You know I only want to please you," she cried.

With gentle force, Phillip placed his hands underneath Paula's armpits and brought her to her feet. "Now, now. I guess the errands were too much for you. Perhaps we should limit your outings during the day. We can't have you forgetting your duties."

Paula shook her head, scared. "Oh, no dear. No. It wasn't too much. I… I just forgot. I'm sorry. I'm so sorry."

Phillip looked at Paula for a few moments before he softened. "All right. I'll forgive it this time. But you must be more careful. Now, please make the coffee."

Like a grateful puppy, Paula nodded and snatched up Phillip's plate of pie before she scurried into the kitchen to make him a cup of coffee. She dumped the pie down the garbage disposal and started the coffee. Five minutes later, she came back into the dining room with a fresh slice of ice cream topped pie in one hand. In the other was a steaming white mug of decaf, the half pack of Sweet'N Low already stirred into the brew. She set both down in front of him and waited.

"I hope it's okay," she said, eager for his approval.

Phillip took a small sip of coffee and put the cup back down on the table. He gave her a curt nod and a relieved Paula could now pick up her fork and eat her own soggy pie, now swimming in a pool of melted ice cream. After dessert, Paula removed Phillip's napkin from his collar and walked him to his favorite chair in front of the television. She flipped it to the all-sports channel before she returned to the kitchen for the first part of her nightly ritual. First, she washed and dried all of the dishes by hand, even though she had a dishwasher. Next, she swept the kitchen floor before she got on her knees and scrubbed it with a hand brush and Ajax, although she had done it that morning.

Wiping the sweat from her brow, Paula moved into the bedroom to prepare it for the evening. While Paula changed the sheets on the bed—Phillip liked to sleep on clean sheets every night—her husband stayed in front of the TV for the rest of the evening. After taking a bath—Phillip didn't like her to come to bed unless she'd bathed—Paula pulled on a long pink flannel nightgown and climbed into bed. It was nine-thirty; Phillip would come to bed at ten. Paula turned on her back and looked up at the ceiling, ignoring her aching knees and the knots in her shoulders. She could hear the low hum of the TV in the other room. She took a sharp inhale, willing herself to stay awake.

She was afraid to sleep, afraid of the dreams that would come. Paula turned over on her side and focused her gaze on the white wall opposite the bed.

"Think about your day today. Think about your day today. Think about your husband. Dream about those things," she whispered to herself in the darkness. Paula continued to mumble to herself before she drifted off to sleep, praying her dreams would be sweet.

• • •

*She was running, her feet stabbing the pavement as she propelled herself forward. The icy wind pummeled her face, chapping her lips and stinging her eyes. But she kept on. Punch, punch, punch, went her shoes. She tried to make out what was around her, but it was too... hard. Too much wind and... snow. Furious white flurries swirled around her, further obscuring her vision.*

*Finally, she stopped, unable to go any farther. She bent over heaving, her breath coming in short, violent bursts. She closed her eyes to shield them from the brilliant whiteness beginning to form in front of her...*

Paula jerked straight up, hyperventilating. She held her hand to her chest and felt her heart jam against her palm with rapid popping movements. Phillip lay sound asleep next to her, oblivious to her torment. She slid back down under the covers and closed her eyes, trying to steady herself. She hadn't had that particular dream in so long.

Except it wasn't a dream, but a horrible truth she couldn't seem to bury.

# TWELVE

Sondra got out of the cab in front of her building, her body wilting with fatigue. It was close to two in the morning and she had to be back at the studio at nine. The narration was done and final mixing was taking up a huge chunk of time. They were on an aggressive editing schedule as the New York premiere was only a few months away, with the nationwide release shortly afterward.

Sondra dragged herself inside and checked her mailbox before falling into the elevator. She opened the door to her apartment and straggled to the bathroom to twirl the faucet on in the shower. Sondra stripped down and climbed in. She stood underneath the blistering needles of water, relishing the chance to power down her brain, even if only for a moment. She scrubbed the day away before washing and conditioning her thick black hair with vigorous strokes. After stepping out of the shower, she rubbed generous amounts of baby oil across her smooth brown skin before she shrugged into a pair of green sweats and a black tank top. She shuffled into her kitchen to make a cup of chamomile tea, and as she waited for the water to boil, she leaned against her counter thinking about the documentary. Overall, she was happy about how it was shaping up.

The kettle whistled and Sondra poured the hot water over the tea bag followed by two heaping spoonfuls of sugar. She stirred it, the clinking of the spoon against the side of the mug the only sound echoing throughout the apartment. Sondra blew into the tea and plopped onto one of her bar stools. That day's *Times* and *Post* were still hanging over the edge of the counter where she'd thrown them that morning. She grabbed the *Post*, not having the mental capacity to handle the

*Times* at the moment. She leafed through it, that day's news only of mild interest now. She stopped on a picture of a pretty blonde girl with doe eyes, from California apparently, and shook her head. Yet another young woman who'd been missing for two weeks, triggering a state-wide search.

"Hmm," Sondra murmured. "She went jogging just like Tracy."

Sondra kept reading, intrigued. When she finished, she pulled her laptop out of her bag and typed the woman's name into Google. Thousands of pages came up, including mentions in *People* and *USA Today*. On a whim, Sondra typed in "Tracy Ellis."

Tracy's obituary from the Chicago papers came up and it looked like her station had run a few stories, though Sondra couldn't access them. No media frenzy surrounding her sister's disappearance. A few outlets had picked up on Tracy's connection to a well-known author and former Olympian, though her parents had chosen not to exploit their fame to spur the search for their daughter. It was just their way. If Sondra had been in the country at the time, she would have raised holy hell. Which was her way. Granted, Tracy had only been missing just shy of a week, so Sondra wouldn't expect there to be a ton of news stories. Still… Sondra glanced back at the *Post* story with half a page dedicated to Sharon Wilson from Cupertino, California.

Sondra continued to click around Google, finding yet more stories about missing women. Sondra's curiosity was piqued by a *USA Today* article questioning the volumes of media ink devoted to finding missing white women versus minority women who vanished. She googled the names from the article and was astounded by the disparity in coverage. Sondra leaned back, her wheels clicking, like they did when she got an idea for a documentary. She re-read Tracy's obituary again.

"Well, baby girl, maybe you won't have died in vain."

# THIRTEEN

Paula folded the last of her husband's brown socks and dropped them on the top of the clean laundry already snug inside the blue plastic basket. Humming to herself, she went into the bedroom and opened the top drawer of the dresser and scooped all eight pairs of Phillip's socks out of the basket and laid them next to each other in the drawer. They were all color-coordinated, the blacks next to the blacks, browns to browns and so on. She moved on to the other drawers, repeating the same meticulous movements of placing his clothes inside. He was quite particular about how his clothes were put away and Paula only wanted to please him. She lived for pleasing him.

She looked at her watch as she picked up the laundry basket. It was Saturday and Phillip always worked a half day at the clinic on Saturdays. It was now eleven and Phillip would be home around one, expecting lunch. As Paula walked through the living room and toward the kitchen, she noticed the window ledges had a thin film of dust.

"Well, if I start now, I should finish in plenty of time to make lunch," she said as she ran her finger along the edge. "Shouldn't take more than a half hour."

Paula filled up a beige bucket with water and pine cleaner and became lost in wiping the smudges from every windowsill in the house with a bright yellow sponge. As she finished, she looked at her watch and panicked. It was twelve-thirty.

"Oh. Oh no," Paula whispered. She'd lost track of time and now would have to hurry to get lunch on the table before Phillip got home. A slender trickle of sweat crawled down the inside of Paula's arm as she hurried into the kitchen.

On Saturday afternoons, Phillip liked two grilled cheese sandwiches with American and Cheddar, creamed corn, a glass of milk and chocolate pudding for dessert. He would then take a nap until three before going into his home office until six, when he would emerge, ready for a dinner of chicken potpies and iced tea.

Paula's fingers fumbled over slicing the cheddar, and she tore holes in three pieces of bread as she tried to butter them. She kept looking at the clock, knowing she wouldn't make it but terrified of what would happen if she didn't at least try. She had just flipped the second sandwich when she heard Phillip's car pull into the driveway. She grabbed a plate from the cabinet and plunked it down on the counter. She slid the first sandwich onto the plate and began to spoon corn next to it.

Phillip's key turned in the lock and he walked in. Paula froze, her fingers still wrapped around the black plastic handle of the pot of corn.

"Paula?"

Paula licked her lips and brought the plate of food out to the dining room table. "Hello, dear. How was your day?" She hoped if she acted normally that he wouldn't get too upset about lunch being late.

Phillip slammed the door shut before he walked over to her. He stood in front of her with his arms crossed. "What is this, Paula?"

Paula looked up meekly, her hands clenched together in front of her. "I'm sorry," she said. "I was cleaning and I—"

Phillip cut her off. "Paula, I work hard, six days a week, and when I come home, I expect to find you at the door to greet me and my meals ready and waiting."

"I know, I know, I'm sorry—"

"You know Paula, you've been doing a lot of things wrong lately."

"Oh, Phillip, no," she whispered. "I've been trying so hard—"

Phillip shook his head. "Not hard enough, Paula. I'm afraid I have to punish you. You've been a bad, bad girl."

Paula's head whipped back and forth in terror as Phillip seized her arm and dragged her towards the hallway. "Please, no, Phillip, please. I'm sorry. I'll do better—I will, I promise."

Phillip yanked open the door to the hall closet and shoved Paula inside. She fell to the floor of the tiny, cramped space and tried to crawl out before he pushed the door closed and locked it.

"Phillip. Phillip! Please, I'm sorry. Please let me out!" She pounded on the door.

"Not another word, Paula," came Phillip's muffled response. "You must learn your lesson. Now. Silence."

Paula clamped her hand over her mouth and cried into it. Even though it was early afternoon outside, it was pitch black inside her prison, save for the tiny crack of light peering through the bottom of the door. Paula drew her legs up to her chin and began to rock back and forth, the cries disappearing into her knees.

• • •

"Paula. Paula, wake up."

Paula felt herself being shaken and she took in a deep breath to bring herself back to life. She had fallen asleep against the wall, and as her eyes drifted open, she saw Phillip kneeling in front of her, shaking her awake. He stood.

"You need to clean the kitchen. And I expect dinner on the table in exactly one hour."

Paula swallowed and nodded. "Yes, dear."

He sniffed and turned to plant himself in front of the TV, which was blaring a documentary about the Titanic. Paula dug the heels of her hands into her eyes to sweep away the crust of sleep and unfurled her knees, wincing from the stiffness. She groaned and stumbled into the kitchen. The creamed corn had congealed in the stainless steel pot and the cheese from the sandwiches had seared itself to the bottom of the heavy black skillet. Paula filled the kitchen sink with scalding soap bubbles, but the hot water was no match for the tears scorching her face.

# FOURTEEN

Cindy Cross stood in the middle of her living room trying to decide if it was too late to run away and join the circus. Looking less like a comfortable space for living and more like the inside of a storage unit, Cindy's living room was bursting with moving boxes, packing peanuts, and newspaper. The Cross family had moved into The Maples three days ago and slowly but surely—mostly slowly—Cindy was getting the house in order.

Cindy's sluggish progress was interrupted by the doorbell. She groaned and stepped around the two huge boxes blocking her path. She opened the door to find a stunning Indian woman in skinny black pants and a snug purple T-shirt standing on her doorstep. She was clutching a basket of pastries and a cup holder with two large cups of coffee.

"I saw you move in a few days ago, and if you're anything like me, you have yet to find the coffee maker," the woman said in a lilting English accent.

"Okay, I will babysit your kids for a month."

"Are you kidding? *I* don't even want to babysit my kids. I wouldn't wish it on you."

The two women laughed as Cindy ushered her new neighbor inside.

"Welcome to hell," Cindy said as she motioned for the woman to follow her into the kitchen, where the small oak kitchen table was littered with discarded bubble wrap and newspaper.

"I swear, I keep house better than this," Cindy said as she swept the packing remnants off the table and onto the floor with the back of her hand. "Of course my husband skipped off to Charlotte this morning for three days leaving me to deal with this mess. It would serve him right if I sat here until he got back and didn't lift a finger. I'm Cindy, by the way."

"Mira," the woman said as she set the pastries and coffee down on the table. She twisted one coffee cup out of the holder and placed it in front of Cindy. "I must say you look rather well put together for someone buried under boxes and with no coffee."

Cindy laughed, revealing Chiclet-white teeth as she tossed back her strawberry blonde highlights. "Well, thank you. I can see I have you fooled."

Mira smiled and lifted her coffee cup to her lips. "Welcome to The Maples."

Cindy sipped her coffee, an almost orgasmic look shading her blue eyes. "Oh, this is tasty. You and I are friends for life."

Mira smiled. "Isn't it yummy? It's from a little bakery in the Pavilion. I get all my sweets there. Carson's. It's divine. So where are you from?"

"A little town in Iowa you've never heard of. My husband and I met in college—we both went to Mizzou. He's from here. He's in IT and we've been married eight years, two kids, four and six."

"Babysitter?"

Cindy nodded. "Babysitter. I mean can you imagine trying to navigate this with two kids tugging after you all day long? I go get them around three. How old are your kids?"

Mira bit off a piece of chocolate croissant. "Eight and five. Remind me to tell you about the park district day camp during the summer. What brings you to the neighborhood?"

"Chris—that's my husband—his company moved offices and it would have been an hour and a half commute from the old house. The neighborhood seems nice."

Mira nodded as she took a sip of coffee. "It is. Everyone is quite friendly. We have block parties, holiday gatherings, that type of thing. Very warm and open. What do you do?"

"Substitute teacher in English at the high school level. You?"

"I do marketing work out of the house. Mostly writing."

Through her kitchen window, Cindy saw Paula drag a broom, bucket of water and mop outside. She watched as Paula took the broom and attacked the concrete driveway with it, sweeping dirt and debris out to the street. Paula then grabbed the mop and swabbed it back and forth across the area she'd just swept. Cindy picked up a muffin and motioned to Paula.

"What's the story with the chicky across the street?" she said as she tore off a banana nut chunk.

Mira looked out the window and laughed. "Oh, yes. Miss Paula. I wouldn't bother trying to talk to her. She and her husband are the official neighborhood weirdos."

"Oh, yeah?" Cindy leaned forward, her interest piqued. "Tell me more."

Mira swallowed more coffee. "Moved in about a year ago or so, couldn't tell you from where. Phillip and Paula. He's a pharmacist, I think, she stays home. No kids. You've seen that 'Stepford Wives'?"

"Yeah."

"Well, if that sort of thing exists, she's got it."

"No kidding?"

"Honest to God."

"Well, I guess anyone who mops a driveway…"

"Precisely. I think that's all she does all day. Clean, I mean. Obsessively." The two women looked outside in unison to see Paula wiping her brow and wringing out the mop into the bucket.

"They never talk to anyone, have made no effort to get to know *anyone*. Never go out to dinner, never take a vacation. They have a guy mow the lawn once a month, but other than that, I don't even think a bloody pizza deliveryman comes. He's home every night at six on the d-o-t, and, from what I can tell, he keeps her on a very short leash. Doesn't even let her drive. She hauls her shopping cart all over the Pavilion."

"Good God."

Mira motioned to the window. "See that housedress she has on?"

"Yeah."

"Not once have I ever seen her wear a pair of trousers. Just those funny old housedresses. She can't be much past thirty and she dresses like my mother-in-law. Worse than my mother-in-law. One day, I stu-pidly locked myself out of the house, and ran over to see if I could use her phone to call a locksmith since Sam was out of town and my old-est had absconded with the spare. Probably buried it in the backyard. I never did bother to look. Anyway, I mean it was like bloody pulling teeth to get her to let me in. Said her husband didn't like strangers in the house. And it's not like she hasn't seen me at the market and around the neighborhood. Finally, she let me in and I have to tell you, the house gave me the bloody chills. I mean, you couldn't tell anyone actually lived there. Stark white, hardly a picture to be found. Not just neat as a pin, but sterile, cold. I couldn't wait to get out of there. I sat outside my house for an hour waiting for the locksmith. Better than sitting in there." Mira shuddered a bit before she resumed eating.

"Wow," Cindy said. "That does sound like Stepford. What do you think the deal is? I mean, seriously."

Mira scrunched up her face. "I can't even begin to speculate. I gave up trying to figure it out." Mira took a sip of coffee. "Of course..." her voice trailed off.

Cindy perked up. "What? What?"

"Well, we're all betting on how long it will be before she snaps and kills him. It's always the people you least expect."

Cindy leaned back, nodding as she considered this. "Interesting."

"Care to lay odds?"

Cindy plunked her chin into her palm. "Based on what you told me, I say she goes postal in a year."

Cindy and Mira looked out of the window again in time to see Paula lug her bucket of water back into her house and shut the door.

"You're on," Mira said.

# FIFTEEN

*She had to get away. She had to get away before they realized what she'd done. The sky above and the ground below were white, but she had to try... had to try and fight her way through the swirl of whiteness around her.*

*She looked down. Thick, syrupy blood was oozing into the stark white snow. She screamed.*

*She had to get away.*

Paula jumped and shot straight up off the couch where she had been dozing.

"Oh, my goodness," she said aloud as she tried to catch her breath. Paula swung her legs around until both feet were planted on her white carpet. She shook her head and jammed her hands over her eyes. The white carpet was too much like the white snow in her dream. She looked at her watch. It was noon, and after her morning chores, which included her weekly mop and sweep of the front walk, Paula had collapsed onto the couch and fallen into an unexpected nap. As she did so many nights, she'd lain awake the night before, staring at the ceiling, trying to stave off sleep. She was confused though. The dreams usually only came at night; she'd never had one during the daytime.

She never told Phillip about the torment sleep brought to her. He would put her back in the hospital and she didn't want that. Anything but that. The constant wails and moans echoing from some far-off room. The medications. The cold that trickled into your bones and stayed, no matter how much you drew that threadbare gray blanket around your shoulders. Shaking her head to wipe away that awful possibility, Paula went to the kitchen for a glass of water. She was still somewhat disoriented from her dream, and as she pulled a glass down from the cabinet, it slipped clean through her trembling fingers and tiny pieces of glass went skating across the floor.

"Oh, dear." She scurried to the laundry room where she kept her mop and broom. She swept up the shards and deposited them into the trash. Her doorbell rang; it would be Carlene coming to color her hair. Distraught, Paula crossed the room to open the front door and found Carlene standing there in a gold tank dress that hugged the rolls of fat jiggling across her hulking frame.

"Hey, girl, how you doin'?" Carlene said in her booming contralto. Her bright red lipstick punctuated the slippery yellow of her teeth and rich mahogany of her skin.

"I'm fine, Carlene, how are you?" Paula asked as she ran her hands down the length of her head to the bun at the nape of her neck.

Carlene cracked her gum and walked toward the kitchen to unpack her supplies. "Girrrl, I had me a date last night with a fine brother. We goin' out again tomorrow. This could be the one," she said as she set up on the table, her ruby lips curling into a smile.

Paula gave a disinterested smile as she leaned against the counter. Carlene always thought she'd found the one, so it was hard to get excited.

"So," Carlene said, her numerous gold bracelets rattling against each other as she sat Paula down into a kitchen chair and draped a smock over her tan cotton housedress. "Are we doing the usual today?" she asked, tapping one long, red airbrushed nail Against the wood trim on the chair

Paula nodded. "Yes, the usual," she said as Carlene began to undo Paula's knot and rake her fingers through the long black strands.

"Why don't we try something different? I could cut it into a really cute flip? Or we could bob it?" Carlene said holding up Paula's silky tresses.

"No. Just the regular touch-up."

"Girl, you got the perfect face for all the really cute styles right now. I don't know why you don't try something different. I'll bet your husband would like it. You know, spice things up a little?"

Paula gave Carlene a feeble smile. "Phillip doesn't like spice."

Carlene took one fingernail and scratched the scalp underneath her own black and blonde flip. "All right girl, we'll do what we always do. But I'ma keep on working on you. One of these days, we're gonna get you a new 'do.'"

Every six weeks Carlene came to the house on Red Rose Lane to color Paula's gray roots black. Phillip had discovered some strands of gray around her temples and commented he didn't like it. He found Carlene in the phone book and paid her double to come to the house and color Paula's hair every six weeks.

"You know I don't think you've ever told me about your husband. What does he do?"

Paula sighed to herself. She always hated people asking her a lot of questions about her personal life. "He's a pharmacist."

"Oh, that's nice," Carlene said as she began to section off Paula's hair. "How did you all meet?"

"We were high school sweethearts."

Carlene nodded her head as she soaked up that bit of information. "How sweet. You been married all that time?"

Paula squirmed in her chair. "No, he was married before, but she died. We reconnected after that."

Carlene's fingers separated the wet black locks of Paula's hair as she worked the color into it. "That's a shame. But I guess if she hadn't died, you all wouldn't have hooked back up." She placed a plastic cap over Paula's head and leaned against the sink. "I guess it's like they say—everything happens for a reason."

# SIXTEEN

It was finally done.

For the first time in months, Sondra felt like she could relax. She'd finished the final edit. Now all she had to do was wait for the madness to commence in the fall: premieres, festivals, award season, press. In the meantime, she was going to get lost on a beach in California for a few weeks.

Sondra ordered up some Thai food and went in search of the box of Tracy's things that she'd gone through a few months earlier. She'd told Mimi she'd bring a few things she figured her mother would want; she'd keep the rest.

Sifting through the photo albums, jewelry and other mementos again was no less bittersweet than it had been the first time. She decided to keep the small purple photo album, the Tiffany necklace and her diaries, setting everything else aside for her parents, making a mental note to take her big suitcase to California with her. The Thai food came, and as she slurped down Soba noodles, Sondra absentmindedly flipped through Tracy's last appointment book before she threw it out, but then stopped at the last appointment. She had seen it the first time she'd gone through the book but hadn't thought about it much at the time. Today, it made her stop and think. There was an appointment for the Monday after she'd disappeared with D.R. at ten A.M.

"D.R. D.R." Sondra wrinkled her nose. "Doctor. Of course." Sondra was about to toss the book in the trash when a thought occurred to her.

"Maybe… maybe it wasn't a routine visit… Maybe it was something she wouldn't have wanted Phillip to know." That would explain what she may have been unhappy about—according to Jack—and why Phillip wouldn't have known about it. Sondra chewed her bottom lip, her heart racing at the awful possibilities.

"Only one way to find out," she muttered, as she looked down at the phone number scribbled next to the initials. She picked up her phone and dialed.

"Damon Randall and Associates."

Sondra was taken aback, surprised there wasn't a "doctor" in front of Randall.

"Oh, uh, hi, yes, may I speak with Mr. Randall please?"

"Who's calling?"

"Sondra Ellis."

"And what is this regarding?"

"Um, following up on an appointment."

"Hold, please."

Sondra munched on a peapod while she waited to be connected with Damon Randall. Finally, a deep baritone came on the line.

"Damon Randall."

Sondra cleared her throat. "Mr. Randall, good afternoon. My name is Sondra Ellis and well this is going to sound strange, but I think my sister may have been meeting you a few years ago and I'm just wondering who you are and why she would have been meeting you."

"I'm afraid I don't follow."

"Sorry. Let me start over. My sister, Tracy Ellis, disappeared about three years ago and I was going through her old date book and found your number in it. She'd made an appointment to meet with you and—"

"Did you say Tracy Ellis?" Damon Randall interrupted.

"Yes."

"Hold on a minute." Sondra could hear him shuffling papers and opening drawers.

"You said three years ago."

Sondra nodded. "Right."

"What month?"

"February."

"Ah. Yes. I was going to meet with Ms. Ellis on Monday morning at ten A.M., February first. She never made it. I do remember now she disappeared and later died, so obviously, we never met."

"Mr. Randall, why was my sister coming to meet you? I mean, what is it that you do?"

There was a small pause. "She wanted to discuss a divorce."

Sondra's heart began to stab her chest. "Whose divorce?"

"Hers."

The box of Soba noodles slipped out of Sondra's hands and spilled onto the floor, lashing her bare foot with thick, brown sauce. "You're a divorce attorney?"

"Yes. A friend of Ms. Ellis' gave her my card and she contacted me and asked if we could meet first thing that Monday. She wanted to file for divorce from her husband."

"Are you serious?"

"Quite. She plainly said she wanted to talk about what steps she would need to take to file for a divorce from her husband. We didn't discuss many details, planning, of course, to do that when we met."

"Mr. Randall, my sister had only been married six months."

"I've seen shorter marriages."

Sondra shook her head. "But... man, this makes no sense," she whispered to herself. "And she didn't tell you anything, nothing at all?"

"I'm afraid not. I'm sorry, Ms. Ellis, but I have a very busy afternoon and I really must go."

"Oh, yeah, right. Thank you."

"My condolences on the loss of your sister. I do recall it being a rather gruesome crime."

Sondra squinted, distracted. "Yeah... yeah it was. Goodbye. And thank you."

"Good day." The phone clicked in Sondra's ear.

Sondra hung up her own phone and winced when her foot squished into slimy, now useless Soba noodles. She wiped her foot and floor as she contemplated this bit of information. A divorce? This was so contrary to... Sondra went in search of Phillip's letter to Mimi, finding it stashed in the black mesh file holder she crammed her bills into. She pulled it out and examined it before she reread it for the first time in a year. She examined the photo of Phillip and his new wife. Sondra looked up, a new thought occurring to her.

Maybe Phillip was cheating on Tracy and that's why she wanted a divorce.

Sondra threw the envelope down on the kitchen counter and went digging for Tracy's last journal so she could re-read the passages. The same rosy picture she'd read before still filled the pages. Of course... she looked at the date again, reminding herself the last entry was three months before Tracy disappeared.

What the hell could have happened in three months' time?

She fished a cigarette out of the box on the kitchen counter and lit up. Her eye fell on Tracy and Phillip's wedding album and she went over to pick it up. She flipped the book open to a picture of the bride and groom smiling for the camera at the reception. Sondra sucked hard on her cigarette and let out a deliberate exhale, the smoke curling around her in a lazy cloud. The happy couple's glowing smiles beckoned to Sondra to figure out what secrets had driven them apart.

# SEVENTEEN

As long as Paula could remember, she had loved Phillip.
It was the first day of sophomore year and she had seen him in the hallway by his locker outside of gym class. He wore a pair of stiff blue jeans, a plaid button-down shirt and thick glasses. She had watched as he unloaded and loaded books into his locker. It turned out they had biology together and became lab partners. They were both shy and quiet, and she spent each day hoping he would look at her as more than someone who could hold the frog open while he cut it. She was in awe of him. He was so smart and nice and Paula fell hopelessly in love.

At the end of the year, he finally asked her if she wanted to see a movie and Paula thought she would die. He had kissed her that night, his soft lips caressing her trembling ones with sweet, gentle pressure. After that, they became inseparable, planning to marry. However, he went off to Chicago to study psychology and Paula stayed behind to go to secretarial school. They tried for a while to keep up the relationship, but it was too difficult and they parted ways. Phillip stayed in Chicago and eventually met and married Tracy. Paula stayed behind and became a secretary at an insurance company. She kept up with Phillip through his mother and wondered if he still thought about her at all. She had dated some, but no one could measure up to her first love.

Paula had been staring out of her kitchen window thinking about her marriage, before she got back to the task at hand. She rinsed the final breakfast dishes and swiped her now-damp dishtowel across the white bowls from this morning's bran flakes before placing them in the rack to finish drying. She hugged herself at how lucky she was to have Phillip back after all these years. She knew that sometimes she disappointed him, and every day when she woke up, she concentrated on how she could be the best possible wife to him. He deserved nothing less. She hated that Tracy had to die for her dreams to come true, but it was like Carlene said—everything happened for a reason.

# EIGHTEEN

Paula didn't like Tuesdays. Tuesdays was meatloaf. Tuesdays was the day the little Mexican man with the gold earring, ponytail, and dirty green t-shirt came to mow the lawn.

Tuesdays was sex.

Every Tuesday and Thursday Phillip and Paula had sex and Paula didn't like it. It was now Tuesday morning and Paula had all day to dread the nighttime custom. At the moment she was scrambling eggs, brewing coffee and browning toast for Phillip.

After arranging the table with his breakfast, Paula went outside to retrieve the morning paper from the end of the driveway. She withdrew the sports section and placed it next to Phillip's breakfast plate before discarding the rest into the trash. She then went to the kitchen and poured herself a glass of orange juice.

"Dear? Dear, your breakfast is ready," she called out.

Phillip appeared and smiled at Paula. "Good morning," he said, walking over to her, preparing to perform the daily morning routine.

"Open wide," he said, holding out his hand, which contained one tiny white pill and one larger blue pill. "Vitamin time."

An obedient Paula opened her mouth and Phillip dropped the vitamins on her tongue. With a swish of her juice, she washed them down into her system. She smiled at Phillip and went to rinse out her glass. Phillip waited for her to seat him and give him the first sip of coffee.

As Phillip read the paper and ate breakfast, Paula packed his lunch. A turkey sandwich on wheat with mustard on one side, mayo on the other; a speared pickle, a thermos of tomato soup and two chocolate chip cookies for dessert. Paula heard Phillip clear his throat and she rushed out to clear the dishes. Phillip continued to sit at the table as Paula gathered up her husband's lunch into a large brown bag and presented it to him with flourish.

"All your favorites," she smiled.

He nodded his approval. "Don't forget my jacket."

She gave him a knowing look. "Of course not, dear." Paula went to the hall closet and pulled out the blazer she had pressed earlier that morning. She helped him into it and turned him around to survey his appearance.

"Perfect," she said, smoothing down the lapel. "Have a wonderful day, dear," she said and smiled.

Phillip gave her a dry peck on her cheek. "Thank you, dear."

With a pivot, Phillip walked out of the door and started up his green Chevy. Paula couldn't remember the last time she'd been inside Phillip's car. Might have been last year sometime. She herself never drove. Paula had never been a good driver to begin with, and then after the accident, she vowed to never again get behind the wheel. Paula shuddered at the memory as she locked the door behind Phillip and set about doing her chores for the day, trying not to think about tonight. Vacuuming, scrubbing, laundry, and dusting made the day pass quickly, and before Paula knew it, it was time to prepare the meatloaf she didn't like. It was her mother-in-law's recipe and she always found it too salty. Once, she decreased the amount of salt and was thrilled with the results. Phillip, however, had a fit and put her in the hall closet for two days, so it was back to the heaping tablespoons of salt the following Tuesday.

Dinner passed without incident and Paula tried to steel herself for the task ahead. She took extra time washing the dishes, swirling the damp dishtowel across the gleaming white plates until they squeaked. She placed the last dish in the rack, her heart about to jump out of her chest over the stress about what was coming.

"Paula?" Phillip called out from the living room.

She gulped. "Yes, dear?"

"Hadn't you better be getting ready?"

"Of course, dear. I was on my way now."

Paula entered their bedroom and rummaged around her drawer until she found her pink flannel nightgown, the one Phillip insisted she wear every Tuesday. She'd grown to hate the soft, prim material and everything it represented. With a heavy sigh, she removed her stiff white bra and thick white panties and slipped into the nightgown. She flipped off the light, lay down in bed and waited, wondering if Phillip could hear the pounding of her heart from the other room. The TV went silent and Paula closed her eyes, listening for Phillip's silent tread down the hallway to the bedroom. The door creaked open and she could see his silhouette illuminated from the glow of the hall light. She tensed up at the familiar jingle of his belt buckle, followed by the whoosh of his pants as they fell to the ground. He took his time undoing each of his buttons and Paula knew he was watching her. She squeezed her eyes tighter and tried to slow the ragged rhythm of her breath.

The bed dipped and groaned with Phillip's weight and Paula tried to keep herself from flinching as the hem of her nightgown trailed up the curve of her thigh and over the flat plane of her stomach. His fingers flicked across her nipples and Paula gulped, hoping the promised tears wouldn't slip out of her eyes. He took both hands and jiggled her breasts haphazardly, rolling them outward, then up and down, the cue for her move. Paula lifted her hand and groped along Phillip's inner thigh until she found his penis, small and flabby against his leg. She took a deep breath and began to manipulate it between her fingers, raking her hand up and down until it finally grew stiff within her palm. Phillip stopped squishing her breasts around and rolled on top of her, pushing himself into the dry, rubbery space between her legs with a soft grunt.

He rammed against her, trying to get comfortable and Paula gripped the mattress to keep from crying out in pain. Finally, he began to jack-hammer inside of her, shaking the bed until it squealed in agony. Beads of sweat slid down Phillip's forehead and splashed against Paula's nose, though she didn't dare wipe the drips away until he was done. His breath started to come in short bursts, Paula's sign that this torture would be over soon. He pushed, up and down, up and down, knocking the top of Paula's head against the bulky oak headboard. He stopped and planted his knees on either side of Paula's head, before shoving himself into her mouth. Paula fought back her tears and tried not to graze against him with her teeth. She'd made that mistake once before and had spent five days chained to the handle of the cabinet and forced to eat the two daily meals he'd allowed her on the kitchen floor. Phillip stopped for a moment and Paula closed her eyes, bracing for the explosion. He shuddered and cried out as the slippery white cream spilled out of him and into her throat.

He waited until he heard her gulp before he pulled back with one long groan, his whole body heaving. He grunted a final time and collapsed onto his back for a few seconds before he cleared his throat and bounded out of bed, headed for the bathroom. Paula waited until she heard the shower cut on before she sprinted to the kitchen and vomited into the sink. She looked at the stove clock. The entire act had taken all of five minutes and for Paula, they were the worst five of the worst ten minutes of her week. She coughed and rinsed out her mouth while trying to swish her stomach contents down the drain at the same time. She ran back to the bedroom and hurried over to the dresser to pull out his blue cotton pajamas and laid them on top of the dresser. She listened to him brush his teeth with his electric toothbrush and gargle as she pulled a fresh set of sheets from the linen closet in the hallway and hurriedly stripped the bed down to the mattress pad. She yanked the fitted sheet across the rounded corners of the bed and flicked the top sheet onto the bed, rushing to tuck the excess fabric beneath the mattress and box spring. She heard the light click off and ran to smooth down the wrinkles and lumps just as Phillip opened the door. She smiled and handed him his pajamas.

"Here you are, dear. Did you have a nice shower?

"Yes, dear. And now, I'm very tired." He gave her a papery kiss. "Goodnight, Paula." Phillip dropped into the bed and rolled over, his signal for Paula to leave and finish her chores for the night. She scrubbed out the tub before filling it up for herself and took a quick bath. She scoured it again before slathering herself in lotion and slipping into the mint green flannel nightgown she'd hung on the back hook earlier that day. She let the hot water from the sink stream out and ran her white washcloth under it until it was drenched in heat. She filled it with a squirt of soap and toothpaste and scraped it across the skin around her mouth, scrubbing it until she felt the familiar tingle. She continued to rub until her mouth went numb and the washcloth was lukewarm. She repeated this three more times before rinsing out her mouth with scalding water, grateful for a reprieve from the rancid tang on her tongue. She ended by brushing her teeth just once, though she wanted to brush them at least four times, but she knew Phillip would be suspicious if he heard the electric toothbrush go on too long. She sighed and patted her face dry, grateful her weekly nightmare was almost over. At least when they had sex on Thursdays, she didn't have to endure the oral assault.

Paula flipped off the light and crawled into bed next to a slumbering Phillip. She rolled onto her back and stared at the ceiling, her limp muscles burning with fatigue.

She really hated Tuesdays.

# NINETEEN

*She was walking fast, trying to keep up. It was snowing, so it was hard to see. There were so many people, so many faces she couldn't make out. She dodged around the faceless splotches, trying, trying so hard to keep her eyes focused. She blinked several times and continued to search the crowd. Finally, she broke into a run and plowed through the blobs. And then she reached her hand out to the one she was looking for...*

*It was a blob with arms and legs and clothes and a voice, but she couldn't hear the voice either. She pushed her hands out and shoved the blob. The blob shoved back and she went sprawling. Angry, Paula charged...*

Paula's eyes flew open and she bolted upright. Her breath came in jagged stops and starts and her cotton nightgown felt like fire next to her skin. Distraught, Paula ran her hand across her forehead, a soft whimper escaping her lips. She pushed back the heavy white comforter, rumpled white top sheet, and made her way to the bathroom. She tiptoed across the sea of white carpet, not wanting to wake Phillip. She closed the bathroom door before she flipped on the light. The sudden fluorescent assault made her stumble backward a bit. Paula gripped the edge of the counter to steady herself before she sank to floor.

"Make it stop," she whispered to herself, a pleading desperation in her voice. "Please, make these terrible nightmares stop."

The walls had no answers to her pleas and with a resigned sigh Paula stood and turned on the cold water to splash her face several times. She patted it dry with the white hand towel hanging on the bar next to the door then switched off the light. She crept back into bed and looked over at her husband. He never stirred. Paula flipped onto her back, staring at the popcorn ceiling and listening to the cricket chirping outside her window. She blinked several times, commanding herself to stay awake, not wanting the dreams to invade her sleep anymore that night.

# TWENTY

Cicely Anderson was having a shitty day. First, she'd overslept and only woken up when her six year-old tapped her on the shoulder to remind her it was her day to take him to school. And then she overcooked the oatmeal. And she was late dropping him off. And on her way to take the car in for the oil change that was two months overdue, she spilled her lukewarm coffee all over her red suit, which she had just gotten out of the cleaners. The oil never got changed, but she did by running back home, which made her late for the luncheon where she was speaking. Now as she sat in the newsroom going over the rundown for the six, every single story in the first block was a rape, shooting, hit and run or child abandonment.

Some days she thought she wanted to get out of the news business altogether and go live on a farm in Wisconsin and sell cheese. Then she would remember she hated the country, was the number one anchorwoman in Chicago and that she was a news junky who thrived on the fast pace of local news and if she had to be stuck on a farm in Wisconsin with just her husband, her six-year-old and wheels of cheese, she'd run screaming for the hills. Cicely shook her head at the thought and continued going over the rundown. Her phone rang.

"Cicely Anderson," she said in her best breathy, disarming anchorwoman voice.

There was slight hesitation before an answer. "Uh, Cicely, hi, this is Sondra Ellis? Tracy's sister?"

"Oh, my God, Sondra, hi," Cicely said, her tone now soft and welcoming. "How are you?"

"I'm okay. Is this a good time?"

"Oh, yeah this is fine. Can't wait to see the new film when it comes out."

"Oh, yeah, thanks. Should be out this fall."

Cicely was silent for a moment. "So what's up?"

Sondra paused. "Um, well, I was wondering… I'm going to be in Chicago day after tomorrow and I was hoping we could have coffee or something while I was there. I wanted to talk to you about Tracy."

Cicely closed her eyes at the mention of her friend's name. Tracy had been an ace producer and the two women had started at the station at the same time. Cicely had come over to Four after ten years at Channel Three and Tracy was fresh from the Philadelphia affiliate. The two became fast friends and had worked on the regular newscasts together. In addition, as a team, they had produced several award-winning specials for the station. It was Cicely who had hosted Tracy's wedding at her Winnetka home.

"Was there something in particular you wanted to talk about?"

Sondra was silent. "I don't really want to get into it over the phone. It's kind of complicated."

"Oh. Are you sure everything's okay?"

"Well that depends on how you define okay."

"Is there anything I can do?"

"If you could spare twenty minutes or so for me within the next couple of days, that would be more than enough."

"What time are you coming in?"

"Flight gets into O'Hare at noon and I'm staying at the Omni."

"Tell you what. I'm on at six and I usually grab dinner about seven. Why don't I meet you in the lobby around that time and we can eat at the hotel."

"Sounds good."

Cicely leaned back in her chair and crossed her legs. "Great. I'll see you then."

"Tomorrow night, seven."

"Have a safe flight."

"I will. And thanks again. Bye."

The phone went dead in Cicely's ear and she replaced the receiver, wondering what Sondra could possibly want to talk to her about. Cicely knew the Ellis sisters had been exceptionally close and how difficult it had to be for Sondra to come to terms with what happened to Tracy. Three years later, the wound was still fresh in the newsroom. Cicely looked over at the framed photo she kept on her desk from a vacation she and Tracy had taken the summer before she met Phillip. They'd gone to Cozumel and spent more time swimming in jumbo margaritas than in the ocean. The photo showed the two women toasting each other with frosty strawberry concoctions, broad, drunken smiles spread across their faces. Cicely smiled ruefully as she looked at Tracy. Shaking herself back to the present, Cicely turned her attention back to her bloody newscast.

# TWENTY-ONE

*There was blood everywhere. On her hands, her clothes, the tops of her leather shoes. What had she done? She had to leave, she had to run, run away from all the blood…*

Paula jumped up from the couch. She ran her hands over her face and whimpered at the moistness she felt. She jerked her hands away from her face and laughed out of relief when she realized it was sweat dripping from her pores and not blood. Paula stumbled into the kitchen and splashed cold water across her face countless times before she sat down at her kitchen table. She stared down at the vast and un-yielding whiteness in front of her. Every day, every night was torture. The dreams, the horrible, gnawing guilt and paralyzing fear over what she had done. Nevertheless, she had to go on, because if she didn't, it would be all over for her.

She looked at the kitchen clock and forced herself to her feet. She had grocery shopping to do and she was a little behind schedule. Paula pulled her shopping cart out of the laundry room and left for the Pavilion.

# TWENTY-TWO

"But mommy, I love you!"

"I love you too baby, but you're not getting it."

"But mommy, I love chocolate poofy puffs!"

"Yeah, and if I let you have them, you'll be bouncing off the walls."

"I like to bounce off the walls."

"Yeah, but Mommy doesn't, because you leave scuff marks. Now put that back and let's go."

Cindy was trying to navigate the aisles of the Kroger in the Pavilion with her six-year-old pulling every sugary cereal he saw off the shelves and tossing them into the basket, while the four-year-old, who was sitting in the child seat of the cart, kept clapping and giggling, her blonde ringlets bouncing in time.

Cindy turned and saw Paula float down the cereal aisle. She was wearing a blue print cotton housedress and her tar black hair was wrenched back into a severe bun. Cindy licked her lips, feeling the need, for whatever reason, to be neighborly.

"Hi, excuse me? Paula, right?"

Paula turned to look at Cindy, her hand wrapped around a box of Grape Nuts. "May I help you?" she asked in a singsong voice.

Cindy held out her hand. "I'm Cindy Cross. I live across the street from you. The gray house with the red door?"

Paula gave Cindy a blank stare. "Oh," she finally answered. "That's nice."

Cindy narrowed her eyes, trying to figure out what was off about this woman. "Well, I thought maybe we could have coffee sometime. You know, since we're neighbors and all."

Paula tilted her head to one side. "Oh, I don't think that will be possible. My husband and I like to keep to ourselves. But thank you for the invitation." Paula turned and gently placed her Grape Nuts in her basket. Cindy looked down and almost laughed at what she saw. Every item was lined up with military precision, not like her own basket, which was a jumble of grape jelly, Wonder Bread and blue boxes of macaroni and cheese.

"You're not from Stepford are you?" Cindy asked.

Paula blinked. "I'm sorry?"

"You know, Stepford? Your basket is so neat. Just like a Stepford wife." Cindy shook her head. "Sorry, bad joke."

Paula wrinkled her nose. "I'm from here. Now. If you will excuse me." With a determined steeliness, Paula shifted her basket past Cindy's and proceeded down the aisle. Cindy stood staring at Paula's retreating back, fascinated.

"What a nut job," Cindy muttered. Her four-year-old's gleeful giggles snapped Cindy back to the task at hand and she continued on with her shopping. Finally, she finished and was on her way, still puzzling over her encounter with the beyond creepy Paula.

# TWENTY-THREE

Paula was consumed with dinner preparations. Now all she needed to do was add the Sweet'N Low to the tea. Paula opened her pantry door and reached into the Sweet'N Low box and was horrified to discover it was empty.

"Oh no," she whispered. She snatched the box out of the pantry, clawing at the bottom of the box for that elusive packet of artificial sweetener.

Paula's face crunched in worry and her hand clamped around her forehead, terrified about what she should do. Phillip always required a half a pack of Sweet'N Low in his iced tea and she'd forgotten to get a new box at the store. Phillip would be home any minute and there would be no time to get to the Pavilion. This was one time she wished she could hop in the car and go.

"What am I going to do?" She looked up. "Maybe she has some," Paula whispered. Smoothing back her hair, Paula opened her front door. There was a silver car in the driveway of the gray house with the red door across the street, so that must mean the woman was home. Holding her hand over her pounding heart, Paula licked her lips and jogged across the street to the Cross house. Reaching the front door, Paula took a deep breath and pressed the doorbell with a timid finger. It was a few moments before the door flew open to reveal Cindy Cross on the other side.

"Oh. Hi," Cindy said. "Did you need something?"

"Do you have any Sweet'N Low?"

"Huh?"

"Sweet'N Low, I need Sweet'N Low. It's for my husband's iced tea and he won't take anything in his tea but Sweet'N Low and I don't have time to go to the store."

Her words were a stream of vowels and consonants crashing into each other. Paula stole a quick glance over her shoulder, fearful Phillip would come driving up and see her talking to this woman. Paula turned back around.

"Please. Please tell me you have it."

Cindy pursed her lips before she stepped aside. "Sure. I have some. My husband likes Sweet'N Low, too. Come on in."

Paula broke down in tears as she rushed inside. "Oh, thank you, thank you," she said as she followed Cindy inside.

Cindy reached into her pantry and brought out the Sweet'N Low box. "I like real sugar myself, but Chris—that's my husband—he likes this crap." Cindy shook the box. How many do you need?"

"A half a packet."

Cindy stopped shaking the box. "Are you sure that's all you need?"

"Yes. Just half a packet."

Cindy rolled her eyes as she reached inside to produce a handful of pink packets. "Here, take all of these," she said. Paula closed her hands around Cindy's, her eyes shining with tears.

"Thank you. Thank you again. I can't thank you enough. I have to go."

Paula rushed out of the house, leaving a gaping Cindy Cross in her wake. She darted across the street back to her house, with barely enough time to measure out the sweetener for the tea and set the glass on the dining room table before she heard Phillip arrive. Paula mopped her face with a dishtowel before she went to greet her husband. She heard Phillip's footsteps on the front walk and assumed her position.

"Hello, dear," she said as Phillip opened the door. "How was your day?"

Phillip frowned when he looked at her. "Fine." They hugged and Phillip pulled back, looking at Paula's face.

"Paula? What's wrong? You're awfully warm."

She hoped he hadn't felt her trembling like a piece of paper flapping in the wind. She was petrified he would find out she had messed up. She didn't want to go into the closet.

Or worse.

"Oh, I was just in the oven pulling out the chicken. It must be from that." Paula was surprised. She had never lied to Phillip and was stunned at how easily that untruth had rolled off her tongue.

Phillip stared at her for a moment longer before he shrugged. "As long as you're not coming down with anything."

Paula chuckled. "Oh, dear, you know I haven't been sick in forever. It's all those good vitamins you give me that keep me well."

They performed their nighttime ritual, and the rest of the evening passed without interruption. As Paula lay in bed that night, trying to stave off sleep, she couldn't stop thinking about Cindy Cross and how grateful she was that Cindy Cross had saved her.

# TWENTY-FOUR

Sondra hunched over her notebook and the papers spread out around her on the kitchen table. She'd been scribbling the sketch of an idea for a documentary about Tracy. She should have been packing for Chicago, but was compelled to keep investigating the thread of her idea. She wanted to examine Tracy's disappearance along with those of other women of color who disappeared and how their cases were treated both by law enforcement and the media. She'd printed out reams of articles and had filled two jumbo three-ring binders with notes and research. As she usually did at the beginning of a documentary, her heart would race and her mind would spin a million miles a minute as she tried to capture her thoughts and images in a semi-coherent fashion.

She had decided to start in Chicago with what had happened to Tracy and had some ideas about the other women she wanted to profile.

First things first, though.

She rifled through one stack of papers and put her hands on the envelope with Phillip's letter, the edges smudged with dirt from Sondra's constant handling. She slapped the envelope against her palm, still debating if she should reach out to Phillip and open a potential hornet's nest.

Maybe he'd been trying to protect Tracy by leading them all to believe everything was rosy between them.

Or maybe not.

Sondra glanced at the return address on his letter, a street in the town of Royal Oak, Michigan.

Chewing on her pen, Sondra pulled her laptop closer and typed Phillip's name into Google. She clicked around a few links, frowning.

His last known address was the house he and Tracy shared, but nothing in Michigan. She sighed and typed in the return address from the letter and gasped at the result.

It was the address of a mailbox rental company in Royal Oak.

Her fingers trembling, Sondra grabbed her phone and dialed the number that came up.

"Thank you for calling Mailboxes R Us. How can I help you?"

"Yeah, hi. I'm wondering, how long have you been a Mailboxes R Us?"

"Oh about six, seven years."

"What were you before that?"

"I think it was a pizza place. Are you interested in mailbox rental?

Sondra looked at the envelope again. "I'm not sure, but do you forward mail for your customers?"

"We do. If you rent a mailbox from us, we'll forward your mail to you anywhere in the U.S."

"Huh. By chance, would you be able to give me an address you might have on file for one of your customers?"

"I'm sorry ma'am, but we couldn't give out that information."

Sondra sighed. "All right, thanks."

"No problem. Have a great day."

Sondra hung up, perplexed. She ran her finger across the address, lost in thought. Why would Phillip have his mail forwarded?

And where was he having it forwarded to?

# TWENTY-FIVE

As Paula scrubbed the windows of her bedroom with a bright pink rag, she thought again about Cindy Cross. She wrung the rag into the bucket, the water sluicing over her raw, shriveled hands. She now thought maybe… she wanted to ask him, but was afraid of the response. Paula thought about asking him while she prepared dinner, formulating the words inside her head while she worked, proposing opening lines, imagining his replies.

After feeding Phillip the first bites of his dinner, Paula paid lavish attention to her baked fish, hoping to find the courage to ask him the question. Finally, she took a deep breath and dove in.

"Dear?" she asked, her voice pitching slightly upward.

Phillip looked up from his asparagus. "Yes?"

Paula bit her bottom lip and focused her gaze on her salmon, afraid to look at Phillip. "Well, I was wondering if I may be allowed to have coffee sometime with our new neighbor across the street?" Paula stopped and let the question hang in the air between them. Phillip set his fork down.

"What?"

Paula swallowed and looked down at the food on her plate, pushing it around with her fork. "It's just that, well, I saw her at the market the other day and she mentioned perhaps we could have coffee sometime and I thought it might be nice to… have a friend."

Phillip leaned back in his chair, incredulous. "You talked to her?"

Paula's face froze as her lips flapped. "It was just a moment, a few seconds really—"

"What did you say to her?"

"Nothing, nothing at all, I swear."

"You know why that's not a good idea," he said, his voice softer than it had been moments before.

"I won't say anything, I swear. I'll be good. I won't tell her anything, I won't slip. I promise."

Phillip shook his head. "I'm afraid I'm going to have to say no. It just wouldn't be wise."

Paula jumped up and ran over to Phillip. She dropped to her knees and clutched his calves. "Oh, please. Please! Nothing will happen. I swear."

Phillip looked down into Paula's earnest face and shook his head. "No, Paula. And that's final."

Paula hung her head and crept back into her seat. The rest of the meal was finished in silence. Paula performed her nightly chores without any of her usual gusto and Phillip seemed not to notice his wife's gloomy mood.

That night, as the water gushed into the tub, Paula cried, her tears ceasing when she turned off the faucet. After she'd put on her mint green nightgown and lain in bed, Phillip came in and stood over her.

"Paula?"

"Yes?"

"I will let you have this one privilege. But no one else and no more. You have too much to do here. If it interferes, even a little, it will be taken from you. Do you understand?"

Paula sat up and clapped her hands together with the glee of an exuberant child. "Oh, yes, yes, I understand," she said.

"And it can't be more than once a week and for no longer than twenty minutes."

Paula's face lit up like a Christmas tree as she threw her body around Phillip in gratitude. "Oh, dear, thank you. Thank you so much. You are so wonderful."

Phillip nodded in agreement. "Yes. Yes, I am."

# TWENTY-SIX

Paula had never been a vain woman, partly because she never thought of herself as attractive or stylish for that matter. When it came to her appearance, practical was the mantra she lived by. In fact, she never went clothes shopping; Phillip ordered all of her clothes online, deeming shopping a "frivolous activity." Besides, he knew what looked best on her. But today, she was going to Cindy Cross' house and she wanted to look extra special. She had decided on a purple dress and was adjusting her stockings when Phillip came into the kitchen brandishing her vitamins.

"Good morning, dear," she said, her voice brimming with cheer as she opened her mouth. Phillip placed the vitamins inside and she downed them with one gulp of her orange juice.

"You're in a good mood today," he commented as he sat down at the table and waited for Paula to serve him.

"I'm going to see Cindy Cross today," she said as she placed a bowl of shredded wheat and an elaborately arranged plate of peaches, strawberries, and cantaloupe in front of Phillip.

She held his glass of juice to his lips and waited for him to sip. She sat down across from him, her eyes shining. "I'm very happy. What do you think about this outfit?"

Phillip held a spoonful of cereal to his lips. "If I were you, I would worry less about clothes and more about making sure things continue to run smoothly in our home. Dinner had better be on time tonight, or I will revoke this privilege."

"Oh, don't worry, dear. It will be. It will be. Meatloaf. Just like every Tuesday." Paula didn't even mind that she had to have sex with Phillip that night she was so excited.

Phillip chewed and nodded. "I hope so."

Paula smiled. "Of course dear."

"Is my lunch ready?"

"Just about. I just need to fill the thermos with soup."

Phillip nodded his approval and popped a strawberry into his mouth. "Very good. Carry on."

Paula walked into the kitchen to finish preparing Phillip's lunch. She put the bag down on the table next to him and waited for him to give the signal that he was done so Paula could clear the dishes. She went to the hall closet for Phillip's blazer and held it up for him. He went to put it on and frowned.

"Paula, you didn't press this."

She looked down. "Yes, I did. This morning, when I woke up."

Phillip ran his index finger under the lapel, highlighting a slight wrinkle near the edge. "No, Paula, I don't think you did."

Paula clutched the collar, her hands starting to sweat. "I promise, I did."

Without saying a word, Phillip grabbed Paula, who dropped the jacket as he yanked her toward their bedroom.

"Phillip, no, no," she said as she tried to drag her feet to make him stop.

Phillip continued as if he hadn't heard his wife's pleas. He stood her in front of the bed and crossed his arms. "Take your underwear off and bend over," he said.

Paula wrung her hands and shook her head. "No."

Phillip sighed. "Do not make me ask you again. Take off your underwear and bend over, or I will do it for you. I think you would prefer to do it yourself."

Crying, Paula lifted up the hem of her purple dress and pulled her thick, white granny panties and pantyhose down until they were pooled around her ankles. Sobbing, she bent over, the bottom of her dress bunched in her hands. She heard the whoosh of his leather belt as he jerked it through the loops of his pants. She jammed her eyes shut and waited, holding her breath. The first slap came with a definitive thwack across her bare skin. She let out a yelp as salty tears fell into her mouth. Another loud smack landed on her bottom, stinging her flesh. Twice more, Phillip slashed her with his belt before he told her to stand up. Paula was hiccupping from crying as she struggled to pull up her panties and stockings and dropped her dress.

"Shut up," Phillip said as he put his belt back on. Paula clamped her hand over her mouth, her shoulders still heaving.

"Go into the bathroom," he said.

Mute, Paula turned and stumbled into the bathroom, tears cascading out of her eyes like a waterfall. He pointed to the floor, her cue to drop down. She winced as her stinging bottom made contact with the icy tile.

Now," Phillip said as he stood over her. "You will stay in this bathroom all day. I will let you out when I return home, at which time you will change the sheets on the bed, bathe, then go right to sleep. Do you understand?"

Paula nodded, too afraid to speak.

"I didn't hear you Paula."

"I understand."

"Obviously, there will be no visits with Cindy Cross today. In light of this morning's problems, I will have to rethink my position on that."

Without a word, Phillip shut the door and locked it from the outside. Paula lay down on top of the white bathroom rug and cried the rest of the day.

# TWENTY-SEVEN

Sondra sipped her club soda while she waited for Cicely. She was desperate for a cigarette, but Chicago, like New York, was smoke-free. She drummed her fingers on the seat next to her and kept an eye out for her sister's best friend. She saw her breeze through the door in all her five foot two, size zero glory. Her pink suit was flawless against her milk white skin, which offset the soft sweep of dark brown hair and flashing green eyes. Sondra threw up her hand to signal to Cicely and upon spotting her, the tiny brunette click-clacked on her teeny high-heeled sandals over to where Sondra was sitting. Sondra rose to greet her.

"Hey, stranger," Cicely said as she gave Sondra a fierce hug.

"Hey, yourself." Sondra said as she returned Cicely's embrace. She pulled back and motioned to her glass.

"Can I get you something?"

Cicely nodded to the bartender. "Whatever the house pinot noir is, please."

Cicely settled into the chair next to Sondra and turned her attention to her friend's sister. "So… how was your flight?"

Sondra nodded. "Oh, it was good. Uneventful."

"So what brings you to town?"

"I'm, um… thinking about doing a film on Tracy and her disappearance."

"Oh. Wow. What brought that on?"

"I was flipping through the newspaper and came across this story about this woman who'd gone jogging—just like Tracy—and disappeared."

"Okay."

"And this story got huge, huge coverage. I mean, you would have thought the Pope had up and vanished. Now, this girl was eventually found dead, but it struck me as kind of interesting how much coverage this got."

Cicely sipped her wine. "Yeah."

"Anyway, I was looking up coverage of Tracy's death and aside from her obits and a few stories you guys did, nada."

"What are you getting at?"

"Okay, so then I found this *USA Today* article about how when white women disappear it's all over the news, but when a black woman disappears," Sondra snapped her fingers, "nothing."

"Sad to say, it happens."

"Originally, I was thinking I would do the documentary about that and Tracy, but now... well, there were some things going on with Tracy before she died."

"Like what?"

"Cicely... did you know Tracy was planning to divorce Phillip?"

Cicely choked on her wine. "Excuse me?"

"I found the number of an attorney, Damon Randall, in her datebook. I called him and he said she wanted to meet with him to discuss divorcing her husband."

"My God. I had no idea."

"She made an appointment to meet with him the Monday after she died."

"You're joking," Cicely said, coughing.

"There's more. Phillip sent a letter to Mimi, telling her he'd gotten remarried."

"Oh, wow."

"Anyway, I wanted to talk to him about Tracy, you know about the documentary and well... everything. I thought maybe he was protecting us by not telling us about the divorce. I just want the full story, right?"

"I get it."

"Well, first I try finding him online and his last listed address is here. Then the address on the letter is some mailbox rental place in

Michigan." Sondra leaned closer. "If you rent a box from them, they'll forward your mail to you anywhere you want them to send it."

Cicely motioned to the bartender for a menu. "Did they give you his address?"

"No, but I have to tell you, I get the feeling he's not in Michigan."

"I'm still trying to wrap my head around the fact she was filing for divorce. Although…"

Sondra sat up. "What?"

"Well, I didn't think too much of this at the time. I didn't think much of it until just now…" Cicely licked her lips. "The last show we worked together, I do remember she kept getting a lot of phone calls that night, and she seemed agitated. I mean the phones are always going crazy and she could handle them like a pro, but this particular night, she seemed really bothered by it."

"Did she tell you who it was?"

Cicely shook her head. "No. Well, she said it was some PR person hounding her, which we get a lot of."

"Who do you think it really was?"

"Jack."

Sondra crunched on her ice. "What makes you say that?"

"Well, a few weeks before Tracy… disappeared, my husband and I were having dinner at Flow, and Jack came over to say hi. Jimmy went to the restroom, and I asked him how he was—really—and he said he still loved her, but that he wished her nothing but happiness. But…"

"But you don't believe him."

"No, it's not that. It's just… sometimes, when you love someone, you'll do things you never thought you would do—good and bad."

"Did you tell her about what Jack said?"

"No. It wasn't my place to tell her that kind of news."

Sondra tapped her finger against the bar, disturbed. "I ran into Jack myself not too long ago."

"Really," Cicely said, surprised. "Where?"

"In New York—he was in town on business. He also said he saw Tracy the night before her disappearance. Told me that she told him she was unhappy."

"Unhappy about what?"

"He said she ran away before she told him anything."

Cicely wrinkled her nose. "Did he tell the police?"

"No. Said he didn't know what difference it would have made and he didn't want to lay that on Phillip. You know, him wondering if his wife was doing her ex, that kind of thing."

"I could see that."

Sondra chewed on what was left of the nail of her index finger. "What did you think of Phillip?"

Cicely shrugged. "He seemed nice enough. I never thought he was her type though. If I'm being honest, I think Jack was her soulmate, but you know, it doesn't always work out with your soulmate. Still, she seemed like she was really in love with Phillip."

"Did you like him? Phillip, I mean."

"Um... he was okay. I mean, it took me a while to warm up to him, but he seemed all right. Like I said, though, I wouldn't have picked him for her, that's for sure."

Sondra snorted. "That's the same thing I said."

"He was... quiet, just... I don't know. Just a different energy from Jack, which we were all used to and loved."

"In that letter he sent my mother, he went on and on and about what a great marriage he and Tracy had."

"Well, maybe it's like you said, he was trying to protect you all from whatever was going on between them."

"I guess."

"Maybe they just realized that they had rushed into things," Cicely said. "I mean they hadn't even known each other a year when they got married." Cicely picked up her wineglass. "Besides, she was probably too embarrassed to talk about any problems. Whatever they may have been. Of course she's not here, so we can't ask her."

Sondra picked up her glass. "There wasn't anything in her journal either." She paused. "Tell me about the last time you talked to her."

Cicely swallowed her wine before she spoke. "Well, we did the ten together that Thursday. And except for that business with the phone calls, she was fine. Anyway, she was taking a personal day on Friday, so we talked about that as we walked out together that night. She said if I wasn't doing anything over the weekend to give her a call and we'd go catch a movie or something. I called her Saturday afternoon and got her voicemail. I called her again on Sunday when I hadn't heard from her and left her another voicemail. Again, at the time, I didn't think anything of it. Like she got busy with other stuff and forgot to check her messages. She wasn't expected back to work until the following Monday. Sunday night, Phillip called and asked if I had talked to Tracy, because he had left her a few voicemails and she hadn't called him back."

"Then what?"

"The police were called and as you know, we did a few stories, Phillip came back, passed out fliers—we all did—and by the end of the week, we got the call her body had been found."

"What did he seem like?"

"He was frantic, I mean just terrified something had happened to her. A total wreck."

"What did you tell the police about Phillip?"

"That as far as I knew, he and Tracy were happy. He was cleared as a suspect almost immediately. He was in Milwaukee at that conference. Probably a hundred people saw him."

"Well, at this point, I don't know what the hell to think. Maybe it's like Gary said... I should just let Tracy go." She paused. "Except I wanna talk to Jack again."

"Can I do anything?"

"I was wondering if you could pull the tapes of the coverage from Tracy's disappearance. I'd like to look at them, maybe use them. I don't know."

"Of course. I can have an intern pull them. Stop by any time after two and I'll set you up in an editing bay so you can look at them. Station is just down the street from here, big red four out front. Can't miss it."

Sondra smiled. "I remember. Cicely, thank you so much. For everything."

"You know, even though we weren't related by blood, I felt as close to her as anyone in my own family."

Sondra sniffed, the all-too-familiar tears welling in her eyes. "She had that effect on people. Just made everyone feel... welcome."

Cicely lifted her glass in the air, and Sondra picked up her now re-plenished club soda.

"To Tracy," Cicely said.

"To Tracy."

# TWENTY-EIGHT

When Phillip arrived home that evening to let Paula out of the bathroom, a fresh wave of tears had unleashed themselves down her already swollen face.

Phillip crossed his arms, disgust smeared across his face. Paula continued to lay crumpled across the bathroom floor like a discarded winter coat in the dead of summer.

"I would have thought you'd have this out of your system by now."

"I'm so sorry I keep disappointing you. I just, I love you so much and want to please you."

"Then why do you insist upon making things so difficult Paula? After everything I've done for you?"

Paula nodded her head as if a puppet master was pulling a string. "You've been so good to me, I know—"

"I've given you my life, given you a good life, certainly better than you would have had otherwise. And what do you do? Treat me like I mean nothing."

Paula's eyes became big watery saucers. "No, no, you're everything. My world, my reason for living."

"I gave up so much to be with you," Phillip continued, as though he hadn't heard Paula. "I had a wonderful life in Chicago. A loving wife who took care of me, a beautiful home." Phillip looked at Paula and narrowed his eyes. "And then you came along—"

Paula jammed her hands over her ears, knowing what was coming. "No please, stop it," she whimpered as her head snapped left to right.

Phillip dropped to his knees and buttoned his hands over Paula's wrists before he wrenched them down by her sides. "And then you came along and threw yourself at me, begging me to take you back, telling me how much better you were for me than she was."

"Please—!"

"And even after I told you I was devoted to my wife, you kept coming at me, pleading and whining—"

"Phillip, no!" Paula squirmed beneath Phillip's grasp, the torrent of water still spurting from her eyes.

Phillip's voice plowed through Paula's protests like a bulldozer. "And then you made her believe we were having an affair, made her want to leave me, and when that wasn't enough, you started stalking her, calling her, following her—"

"Oh, God!"

"And then you killed her! You followed her that night and you smashed that rock into her beautiful face and killed her!"

Paula let out an anguished yelp and tried again in vain to twist away from Phillip's rough grasp on her wrist and the ugly truth that had pushed past his lips.

"But I had to! I had to kill her!"

"And then because I felt sorry for you, I covered for you, kept you from going to jail, put you in the hospital instead. And all I asked in return was that you take care of me, be good to me." Repulsed, Phillip flung Paula's hands down until they hung by her sides like limp strands of spaghetti.

Paula collapsed across the edge of the tub, her tears slippery against the fiberglass. Phillip had verbalized the worst nightmare of them all. She often saw herself running after Tracy that snowy night, her feet crunching into the fresh flakes. She had finally caught up to Tracy and swung her around to face her. The two women had argued and in a rage, Paula had pushed her down onto the ground and slammed that rock into Tracy's face until she finally stopped screaming and writhing. Horrified by what she had done, Paula had called Phillip and begged him to help her. He had agreed, saying it was obvious Paula wasn't well and he would take care of everything.

And he had.

But every day Paula was reminded of what she had done. Phillip had saved her life and she was determined not to let him down.

Phillip was leaning against the doorjamb. "I think you should stay in here the rest of the night. Maybe that will teach you a lesson." For the second time that day, Phillip slammed the door shut behind him and locked it with a strident click.

# TWENTY-NINE

True to its name, Dive's décor boasted an aquatic theme. A water wall separated the bar from the restaurant and water swirled beneath the light blue Plexiglas floors. The deep azure walls were interrupted by stark postmodern black and white prints of various water images. Each table was draped with crisp white linen tablecloths and small cobalt colored vases with white tea lights floating inside. Located in River North, a neighborhood renowned for its upscale restaurants, Dive had been a roaring success with its soul food tapas concept and its sister restaurant, Flow, tucked off the Magnificent Mile on St. Clair, had come on the scene a few years later as a wine bar. Both had made Jack Turner a rich man and a minor celebrity in Chicago.

Sondra now sat inside the dimly lit restaurant waiting for her sister's former boyfriend. Sondra checked her watch. She had called earlier and was told he would be in around eleven. It was now a few minutes past. As was her way, Sondra was growing impatient and let her gaze wander across the vast expanse of blue as the staff bustled around her getting ready for the lunch rush. At eleven-fifteen, Jack came bounding through the door in full deal-making mode, cell phone glued to his ear, shades pulled down over his eyes, and talking a mile a minute. He was swathed in a cream linen shirt and trousers with black leather man sandals or mandals, as Sondra called them. He came to a dead stop when he saw Sondra sitting at the bar staring at him. He hung up and ambled over to her.

"Sondra? Hey, what are you doing here?"

She ran her tongue across her teeth. "I'm in town for a few days. I need to talk to you and it's important."

"Yeah, sure, my office is in the back."

He motioned for Sondra to follow him, and she hopped down off the black iron bar chair. She jogged to catch up to Jack, who was unlocking the door of his office. He turned on the light and set his briefcase, keys and cell phone down on the tempered glass desk.

"Have a seat," he said, gesturing to a straight backed, hammered metal chair with a deep blue cushion. Jack pulled his desk chair around so that he was sitting face-to-face with Sondra.

"So, what's up?" he asked. "What brings you to town?"

Sondra sniffed. "A few things. I saw Cicely Anderson last night." She waited to see what kind of reaction she got from him.

"How's she doing? I haven't seen her in a while."

She pressed her lips together into a thin line. "I want to know what was going on with you and my sister."

Jack frowned. "What do you mean?"

"Were you having an affair?"

"What? No, of course not."

"She was leaving her husband and Cicely said you told her you still loved Tracy and Tracy was going to file for divorce—"

Jack held up his hands in protest. "Whoa, whoa, whoa, wait just a minute, she was getting a divorce?"

"Yes, she was—"

"Just what, exactly, are you getting at?"

"Were you and Tracy having an affair?" Sondra repeated.

Jack licked his lips and looked Sondra dead in the eye. "Not only no, but hell no."

"Cicely said Tracy had been getting a lot of phone calls that upset her right before she disappeared. Was it you?"

"Sondra, I am telling you, there was nothing going on between me and Tracy. It's like I told you, I ran into her, she said she was unhappy and that was it. That was the last time I saw her."

"Why didn't you tell the police?"

"I already told you why."

"Where were you the night she disappeared?"

Jack didn't say anything, merely stared at Sondra. "Excuse me?"

"How much did you want her back?" She licked her lips, drops of sweat snaking across her upper lip. She hadn't intended to get so worked up, but the more she thought about things, the angrier she got. "Did you get so upset that you killed her? You blew your chance with her and so nobody could have her?"

"How could you even ask me that?"

Sondra looked at Jack, searching for any sign that he was lying. She saw nothing. She broke her gaze and let her head plummet to her chest.

"I'm sorry, Jack, it's just, when I found out she wanted to divorce Phillip and Cicely said you wanted her back…"

Jack looked up at the ceiling, trying to choose his words carefully. "Yes, I loved Tracy more than anything in the world," he said. "I would never hurt her like that. We weren't having an affair; we weren't talking about an affair. Nothing like that at all. Before that last time, I hadn't seen or talked to Tracy in over a year." Jack brought his head back down and focused his eyes directly at Sondra. "And that night? I was here at the restaurant. I came in at three and didn't leave until well after two A.M. Then I went home and slept for ten hours."

Sondra looked at Jack for a few moments. "Okay," she said. "I believe you."

Jack looked down at the floor. "Thank you."

"I just want to know what happened to her. I need to know."

Jack shook his head. "You may never know."

# THIRTY

Paula had slipped out of bed quiet as a mouse. Phillip had finally let her out of the bathroom, but not before he had forced her to her knees and made her tell him over and over how much she loved him before he allowed her to crawl into bed, limp as a rag doll.

This morning, she was determined to show Phillip she was worthy of his love. She pressed his blazer four times, almost burning a hole into the thick fabric. She made him three slices of French toast instead of his customary two and four slices of turkey bacon rather than three. She just wanted to make him happy, because when he was happy, she was happy. She spread the peanut butter for his lunchtime pb&j sandwich across the fluffy white bread, mindful not to tear holes in the delicate slices. After packing Phillip's lunch, Paula forced her trembling fingers to assemble the breakfast food on the table. She waited for him to emerge from the master bedroom, her nerves tight as a drum. Finally, the door creaked open and she heard him pad across the abundant white carpet. He gave her a stern look before his eyes swept across the table.

"I made extra breakfast this morning," she said. "I hope it's okay."

Phillip set a cold stare on Paula. "I've been forced to have fast food for my dinner the past few nights. You know how much I hate that."

Paula's eyes dissolved into pools of water. "Oh, I am so sorry you had to do that. Can you ever forgive me?"

"You will have to do a lot to earn my trust back, Paula. Are you prepared to do that?"

"Oh, yes, anything, anything at all."

Phillip gave her a curt nod of approval. "Good. We can start today. I would like you to start by disinfecting the walls from top to bottom. Then scrub the tiles in both bathrooms with a toothbrush. Afterwards, I want you to sweep and mop the garage. And I still expect dinner to be on the table at six when I get home. If I find any of those things not done when I return, you will be punished."

Paula stood in front of her husband, her eyes bolted to the floor before she nodded her agreement. "Yes, dear. I will do all those things," she whispered.

Phillip threw back his shoulders. "I'm glad we understand each other. Oh. And one more thing. You will feed me my entire meal this morning."

Paula pinched her lips shut. "Yes, dear."

"All right then. Now. Open wide."

Obediently, Paula held out her tongue for her vitamins and followed them with a glass of water. Phillip waited for Paula to seat him at the kitchen table. She started to pull up a chair next to him when he held out his hand.

"Standing," he said.

With a plaintive inhale, she stood in silence next to Phillip and fed him each forkful of his breakfast. She managed not to spill anything, and when he indicated he was done, she dabbed the corners of his mouth with the soft fabric of the white linen napkin she'd tucked into his collar. Paula went into the kitchen to retrieve the lunch she had made for Phillip, who stood by the closet, impatient for his blazer. She handed him his lunch and got the blazer out of the closet. As she started to put it on him, he grabbed it from her and held it up for inspection.

"Much better job today. You are already improving."

"I just want you to be happy, dear," she murmured as she helped him into the jacket.

He smiled and gave her a cold peck on the cheek. "We haven't had relations yet this week. Expect to have them tonight."

Paula swallowed. "Yes, dear. Have a good day."

Phillip turned on his heel and left the house. Paula stood rooted to the spot until she heard his car pull away. With an audible sigh of relief, Paula fell against the couch for several minutes before she began her chores for the day.

# THIRTY-ONE

After her visit with Jack, Sondra was still worked up and had smoked two cigarettes in six blocks.

Needing to get out of her head for a few hours, she wandered into a nearby movie theatre to watch some inane comedy that elicited few laughs. Still, it felt good to focus on something other than the persistent questions swirling around her head about Tracy. She was about to walk back to her hotel when she changed her mind and hailed a cab instead.

"Belmont Harbor please," Sondra said. The cab merged onto Lake Shore Drive and headed north. As soon as she got out, she lit up and began walking east toward the lake. This particular stretch of Belmont was filled with an endless assortment of trendy boutiques, glittery yogurt shops and cramped convenience stores filled with the pervasive musk of incense. It was ironic that Sondra lived in a swanky Manhattan high-rise while Tracy had lived in a funky Chicago neighborhood.

Sondra reached the trail and began to stroll along the lakefront, where summer was in full swing. Sailboats dotted the brilliant blue waters of Lake Michigan; young mothers pushed strollers where their sleeping babies dozed; rollerbladers whizzed by and joggers bopped down the trail. Sondra enjoyed the warm summer winds washing over her, though she hated the reason she was here.

Just ahead of her, Sondra could see the rocks where Tracy had been found. She quickened her pace before breaking into a run. Hyperventilating, she finally reached the spot where that dog walker had found Tracy. She knelt down and looked at the jagged and broken boulders. Sondra shuddered, the hairs on the back of her neck standing at attention. The points of the boulders jutted up at varying angles, like pins jammed into a pin cushion. Sondra stared at them and let her fingers trail over the rocks, wincing in pain as she thought about one of those spiky edges driving into her sister's face, splitting it open. Had that maniac been watching her, planning what he would do to her? Was it spontaneous? Had he grabbed Tracy from behind? Maybe he'd asked for the time or directions. When had she realized he meant to harm her? How long had they struggled before she understood that she would suffer a painful and violent death at this man's hands?

Sondra began to twitch with violent sobs as all the horrific possibilities of those last few moments of her sister's life danced in front of her. Sondra looked out over the horizon at Lake Michigan, her eyes brimming with tears, and tried not to picture how it must have been. Sondra stood and let her cigarette drop, watching it roll away from her. It got caught on the sharp corner of a rock before falling over the edge and out of sight.

# THIRTY-TWO

Sondra wasn't sure how long she sat at Belmont Harbor. She just wanted to be lost in her thoughts, even though she couldn't make sense of all the emotions churning inside her. With a heavy grunt, Sondra got to her feet and started walking until she found herself back on Belmont. Sondra thought about Tracy's house not too far away. Maybe… maybe she would stop by and see… Well, she didn't know what, but something was drawing her to it. A few short blocks later, she found herself standing on the sidewalk out front.

Sondra took a deep breath, climbed the stairs and rang the doorbell. It was a few moments before a short, slightly overweight woman with frizzy blonde hair and red acne scars coloring her cheeks answered the door.

"Can I help you?" she said with the cautious tone of a woman who had perhaps shooed away one too many salespeople.

Sondra bit her bottom lip and smiled. "Hi. My name is Sondra, and my sister owned this house before you, and I was wondering if it might be okay if I took a look around."

"Yeah, I don't think that's a good idea. Goodbye." She went to shut the door before Sondra called out.

"Wait!" The woman stopped and gave Sondra another wary stare.

"Okay, that sounded stupid. Let me start over. My sister and her husband lived in this house a few years ago. She disappeared and later di… died…" Sondra swallowed, trying to compose herself. "And, I'm just trying to get some closure, and I wanted to take a look around… to say goodbye."

The woman narrowed her eyes, trying to decide if she believed Sondra's story. "What was your sister's name?"

"It was Tracy. Tracy Ellis. Her husband was Phillip Pearson."

This seemed to reassure the woman. "Yeah, we used to get their mail for a while."

Sondra swallowed. "Did you get a forwarding address by chance?"

"No, we were just told to send anything we got to the guy's—Phillip's—attorney and he'd make sure he got everything."

Sondra cocked her head. "Do you still have the name of the attorney by chance? I'm sorry to be asking all these questions, I'm just trying to sort through some things. I was out of the country when my sister disappeared, and then had to leave again after her funeral. I've got a lot of loose ends."

The woman softened her stance somewhat. "Um, yeah, probably. If you come in for a minute, I can look for it."

Sondra smiled. "Thank you," she said as she stepped inside. She carefully closed the door behind her and looked around. It was jarring to be in Tracy's house and see that it was now someone else's. The formerly rich red walls were now butter yellow and the décor had transformed from urban chic to French country. The maple hardwood floors were buried under a swath of beige Berber carpet, a bright yellow baby swing stood where the TV used to be, and toys littered the floor. The living room reeked of spoiled fruit juice, kitty litter, and dirty diapers. Sondra stopped breathing through her nose. The woman reappeared holding a card in her hand and handed it to Sondra.

"I think this guy was handling the sale of the house and a bunch of other stuff for the guy—Phillip. You know, come to think of it, there was a box of stuff that got left here. I tried to give it to the lawyer to send on, but the guy said he didn't want it. We just never got around to getting rid of it. It's out in the garage if you want to take a look."

"What's in there?" Sondra asked as she shoved the card into her back pocket.

The woman shrugged. "Some books, other odds and ends. We found one of the books shoved behind a panel in the garage. I think it was a diary, so we threw it in there, too."

"Uh, yeah," Sondra nodded. "I'll take whatever you've got."

"My name is Maureen by the way," the blonde said as she led the way to the garage behind the house. "We moved in a little over a year ago. It's a beautiful old house."

"Yeah. Tracy loved living here."

Maureen clicked the remote for the garage door, which yawned open. Maureen went in and maneuvered around a dusty red SUV before she came out holding a medium-sized box. She set it down in front of Sondra. "Do you have a car?"

"No. I'm staying downtown, so I'll get a cab." Sondra nudged the box with her toe. "It's not heavy, is it?"

"No, not really. You can walk out here to Belmont and you should be able to get a cab pretty easily."

"Thanks. I'll do that." She shot her hand out to Maureen, who returned Sondra's firm grasp. "I appreciate your time."

"Sure."

Sondra smiled and reached down to pick up the box, which was relatively easy to handle. Maureen went back into the house and Sondra made her way out to the street, where she quickly hailed a cab.

# THIRTY-THREE

"So she flipped out over some Sweet'N Low?"

Cindy nodded and swabbed an arm across her forehead. "Yup. Totally nuclear. Kind of scared me, to tell you the truth."

Cindy and Mira had become jogging buddies and were coming up on their fourth of six miles. Cindy had relayed the story about the grocery store and the Sweet'N Low episode.

"He's got to be hitting her. I really think this could be some kind of domestic situation," Cindy said.

"You really think so?"

"You saw that movie, what was it, with Julia Roberts? Enemy something? Remember, if she didn't have things exactly the way he wanted them, he'd beat the shit out of her?"

"Oh, God, you're right. This sounds exactly like that movie. We should go to the police."

Cindy nodded her head slightly as she continued to pump her arms and search for the final surge of adrenaline she needed to finish the last two miles.

Cindy looked over at Mira. "You could go. You've known her longer."

Mira snorted. "Have you forgotten the bloody locksmith story?"

"Oh, right. Still, though…"

The two women continued jogging for a few moments, the only sounds they made being raspy breaths.

"Maybe it's like you said," Mira finally wheezed. "She's not all there and he's trying to protect her."

"I don't know," Cindy said, defeated. "I just don't know."

The two women kept jogging down the trail, unsure of what to do about Paula.

# THIRTY-FOUR

It was as Maureen said; a box full of odds and ends. A small black lampshade; an alarm clock, some books Sondra knew must have been Tracy's; an umbrella; a few old purses. It wasn't until she had taken everything out of the box that Sondra noticed one last book at the bottom. She reached in and picked it up, turning it over in her hands. It was red silk with a swirling, gold Asian-inspired design and a lock across its opening.

She flashed back again—that last journal ended three months before Tracy died.

"*This* must be her last journal," Sondra said, turning the book over in her hands. Was this the one Maureen said had been stuffed in a garage panel?

Sondra searched to see if there was a key for it and found none. After looking around her room for something to use to pick the lock, she finally resorted to slamming the hotel hair dryer on top of it several times before it burst open.

"Whatever works," she mumbled as she carried the book back into the bedroom and sat on the edge of the bed. Sondra flipped back to the front of the book and began to read.

The first words stopped her.

*I made a mistake.*

"Oh, God," Sondra whispered as she licked her lips, afraid of what she would read next.

*"I feel like Phillip lied to me. When we were dating, we talked about having children and he said nothing would make him happier. So now, here we are, three months into our marriage and I asked him what he thought about trying to have a baby in another year, year and a half. And he fucking freaked out.*

*He said it was way too soon to be thinking or talking about this and why was I bringing this up and that he'd been thinking about it and he really didn't want children after all. I was stunned. I mean, I thought that's what we both wanted. He SAID that's what he wanted. And now this??? I feel like I got sucker punched.*

Later passages revealed jealous rages, obsessive behavior, temper tantrums, crying fits, and Tracy's growing disillusionment and downright disgust with the man she'd married.

*"I don't know how much more of this I can take. I pictured a long and wonderful life with this man, of growing old together but now… it's time to look for the exit row. I suggested counseling. All that got me was crying and begging and 'I love you's' and please don't leave me, he just needs me, not a shrink. He's driving me fucking crazy. Every day is a new drama. It's not like when we first met. He hangs on my every move. It's almost like… like he can't function without me. He calls me constantly, questions everything I do. In fact, I'm pretty sure he's been snooping through my diary. I didn't see him, but the way it was turned in my nightstand drawer… I don't know; it just didn't look right. I didn't dare confront him about it, 'cause God only knows what kind of havoc would have rained down on my head. To be on the safe side, I bought this new one and am hiding it in a panel in the garage he doesn't know anything about. I don't know what happened. It was never like this.*

*Yesterday, I had lunch with Cicely and didn't hear my cell phone. So by the time I got home, he was furious, accusing me of having an affair and telling me what a liar I was. I checked into the Park Hyatt and turned my phone off. I turned it back on and he'd left me fifty messages. FIFTY. I CANNOT live like this.*

Sondra put down the diary, stunned. Her mind whirled like a

vigorously shaken snowglobe. And like a snowglobe, the bits of fake snow began to settle down inside Sondra's brain and the scene became clear.

Phillip.

Tracy.

Tracy was leaving Phillip.

And that's why she'd told Jack she was unhappy.

Not because there was infidelity.

Because she wanted out of her miserable marriage.

She flashed back to those awful days after Tracy had been found. Phillip, so broken up over his wife's death. Phillip, so guilty that he'd been gone when she disappeared. Phillip, so supportive of Sondra and her parents during and after the funeral. Phillip, weeping about how he didn't know how he would go on without Tracy.

"He lied," Sondra whispered. "It was all a lie."

# THIRTY-FIVE

He had spent hours practicing in front of the mirror. They always looked at the spouse first, so he had to be convincing when they questioned him. He had written down a list of questions they might ask him on a yellow legal pad and rehearsed his answers in front of his reflection.

"Mr. Pearson," he said aloud in a voice a good three octaves lower than his own. "When did you say the last time was that you spoke to your wife?"

Phillip took a deep breath and said in a shaky whisper, "Saturday. We talked Saturday."

"What'd you talk about?"

"Um, I don't know. I told her how the conference was going; I asked what she'd done that day. She told me she was going jogging and would call me when she got home."

Okay, good. Good tone, the definite sound of a worried husband who was still holding out hope that his wife would be found alive and well.

"Was that something she did often? Jogging, I mean. At night?"

Phillip cast his eyes down then looked back up at his likeness in the glass. "Sometimes on the weekends, yes. Not late at night. She works nights during the week. But occasionally she goes jogging on a Saturday evening before we go to dinner or a movie."

That was a lie, but no one would know any different.

"And the last time you talked to her, what was her mood?"

Phillip shrugged in confused disbelief. "She was fine. Her usual happy self. Tracy is a very upbeat person."

For good measure, he wrung his hands, but not too much. He didn't want to seem too nervous, tip them off that something was up. Just enough to seem worried, but not suspicious.

"What's her jogging route?"

"Usually down by the lake, right along Belmont Harbor, up to Oak Street Beach."

That was good. It wouldn't seem weird when she was found along the lakefront.

"Mr. Pearson, what was your marriage like?"

"God… we're basically still newlyweds… we're happy… happy… we have a good marriage…" Dissolve into tears, but don't overdo it. Don't want too seem phony. And refer to her in the present tense. That was key.

"Can you think of anyone who would want to hurt your wife?"

Give incredulous laughter. "God. No. Everyone loves Tracy."

Fight back the tears as you think about the fact that her life could be over. Wring hands some more.

"Please, you have to find her. It's cold and she could be hurt… hungry… alone. Please. Please find my wife."

Let his voice tremble ever so slightly on that last bit. Hold the gaze of the detective and then ask feebly if they were through; he wants to get back to passing out fliers around the neighborhood.

The detectives would give him a sympathetic smile and nod. Of course, they would say. We'll let you know if we have any more questions. He would put on a brave face and usher them out the door. The detectives would compare notes on his demeanor, check his alibi and determine that he had nothing to do with his wife's disappearance. Phillip straightened up and smiled.

This would be so easy.

# THIRTY-SIX

Cindy sat inside her silver Honda in front of the police station for a good thirty minutes, still trying to talk herself into going in. The more she thought about it, the more something just seemed so… *wrong* with Paula; she couldn't get over her neighbor's wackadoo behavior. Cindy would never forgive herself if Paula really was in danger from her husband and she could have done something to stop it and didn't.

Taking a deep breath, Cindy grabbed her bulky brown leather purse from the passenger seat floor and slung it over her shoulder as she stepped out of the car. She pushed open the heavy glass door and strode up to the desk sergeant with false bravado.

"Excuse me."

"Yeah," the sergeant replied, never looking up from his computer screen.

Cindy pursed her lips. "I'd like to talk to someone about my neighbors."

"What about 'em?"

Cindy went to answer then stopped herself, not sure what to say. Well, the wife mops her driveway and is terrified of not having enough Sweet'N Low? Cindy shook her head at how goofy it all sounded and focused her gaze once more on the bored face in front of her.

"My neighbors who live across the street. I think the husband might be hitting the wife."

The desk sergeant looked up, bored. "Have you seen him strike her?"

"Well no, but—"

"Ever heard them get into any violent arguments, or seen any bruises on her?"

"No…"

"So what is it, *exactly,* that leads you to believe he's abusing her?"

Cindy shifted in her brown leather flats, feeling even more foolish than when she'd walked in. "I mean nothing specific, just a feeling."

"Ma'am, unless you actually witness an assault, there's nothing we can do. And besides, she would have to be the one to press charges."

"You're telling me you're just going to sit there and do nothing?"

The sergeant held up his hands as if to ask what Cindy expected him to do. "Ma'am, like I said, unless you actually see something, our hands are tied by the law. If you do see something, call us, we'll pay them a visit." The phone rang and the sergeant turned away from Cindy and began to dispense more by-the-book cynicism to yet another helpless citizen.

Cindy stood in front of the sergeant for a few moments more before finally letting out an exasperated sigh and walking out of the police station.

# THIRTY-SEVEN

He had known they were watching him. But he had been prepared for the scrutiny. When his in-laws had flown in and were staying at the house, he would sit in the living room clutching one of her sweaters. When he heard them approach, he would comment quietly that he hoped she wasn't cold before he would break down in tears. His mother-in-law would rush over and comfort him, murmuring that she would be found, that she would be all right, they just had to keep believing, keep the faith. His father-in-law would paw his shoulder in an attempt to disperse quiet strength. Finally, he would say he was okay and how much he appreciated their being there.

He stopped eating in order to give himself a gaunt appearance and took caffeine pills at bedtime, leading people to assume he was struggling with endless sleepless nights. It had worked. Everyone the police questioned all said the same thing; he was extremely distraught, working round-the-clock to spread the word. Coupled with his alibi... no one would ever suspect a thing. Sometimes he felt guilty, but he would swat it away like an annoying gnat. After all, the most important thing was that no one ever figure out the truth.

# THIRTY-EIGHT

Though she was half-white, Sondra had been blessed with some booty. However, it wasn't doing her any good at the moment, as the hard wooden bench she was sitting on pressed uncomfortably against her tailbone. She crossed her legs for the umpteenth time that afternoon, wondering how much longer she would have to wait. Sondra had skipped meeting Cicely at the station after the revelation of what was really going in her sister's marriage; she was simply too drained to leave her room. So she'd ordered up a hot fudge sundae and spent the night not watching a *Law and Order* marathon. It was now morning and Sondra had told Cicely she would be by later.

"Miss Ellis?"

Sondra looked up at the mention of her name. A tall woman with a badge, short dark hair, a boxy, sand-colored silk blouse and matching pants was standing in front of her.

"Detective Wallace?"

The woman held out her hand to Sondra. "Yes. Good to meet you."

Sondra gave a small smile. "I wish I didn't have to meet you."

Detective Marion Wallace gave her own wan smile. "Well, let's hope our time together is brief. Right this way."

Marion took long strides towards the back of the station house as Sondra lollygagged behind her, absorbing her surroundings. She'd never been to a police station before and was fascinated. Junkies, prostitutes and thugs filled the waiting room—some screaming profanities as they protested their innocence, others slack-jawed and glassy-eyed as they sat slumped over in the hard metal chairs waiting for who knew what. She wondered what stories lurked behind the sad, droopy gazes. Sondra shook her head and caught up with the detective.

"Tell me," Marion said as she gestured to a chair in front of her desk, "what can I do for you? You really didn't say much when you called."

Sondra cleared her throat. "I understand you were the lead detective looking for my sister, Tracy Ellis."

"I was."

Sondra leaned forward, propping her elbows on the edge of the gray metal desk. "Well, I was hoping you could fill in some blanks for me."

Marion clasped her fingers together in front of her. "I'll do what I can."

Sondra took a deep breath and plowed through. "According to a friend of Tracy's, the last time anyone talked to her was my brother-in-law on Saturday evening?"

Marion picked up the case notes from the file in front of her and nodded. "Phillip Pearson talked to his wife Saturday evening on January twenty-seventh for fifteen minutes. He left her two subsequent voicemails, both on Sunday the twenty-eighth, neither of which she returned. Called her friend, Cicely Anderson, Sunday afternoon when Tracy still hadn't called back, to ask if she had heard from Ms. Ellis. Mr. Pearson called to report his wife missing that same day. Ms. Ellis' body was found behind the rocks of Belmont Harbor that Thursday, February second. Autopsy declared her death to be from blunt trauma to the face." Marion set her notes down and looked up at Sondra. "As far as we were able to determine, your sister went jogging, something we were told she did often, and was in the wrong place at the wrong time."

"It took almost a week to find her body."

Marion looked at her notes again. "We had two major snowstorms that week—one Saturday night and another on Monday—followed by deep freezes that lasted a day or two. Kept most people off the lakefront. It wasn't until the warm-up and thaw a few days later that she was found."

Sondra leaned back in her chair. "Who goes jogging in a snowstorm?"

Detective Wallace snorted. "In this town? You'd be surprised."

Sondra shook her head, trying to wrap her head around this concept. "And the police believe...?"

"That Ms. Ellis went jogging Saturday evening and was mugged and killed."

"Okay, so, she got mugged. But she wasn't raped or anything? Don't muggers usually carry guns or knives? And aren't most women who are killed usually raped? Why would he smash her face in with a rock?" Sondra struggled to keep from crying as she thought of that concrete shattering Tracy's skull.

Marion twisted her lips into an uncomfortable bow. "We believe your sister's assailant came up behind her and attempted to assault her. She threw her wallet at him. She fought with him and they struggled. She was probably screaming her head off and he couldn't get her to stop. If he was planning to sexually assault her—which not all of these creeps even want to—at this point wasn't worth it—not to mention how cold it was—and used the rock to keep her quiet. He took the cash from her wallet, flung it on the beach as he fled. Happens all the time."

Sondra leaned back against the wooden chair, digesting what Marion had told her. "And no witnesses? No one heard or saw anything?"

Marion shook her head. "No. Nothing. We did an exhaustive canvass of the area, didn't turn up anything."

Sondra closed her eyes, tears beginning to well beneath the lids. She wiped her eyes and looked at the detective. "Did you have any suspects? Any at all?"

Marion handed Sondra a Kleenex from the box on her desk. She waited for Sondra to dab her eyes and blow her nose before she continued.

"There wasn't any physical evidence to link Tracy Ellis to any suspect. Unfortunately, the snow and her being frozen like that… the trail started and ended cold. No pun intended." She cleared her throat and looked down, embarrassed. "Sorry."

"What about Phillip? What was his alibi?"

Marion looked back down at her notes. "At a conference in Milwaukee. Left the Thursday before your sister disappeared. Hundreds of people saw him over the course of the conference. His cell phone records indicated he talked to your sister when he said he had and the signals were bouncing off the right towers. The lobby cameras of the hotel he was staying at recorded him leaving for dinner Saturday evening with two people and came back with those same two people around ten. He was ruled out as a suspect immediately. Why?"

Sondra looked down at the desk, wondering whether to share the little bits of information she'd found out over the past few days. She herself still wasn't sure what to make of things.

"I'm just trying to understand what happened," she finally answered, deciding to hold on to what she had learned just a little bit longer.

"Besides, no one we questioned said anything about problems between the two. By all accounts, he was frantic over what may have happened to her."

"Yeah," Sondra sighed, tired by now of hearing that, especially after reading Tracy's diary and knowing about the imminent divorce. "I know."

"I've been doing this a long time, seen a lot of guilty husbands. Your brother-in-law didn't fit the profile. As hard as this is to hear, trust me when I tell you this was a senseless, random act."

Sondra chewed her bottom lip, not believing it was random at all. Her gaze drifted down to the case file open in front of Marion. "Are…" Sondra swallowed. "Are my sister's… pictures in there?"

Marion hesitated as she looked down at the file underneath her palm. "Yes, but Ms. Ellis—"

"Please? I just… I think it will give me closure."

Marion paused again before she relented. "Ok, but I have to warn you—these are pretty graphic."

"That's okay. Please. I want to see them."

Marion pressed her lips into a thin line as she looked at Sondra. Finally, she reached underneath the sheaf of papers in the case file and began to gather the last photos ever taken of Tracy Ellis. She handed them to Sondra gingerly.

"You don't have to do this—"

"I know," Sondra cut her off. With wobbly fingers, Sondra picked up the glossy stack. The picture on top was a front-facing shot. Having been under snow for so many days, the pictures revealed an eerie, frozen death mask. The pink flesh and what had once been bright red blood, now an icy black sludge, mingled with the exposed white facial bones. One eyeball had fallen out of the socket and hung to the side and the whole thing looked like a big black hole where a face used to be.

But it wasn't the colors or intensity of the photos that made Sondra gasp.

"Ms. Ellis, I told you, this would be hard—"

"That's not it," Sondra whispered, her heart stuck in her throat. She looked up at Marion, tears cascading down her cheeks. "That's not Tracy."

"Ms. Ellis, faces look different in death, not to mention how brutal this was—"

Sondra's tears were flowing now as she continued to examine each photo, knowing it wasn't Tracy. "I'm telling you—that's not her. I looked at her every day for fifteen years until I left home for college." Sondra wiped her eyes. "And it's not her."

"Mr. Pearson positively identified her."

Sondra let out a bitter laugh as she tossed the stack onto the desk. "I don't care. It's not her." Sondra thumped the photos with her index finger. "I guarantee you, if my mother saw these photos, she would tell you the same thing."

Marion ran her tongue along her teeth. "You are absolutely positive about this?"

"I'm as sure of this as I'm sitting here. It's not her. It's not Tracy."

"So what are you saying?"

"I don't know, I don't know!" Sondra looked down at the dead woman's photos again. "And son of a bitch, the body was cremated," Sondra murmured. Sondra looked up. "Detective Wallace, I'm not sure what's going on, but I know my alarms are going off like crazy. I think yours should be too." She stood up and looked back down at the mangled woman in the photos.

"That woman is not my sister. I suggest you find out who she really is. And I don't know if that means my sister is dead or alive or what. All I know is, I have to find her, no matter what."

Sondra turned on her heel and walked out of the station.

# THIRTY-NINE

He had just started driving, with no real idea of what his next move should be, when the solution came to him. He stopped at a gas station and found a pay phone.

It was time to call in a chit he never knew he'd need.

"Dr. Keegan."

"Keegan. Phillip Pearson."

Silence on the other end, but Phillip had expected that.

"Phil. It's late. What do you want?"

"I'm calling in that favor you owe me."

An anguished, exasperated sigh from the other end. "Jesus Christ," he muttered.

"I'll bet you thought I was going to forget, didn't you?" Phillip laughed, his breath puffing out in the bitter air like a plume of chimney smoke. "Or I guess a better way to put it is that you were *hoping* I would, huh?"

"Just spit it out, Phil."

"I need you to admit a patient for me. Tonight."

"Are you crazy? It's almost midnight."

"Oh, like you don't check people in at all hours of the night. Consider it an emergency. Oh, and you're the only one I want handling this. No shoving this off onto one of your lackeys."

"There are protocols, Phil, certain way these things have to be done—"

"I don't care. You'll figure out a way around it. You're good at getting out of things."

"Forget it. You're gonna have to come up with something else."

"Nope. This is it. This is the favor I told you I would want one day." Phillip hopped from one foot to the other, trying to keep the blood circulating. He looked at his watch. "I'm about an hour away, which should give you enough time to get out of bed and meet me over there."

An angry sigh this time. "Fine. Fine. I'll meet you there."

Phillip smiled. "See you then."

He hung up, let out a short breath and started walking back to his car. He glanced behind him. She was sedated in the backseat and he estimated she would be coming out just about the time they reached their destination. He'd give her another dose when they got there and instruct Keegan to keep her sedated—among other things. It wouldn't be easy, but it was the only way. He slid behind the wheel and pulled out of the gas station as he turned up the easy listening station and settled in for the drive.

# FORTY

She knew without a doubt the woman in those photos wasn't her sister.

So who the hell was she?

Sondra was sitting at a coffee shop, scrawling all types of questions, answers and narrative into her notebook, trying to make sense of everything. Truthfully, she didn't know what to think anymore, but she knew that she had to keep going in order to figure out the trail, no matter where it led. Sondra looked at her watch and realized she was late for her appointment with Carl Fisher, Phillip's lawyer. She hailed a cab, and within minutes she was in the lobby of his Loop office and the receptionist was taking her to see him.

The stout silver-haired gentleman rose when he saw Sondra and held out his hand. "Ms. Ellis," he said, his thick Midwestern twang ringing in Sondra's ears as he shook her hand. "Nice to meet you."

"Yeah, you too."

Carl sat down and folded his hands in front of him. "What can I do for you, Ms. Ellis?"

"I'm looking for my brother-in-law, Phillip Pearson."

"I'm afraid I don't know where he is. Haven't spoken to him in about a year."

"Well, where was he then?"

"Back in Michigan from my understanding."

"Hmm. What kind of work were you doing for him?"

"Ms. Ellis, you understand I can't divulge the exact nature of my business with Mr. Pearson. What I can tell you is that I settled your sister's estate."

"All right, all right, how about this… I ask vague questions and you nod. Will that work?"

Carl raised his scraggly white eyebrows. "Well, we can try that."

"Did my sister have a life insurance policy?"

"Yes."

"Phillip got all the money when she was declared dead?"

"Yes, he was the beneficiary."

"What about the house? He made money on that, even though it was Tracy's house?"

"Ms. Ellis, your sister and her husband sat down with me right after they got married and drafted their wills. They made themselves the executor of each other's estate, which included all life insurance policies, retirement accounts, investments, etc. So, to vaguely answer your questions, yes, Mr. Pearson was left all of your sister's assets. Your sister wasn't wealthy by any means, but she was careful with her money."

Sondra tapped her finger on the edge of the desk. "And you said the last time you talked to him was about six months ago. Do you have his address?"

"Mr. Pearson preferred to conduct all of our business in person. He would come to my office to collect his mail, sign any papers, and pick up any checks. He would call me periodically to see if we needed to meet, and that's what we would do."

Sondra bit her bottom lip. "So you never had a phone number or address for him? Didn't you think that was strange?"

"Oh, people handle these kinds of things all kinds of ways. I had one client who would only meet with me on the third Sunday of each month in the parking lot of the Jewel on Clark and Division. People are strange. Besides, he always paid me in cash, so I didn't much care how he wanted to conduct our business." Carl paused. "Why are you looking for Mr. Pearson?"

Sondra ran her tongue across her teeth. "Just some family business I wanted to discuss with him. Do you think he'll be calling you anytime soon?"

Carl shook his head. "Doubtful. We concluded business rather swiftly since your sister's estate was pretty well in order."

"If by chance, he does call you, could you call me? Don't tell him I was looking for him, though."

Carl frowned. "Why not?"

"I'd prefer to discuss that with him. Confidentiality. You understand."

Carl gave her a tight smile. "I suppose I could do that."

Sondra scribbled her cell phone number on the back of one of Carl Fisher's cards from the holder on his desk. "I really would appreciate it if you let me know." She stood up and handed Carl her phone number.

"Thanks, Mr. Fisher. You've been very helpful."

"Good day, Ms. Ellis."

Sondra gave him a curt nod and left the office.

# FORTY-ONE

He had always hated going out with her. The stares they would get. Women would figure he must be rich and the brothers would wonder how in the hell a guy who looked like him landed a fine sister like her. He sometimes wondered himself. He would never know what made him call her that day. He was so shy around women, no matter what they looked like. Tall, short, beautiful or ugly—his mouth would explode with cotton and his bowels would churn. Girls had made him nervous his whole life. He was a nerd, plain and simple. He was smart, but that didn't count for much with the pretty girls. Or the ugly ones, since they both pined for the handsome jocks. He'd never been the most handsome or most athletic or "Most Anything." Even if you weren't good looking, if you were at least "Most Anything," you could get the girl.

But not him. His clumsy attempts at dating were laughable. He'd had a few short-term girlfriends. Nothing of note, really. Nevertheless, for whatever reason, that day, he decided to take a chance and just see if maybe, he might be able to know more about her. His fingers wobbled like Jell-O as he dialed her number under the pretense of seeing if the Vicodin was working for her. He had already rehearsed in his mind how the conversation would go. He would remind her that he had been her pharmacist the other day and he just wanted to see how she was doing. She would sound surprised and say, "Yes, thank you for calling" and "Wow, she didn't think pharmacists made follow-up calls." He would chuckle and say he always liked to give good service. Then he would swallow and suggest going to get an omelet. She would pause and say, "Oh, thank you but no, I've already got a boyfriend," or "I'm not interested," or "I'm really busy, but I'll call you sometime," but never would. She would somehow find a way to gently, but firmly shoot him down.

But to his immense pleasure and utter surprise, she'd said yes.

She'd said yes.

And they hit it off. It wasn't so much that they liked the same things, but more that they had the same outlook on life, thought the same way. He was shocked when she agreed to go out with him again. And when she continued to go out with him. He worked so hard to win her love. He was attentive and sensitive. He masked how oh-so-desperate he was to make sure he wasn't a nice guy who finished last. And it worked. She fell in love with him and told him she wanted to spend the rest of her life with him.

Except, every day, he lived in fear. The constant attention she got from other men. He didn't fit in with her friends. Her sister didn't like him. He even felt distance from her parents. He was terrified they were talking about him, whispering in her ear that he was weird, why was she with him, that she could do better. Another man would come along, better looking, smarter, with more money and she would leave him.

Or her ex, the tall, dark, and handsome Jack would sweep back into the picture and take her away from him. He would say all the things she'd wanted to hear when they were together and she would tell Phillip she was leaving. He became frantic. Marriage was the only answer. After they got married, they'd be together forever.

Until death did they part.

# FORTY-TWO

Sondra was walking down Michigan Avenue on her way to Channel Four, a cigarette already clamped between her fingers.

It was early evening in Chicago, and Sondra was struck by how much she liked the city. New York was home, no doubt, but if she had to live somewhere else in America, this would probably be it. Or maybe Boston. It was a hot and sticky summer evening, though the breezes coming off Lake Michigan helped a little. Rush hour traffic whooshed down the Magnificent Mile and throngs of people crowded the sidewalks on their way to dinner or one of Chicago's many tourist-friendly destinations. Sondra took a final drag and dropped the cigarette on the sidewalk in front of her, the orange embers glowing briefly before she stubbed them with the toe of her flip-flop. She breezed through the revolving glass door of Channel Four and right to the front desk.

"Sondra Ellis to see Cicely Anderson."

"Sign in, please," the guard said as he motioned to the guest book and called Cicely. Moments later, Cicely came bounding through the gray doors and waved her hand for Sondra to follow her to the back.

"Hey, how was the police station?" Cicely asked.

"I saw the autopsy pictures."

"Oh, God, that must have been awful. I'm so sorry."

Sondra shook her head. "No, no. I mean it was awful, yes, but that's not it. It wasn't Tracy."

Cicely blinked. "Come again?"

"It wasn't Tracy in those photos. It was another woman."

"Are you sure? I mean, people look different in death..."

"Jesus, now you sound like the detective," she muttered, annoyed. "No, I'm telling you, if you saw them, you'd say the same thing."

Cicely shook her head, not sure what to make of this information. "But Phillip IDed the body."

"Right. And he also had the body cremated." Sondra raked her fingers through her hair. "And that's not all. I went to Tracy's house. Turns out, Phillip left a box of things there and the lady who lives there now gave it to me. I know what was going on with her, why Jack said she was 'unhappy'."

"Why, what?"

"Tracy's diary was in there. Apparently, Phillip had turned into some psycho freak, totally possessive, jealous, said he didn't want kids after he had told her he did, all kinds of craziness. That's why she was getting a divorce. She wasn't having an affair, he wasn't having an affair—he was just a crazy fucking psycho."

"Whoa."

"I just... the pieces still don't fit." Sondra's frustration continued to gnaw at her. "Did he find out she was leaving him and then he killed her? And if so, where the hell is the body? And who was that other woman? Did she and Tracy know each other?"

"You're starting to sound like this is some sort of conspiracy or something."

"I don't know. All I know is that none of this makes any sense. Does it make any sense to you?"

"Well, no, but everything you're saying sounds so crazy—"

"Listen, Cicely, with all due respect, don't patronize me."

"Sondra, you know that's not what I was doing."

Sondra took a few deep breaths. "Something happened to Tracy and I have to know what it is." Sondra softened her voice. "Cicely, this is my baby sister I'm talking about. You have to understand that."

Cicely folded her arms across her body and looked down at her shoes for several moments. Finally, she brought her eyes up to Sondra's. "Okay. I told you I would help you any way that I could, and I meant that. But, Sondra, honey, you have got to get a grip."

Sondra's shoulders wilted and she leaned against the wall opposite Cicely in the tiny hallway. "I'm sorry," she sighed. "I know I'm really emotional about this and it's making me a little nuts."

"No worries," Cicely said as she straightened up. "I pulled those tapes for you and I've put you in one of our editing bays. Come on." Cicely walked in the direction of the newsroom when Sondra put her hand on Cicely's elbow.

"Thank you, Cicely. You'll never know how much I appreciate all of this."

Cicely nodded and grabbed Sondra's hand. "It's okay."

The two women walked over to a small cubicle with a computer and dozens of tiny blinking red, green and orange lights. A stack of tapes sat on the small metal chair directly in front of the editing bay being manned by a lanky, young Latino guy.

"Ricky, this is Sondra. Sondra, Ricky."

They shook hands and exchanged pleasantries and Ricky offered her a seat next to him.

"So, what have we got, Cicely?" Ricky asked.

"Sondra's working on a documentary about what happened to Tracy."

Ricky snapped his fingers. "Of course, Sondra Ellis. I love your work."

Sondra managed a feeble smile, anxious to get down to it. "Thanks."

"I had everything pulled from our first story when she was reported missing to the memorial service. It's probably about twenty stories in all, since we do packages on some newscasts and live shots, readers or voiceover/sound-on-tape for others." Cicely handed Ricky the first tape on the pile and he popped it into the playback machine.

"Ricky'll take care of you. When you're done, just follow the hallway, turn left, and you'll be in the main part of the newsroom. I should be there," Cicely said as she stood up to leave.

"Thanks," she murmured as Cicely smiled and went down the hallway and back into the newsroom.

Taking a deep breath, Sondra looked at Ricky. "All right. Let's hit it."

"Here we go," Rick said as he hit the play button and waited for the tape to cue up.

The opening music for the Channel Four news shot out of the speakers and a montage featuring all of the anchors for that show, including Cicely, splashed across the screen. Sondra bit her lip, waiting. A somber Cicely appeared.

"Good evening. Topping our news tonight is a story that hits close to home for us here at Channel Four. Yesterday, Tracy Ellis, executive producer of this newscast, was reported missing. She was last seen Friday morning here at the station, and her husband spoke with her by phone early Saturday evening. Channel Four's Adam Lewis is live in Lakeview with the latest. Adam?"

A hunky blond reporter appeared, shivering in the bitter wind as he stood in front of Tracy's house.

"Cicely, as you said, this is an extremely difficult story to report. Tracy has been at Channel Four for five years, and during that time she has proved herself to not only be a superior producer, winning numerous awards for her work, but truly, one of the lights of the newsroom, always smiling, always laughing, always full of energy, which is astounding, considering how grim this job can sometimes be. She's always taken interns under her wing, mentored young writers and producers and, as we can all attest, is one of the biggest pranksters in the building. Not only are we in shock here at Channel Four, her Lakeview neighbors are stunned as well."

The story cut to a pre-taped news package about Tracy's disappearance. There was a picture of Tracy from some station function, all glorious white teeth and happy times. Many of her neighbors expressed their fervent hope that she was found safely soon. They were shown taping bright pink fliers to metal poles and community bulletin boards at churches, grocery stores and even inside the doors of El trains. A shot of Phillip standing on a street corner flashed on the screen. He was holding a stack of flapping fliers, handing them out to shivering pedestrians as they rushed down the crowded city street.

"Tracy's husband, Phillip Pearson, has been passing out fliers around the neighborhood non-stop since yesterday, searching for any glimmer of recognition from anyone about his wife's whereabouts."

Sondra leaned in closer to the computer screen to examine Phillip. January's biting winds produced a small crust of white around his lips and he licked them repeatedly for moisture. His eyes were red behind his thick-rimmed glasses, though it was hard to know if that was from crying himself to sleep over his wife's disappearance or from the brutal wind whipping around him. He adjusted his glasses several times and stopped every person who passed him to press a flier into their gloved hands and ask, "Have you seen this woman?" The story then cut to a shot of Phillip talking to Adam.

"I beg anyone who has any information, no matter how insignificant they think that it might be, to please, please call the police. We love her and we miss her and we just want her home safe with us. Anything that anyone can do to help us find her, we appreciate. We just want her home."

Sondra narrowed her eyes as she studied Phillip, searching for any sign of insincerity or falsity. She had Ricky rewind this part several times and was dismayed to realize that it was just as Cicely had said; he was frantic to find Tracy.

With a terse sigh, Sondra continued to watch the story. The reporter came back on with a picture of Tracy and a description: African-American, five-eight, one hundred twenty-five pounds, hazel eyes, brown hair, and anyone with any information was asked to call Area Three police. Sondra watched the rest of the tapes in silence. Most of the stories were the same until the discovery of Tracy's body. Phillip was shown on TV with a brave and stoic face as he talked to neighbors offering their condolences.

Maybe she'd been wrong. No one was that good of an actor. Phillip was genuinely worried about Tracy and had moved heaven and earth to find her. But she kept coming back to that poor woman in those photos. Maybe in his grief he really *did* think it was Tracy. Once she was done, Ricky pushed 'stop' and Sondra slouched down in her chair, a mixture of sadness and frustration knotting her shoulders.

"You okay?" Ricky asked.

Sondra shook her head. "No. It's just really hard to watch this, you know?"

"I get it." Ricky looked down. "Looks like there's one more tape. You up for watching it?"

"Might as well chug to the finish line."

Ricky shoved the tape into the machine and waited. Another anchor, a man, came on the screen. "A Hyde Park woman is missing tonight. Thirty-two year old Carol Henderson went out Tuesday night to walk her dog near her home. Neighbors are mobilizing search teams hoping to find her soon, but fear the worst."

Sondra frowned and leaned closer. Cicely's intern must have included this tape by accident.

"Carol Henderson is African-American, five-eight, one hundred thirty pounds with hazel eyes and brown hair."

Sondra almost fell out of the chair when Carol Henderson's picture flickered in front of her.

It was the woman she'd seen in the autopsy photos.

# FORTY-THREE

Nothing had gone the way he thought. He was certain that once they got married, she would want to stay home. He made good money—great money. She didn't need to work. Isn't that what women wanted? Find a man to take care of them so they could stay home and look after the house? His mother had done that, and she had been perfectly happy to do so. His father's word was law and no one questioned it. The house was always spotless, his clothes neatly pressed, breakfast on the table the same time each morning, dinner on the table the same time each night. It had been a wonderful way to grow up.

But she didn't want that. So she continued to work, to spend time doing things that didn't include him. And he hated it. All he could think about was all those men hitting on her, all that temptation.

How long would it be before she looked at him and thought she could do better? Though it was his ring on her finger, that question haunted him daily. It made him crazy to have those thoughts jabbing into his brain like a boxer on the rampage.

Then she mentioned having a baby. That had sent him screeching over the edge. He could barely stand to share her with her friends or her family; if they had a baby, he'd lose her forever. The baby would take all her time; the baby would consume her and she would forget all about him. And that was when the fear really set in. He was sure she was plotting to leave him. He'd even read through her diary, thinking he would find a clue there, but nothing. The pages were filled with nothing but love and adoration for him.

He didn't buy it though. He couldn't. As much as he tried, he just couldn't. And even though he knew he shouldn't act so irrational, shouldn't pepper her with constant questions about what she was doing and where she was going and who she was with, he just Could. Not. Help. Himself.

Why couldn't she just devote herself to him the way he had to her?

# FORTY-FOUR

"Oh, my God," Sondra whispered.

"Wow. She looks just like Tracy. They could be twins," Ricky said.

"Pause the tape," Sondra said as she peered in for a closer look. She studied each detail of the smiling woman's face from a picture taken at what looked to be a family function, stunned at how much Carol Henderson looked like Tracy. Same coloring, hair in a similar style, almost identical.

"Hang on a sec. I'll be right back."

Sondra ran towards the newsroom to find Cicely. She found the tiny newswoman dwarfed behind a huge computer monitor, where she was pounding away on her keyboard.

"Cicely, I need you to come back and look at something."

"What's wrong?"

"Just, please, come look at this," Sondra said as she began to walk back to the editing bay. The two women sat down and Ricky cued up the tape. Much like Sondra and Ricky, Cicely almost fainted when she saw Carol Henderson.

"My God, they could have been twins," Cicely murmured.

"That's what I said," Ricky chimed in.

"This is the woman I saw in the autopsy photos. No question in my mind."

Cicely leaned back in her chair. "Jesus. This is just… unreal. I can't believe no one made the connection at the time,"

"Ricky, can I get a dub of this?"

"No problem," Ricky replied, his fingers springing into action as he worked to do the transfer.

"Can you tell me if you have any more stories about her?" Sondra asked.

Cicely turned to the computer next to the editing bay. "Yeah, I can check the archives. Hang on." Cicely tapped out a few words into the computer and waited. She shook her head, a resigned look on her face.

"Just that one. Now that I think about it, that was about the time of those bombings in L.A. and then the sniper attacks in New York. Pretty much pushed everything else off the page." She leaned back in her chair and looked at Sondra. "Looks like Carol Henderson's disappearance fell through the cracks."

Sondra rolled her eyes. "Doesn't surprise me. Being black and all."

Ricky snorted in agreement as he handed Sondra the DVD.

"What now?" Cicely asked.

Sondra simultaneously dropped the dubbed DVD into the bottom of her bag and pulled out her cigarettes.

"I'm going to see what I can find out about Carol Henderson."

"Shouldn't you let the police know about this?"

"I will. Soon." Sondra shook her head as she extracted a cigarette from the pack. "Of course, they're the ones who fucked this up to begin with. I just want to search out a few more things first."

Cicely folded her arms across her chest and looked at Sondra. "Do you think she's still alive?"

Sondra let out a deep sigh and shook her head. "I don't know. Sondra looked at her watch. "Listen, I gotta go. I'll call you. Thanks Ricky." Sondra stood and rushed out of the station.

# FORTY-FIVE

"I need to see Detective Wallace. Now."

"Have a seat."

"Tell her it's Sondra Ellis and that it's a matter of life or death."

"Aren't they all? Have a seat," the desk sergeant repeated.

Frustrated, Sondra plopped down into what was probably the same rock-hard wooden chair she'd sat in before. To her surprise, Detective Marion Wallace appeared within moments.

"Ms. Ellis?"

Sondra jumped up. "I have something you need to see. I found the woman in those pictures."

"Ms. Ellis, I know you want it to be a different woman in those pictures—"

Sondra held up the DVD from Channel Four in front of Marion. "Just look at it. You'll see right away that I'm not nuts."

Marion narrowed her eyes at Sondra for a moment before she flashed a look at her watch. "This better be good," she muttered.

"I promise you, this is going to change everything."

Sondra followed Marion toward an interrogation room where there was a DVD player. Sondra handed the DVD to Marion and watched her load it. Sondra held her breath as she waited for Carol Henderson to appear.

Marion was perched on the edge of the table in the room, arms crossed. One look at Carol Henderson and her hands dropped to her sides as she stared at the screen.

"Holy mother of God," she whispered. She paused the DVD several times and rewound it. Finally, she looked at Sondra.

"Where'd you get this?"

"Cicely Anderson at Channel Four. Actually, I had her pull all the stories about Tracy and this one wound up in the pile by mistake." Sondra began to tick off the facts on her fingers. "Carol Henderson was from Hyde Park, disappeared about the time Tracy did, hasn't been seen since. Maybe Carol and my sister were connected somehow, I don't know, but—this means Tracy is out there somewhere."

Silently, Marion began to walk back to her desk and Sondra found herself experiencing déjà vu as she swore she saw the same junkies, thugs and prostitutes today that she'd seen before. She sat down in the same chair.

"What are you doing to find my sister?"

"Well, we'll reopen the case, but I have to tell you, the chances of finding her—"

"What? You think she's dead?"

"Ms. Ellis, it's been three years. The chances that your sister is still alive are slim to none."

Sondra looked at Marion, the slender thread of hope snapping inside her before she finally averted her eyes. "What now?"

"We'll get Carol Henderson's family in here to ID the photos—"

"Are you going to start looking for Phillip?"

"We'll find him to notify him that we are reopening the case."

Sondra's eyes widened. "That's it? You aren't going to bring him in for questioning?"

"Ms. Ellis, I already told you, he had a rock solid alibi—"

"I don't give a shit what he had. He lied about that woman—I took one look at those pictures and knew it wasn't her. You took one look at Carol Henderson and there was no doubt in your mind. And then he had the body cremated?" Sondra shook her head and took a deep breath. "You've got to be kidding me."

"Miss Ellis, I know this is hard, but you've got to let us do our jobs."

Sondra was silent for a few moments. "Did you do a DNA test on the body?"

Detective Wallace pulled out the case file, searching for the information before shaking her head. "No. Your brother-in-law refused the test, saying he was positive it was his wife."

Sondra started to pace the room. "Listen, he wrote my mother a letter not too long ago and told her he'd gotten remarried. It came from an address in Michigan, which turned out to be completely bogus. I couldn't find any record of a current address for him. So where the hell is he?" Sondra sat back in the chair and raked her fingers through her hair, trying to stave off what she knew was coming. She couldn't help it. She dissolved into a quivering mass of salty tears and raw nerves. Marion handed her yet another fistful of Kleenex from the box on her desk.

"Like I said, we'll let him know we're reopening the case. Right now, that's the best I can do."

Sondra dabbed at her eyes and blew her nose as she stood up. "Yeah, well that's not good enough."

Without a word, Sondra turned and stalked out of the station.

# FORTY-SIX

The waiting had been excruciating. Every time the phone rang, he jumped, hoping it was the police telling him he needed to come in and ID his wife's body. Of course, people assumed it was because he was *afraid* it was a call telling him it was his wife's body. However, each time he answered, he always called out his wife's name, with just a touch of hope and hysteria.

Finally, early that Friday morning, the police showed up at his door to escort him to the morgue.

*Mr. Pearson, we're so sorry, but we need you to come down. We may have found your wife.*

He would look at them with quiet desperation. His in-laws would exchange nervous glances and clutch each other's hand. He would take a deep breath and ask the detectives if they were sure and they would nod uncomfortably and say that yes, they needed him to come down. Fighting back tears, he would hug Mimi, put a hand on Gordon's shoulder and whisper that he would be back soon. His father-in-law would offer to come with him, and he would shake his head and nod toward his mother-in-law and say no, stay here, she needs you.

He would ride in silence in the back of the car, watching the scenery whiz past him. The detectives would lead him to the room full of metal drawers, their voices echoing in the cavernous space even though they were speaking in hushed tones. One detective would nod to the coroner who would grasp the handle firmly and pull the drawer out. He would peer for just a moment at the woman's face, and manage to choke out that yes, it was her, it was his wife. He would refuse the DNA test, saying he was positive it was Tracy and they just had to accept it.

Then, he would break down completely, the sobs coming like a gale force wind. The detectives would hold him up, one at each elbow and take him to another room, offer him some water or was there someone they could call? He would refuse and ask what happened.

*Well, Mr. Pearson, she was found down on Belmont Harbor. We found her wallet nearby and she was wearing the jewelry you described. We think a mugger attacked her then smashed the rock into her face.*

He would hunch over, unable to turn off the tears, moaning and wailing, asking how could this happen. If only I'd stayed home that weekend. Eventually, he would work himself into such a state that a shrink would come in and give him a sedative. The detectives would take him home and he would look at his in-laws and confirm their worst fears. Yes, their daughter was dead. In halting, wispy tones, he would relay what the police had told him about how she died. His mother-in-law would lose it completely, and his father-in-law would cry silent, pained tears. And he would cry too, careful not to overdo it, because that would be suspicious.

The body would be cremated and a memorial service would be planned. People would tell funny stories, people would cry.

And they would all be watching him.

He would play the role of grieving husband to the hilt.

They all thought he was some stupid nerd that got lucky when he scored her.

He fooled them all.

# FORTY-SEVEN

Sondra added yet another cigarette butt to the impressive pile at her feet. She was sitting on the concrete risers at Oak Street Beach, trying to calm down. Ever since her encounter with Detective Wallace, she'd been trying to quell the wave of emotions running rampant inside her—anger, fear, frustration, desperation, confusion, and sadness. In Sondra's world, that meant chain smoking and today she was setting a record.

Phillip's face floated in front of her. He'd done something—she just knew it. But what? She didn't trust the police. She didn't trust him. She didn't trust anybody.

Sondra jerked a hand through her matted waves, her mind on point. And then, it came to her and she couldn't believe she hadn't thought of it before. She pulled up the number on her phone.

"I need a favor."

"Which would be…"

"I need Nicky's number."

"I always knew you had a thing for him. I guess now that I'm out of the picture you have clearance."

"In his dreams. Yours too, apparently."

"I always was a vivid dreamer."

"Seriously, I need him to find someone and you said he's the best."

"Looking for a new husband?"

"As if anyone could replace you."

"True. All right, I'll play along. Who are you looking for?"

"Phillip."

"Ah, yes, the oh-so-odd brother-in-law. And why are you looking for him, love?"

"Ugh, it would take me forever to explain. I'll tell you all about it one night over dinner at Le Colonial."

"Love, you'd have to put on a dress for that. Do you even own one?"

"One. I'll wear it just for you."

"My, my. I am atwitter with anticipation. Mostly about seeing you in a dress. I think our wedding was the last time."

"Ha, ha. Now are we gonna dance around all day or are you going to give me Nicky's number?"

"Oh, but I'm having so much fun."

"You're the only one."

"Hardly. Do you have a pen?"

"Yup."

"800-555-9170."

"Thanks, Gary. I owe you big."

"Which is why you're taking me to Le Colonial."

"Talk to you soon."

"Goodbye, love."

Nicky was a bounty hunter whom Gary had met over twenty years ago in Las Vegas after Gary pummeled him in a back-room poker game. Each spring, the two men—who on the surface couldn't have been more opposite—would take a jaunt down to Cabo for a week of tequila-fueled bonding and endless rounds of poker with the locals. That was the extent of the relationship. There were no phone calls exchanged throughout the year, no occasional emails inquiring how the other was, no Christmas cards with hastily scribbled good tidings. They would simply each show up the second week of April at a little bungalow on the beach and take turns buying the booze. Sondra had never even met him.

Nicky picked up on the first ring. "Yooooo. Who dis?"

"Nicky, it's Sondra. Gary's wife. Well, ex-wife."

"What's up girl? How's G doin'?"

"Same old Gary. Listen, I need a favor and you're the only one I know who can help."

"Shooooot."

"I need to find my brother-in-law. It has to do with my sister's disappearance and just a whole lot of things I can't really get into, but I need to you to find out where he is. I'll pay you whatever."

"Awww, for you baby, this one'll be on the house. What's his name?"

"Phillip, Phillip Pearson. I don't want you to confront him or anything, just find him and tell me where he is."

"Consider it done. Now, tell me what you know."

# FORTY-EIGHT

Carol Henderson's family had been notified and asked to look at the autopsy photos that had been identified as Tracy Ellis. They confirmed that, indeed, it was Carol.

Tracy's case had been reopened, and though the police were taking extra care to keep the story quiet, Sondra knew it was a matter of time before the shit hit the fan and the story was everywhere. Mimi had fainted when Sondra called her to tell her what was going on and Gordon could only respond in sputtering disbelief.

Sondra was determined to talk to Carol's husband on her own and though Detective Wallace had told her to stay out of it, she took it upon herself to track him down and get in touch with him. It had taken Sondra a few tries, but she had finally gotten a hold of Kevin Henderson.

Sondra sipped her iced coffee and checked her watch again. Kevin had said he would meet her at two-thirty and it was already three. She hoped he hadn't changed his mind. Sondra took another swallow and waited. Finally, a handsome, mahogany-colored man with a shiny dome of a head pushed open the door to the Starbucks. That had to be him. She threw up her hand to signal to him. He gave her a stiff nod and made his way over to the table.

"Ms. Ellis?"

Sondra nodded and held out her hand. "Yes, please, call me Sondra."

The pair shook hands and Kevin eased his army green newsboy bag to the floor and sat in the chair opposite Sondra. "I'm sorry I was late. I... I was at the police station."

Sondra was quiet. "I'm so sorry," she finally said.

"Yeah, well, now at least I know what happened to her," he said.

She gestured to the front counter. "Did you wanna grab something?"

Kevin twisted around. "Yeah, if you don't mind waiting." He chuckled, catching himself. "I mean, any more than you already have."

"Go right ahead."

A few moments later, he came back with some mocha tall grande cinnamon something or other. He slid back into the chair and stared at his drink without touching it.

"Do you mind my asking why you wanted to meet with me?" he inquired, never taking his eyes off his coffee. "Since you never really said on the phone."

Sondra sighed. "I'm trying to figure out if there was some connection between your wife and my sister."

Kevin sighed and went to take a sip of his drink when he stopped and snapped his fingers. "Wait a minute. Sondra Ellis. You're not the filmmaker, are you?"

"Guilty as charged."

Kevin leaned back in his chair, grinning, his demeanor suddenly much more pleasant. "Awwww man! This is crazy! I saw *The Deepest Cut* with Carol—" Kevin's face clouded momentarily as he mentioned his wife's name. "Carol and I saw it when it came out. We both really enjoyed it. Damn. I'm sorry."

"I wish I knew what to say," Sondra said.

Kevin looked down at the table, his finger running up and down the length of his coffee cup. "Yeah, well..."

Sondra was silent for a moment before she spoke. "Would you like to see pictures?"

He smiled and nodded.

Sondra pulled Tracy's small purple photo album from her bag and flipped it open to the first picture of the family at Christmas. She tapped her finger on Tracy's image.

"That's her. That was taken probably four years ago."

Kevin did a double take as he lifted up the small book. "Oh, she looks just like Carol," he uttered in stunned disbelief.

"Yeah. What is it they say? Everyone has a twin? I couldn't get over the resemblance myself when I saw Carol's picture on that tape."

Kevin frowned. "What tape?"

"Well, that's how this whole thing started. I'd been thinking about doing a documentary about Tracy's death and was looking at some footage from her news station from when she disappeared. One story about Carol's disappearance popped up. I told the police and... here we are."

"Police didn't mention that. All they said was they wanted us to come down and look at some photographs."

Kevin continued to turn the pages of the album with careful fingers, almost as if he were afraid they might crumble beneath his touch. "It's crazy, how much they looked alike," he said, shaking his head. Finally, he closed the book and placed it on the table. "She was beautiful." He looked down sheepishly, before he reached into his back pocket and withdrew his wallet. He flipped it open and pulled out a tiny photo.

"This is Carol," he said, his voice so soft, Sondra almost didn't hear him. She picked up the picture and looked at it, almost unable to keep it together. Carol had the same sparkling white teeth and clear, smooth skin as Tracy. She was in a black leather recliner with her feet curled underneath her and one palm cradling her cheek.

"You know, it's more than just looking alike. She reminds me of Tracy because she looks so happy." Sondra slid the photo back across the table to Kevin. "Tracy was always a very up person."

"Man, you hit it on the head. That's exactly how Carol was. Just so... full of life and positive. She'd do anything for anybody and that's what makes it so hard to believe... that someone would do that to her..." Kevin's voice trailed off as he looked at the picture one more time, before sliding it back into his wallet.

Sondra cleared her throat and leaned forward, an intense look on her face. "Like I said, I'm trying to figure out if there might have been a link between Carol and Tracy."

Kevin slumped back in his seat, his frosty reserve melted. "You know, I wracked my brain over and over to see if I could come up with anything, and so far, nothing."

"Well, maybe you can tell me a little about Carol and we can work from there? Like, for example, what did she do for a living?"

"She was a loan officer with Chicago National. She'd been working there, man, eight years. There are branches all over the city, but she worked downtown—the main branch."

Sondra pulled her notebook from her purse and scribbled the name of the bank. "I don't know if Tracy banked there or not. Easy enough to find out." Sondra continued, "My sister was a producer with Channel Four news. Is it possible she did a story on the bank or something where Carol might have been involved?"

Kevin considered it for a moment before he shook his head. "No. No she would have told me about anything like that."

Sondra bit her bottom lip. "You live in Hyde Park, which is on the South Side of the city, right?"

"Right."

"Well, Tracy lived in Lakeview, which is north."

"Hmm, mmm."

"So, Carol was found near where Tracy lived. Did you all know anyone in that neighborhood? I mean, is there any reason she would have gone up there?"

Kevin shifted in his seat and shook his head. "Naw. Carol and I both grew up on the South Side and that's where all our friends and family are. We don't know anyone up north."

Sondra shook her head. "It just doesn't make sense," she murmured to herself.

"Believe me, I can't figure it out myself."

She looked at Kevin. "What happened? That night?"

Kevin let out a deep breath and closed his eyes. "You don't know how many times I have thought about that night. If only I'd taken the dog out instead. If she'd taken him five minutes earlier, or five minutes later… it could have changed everything." He took a gulp of his drink before he resumed his story. "It was Tuesday night—we had a huge blizzard that night. I mean, the snow had been coming down all day, just non-stop. So, it was about eight-thirty, eight-forty-five, and I was watching some ballgame—it was really important at the time—and now I couldn't tell you what sport it was, what teams were playing, nothing."

"Then what?"

"Carol yells out from the kitchen that she was going to take Rusty out to do his thing. She would normally take him out at that time, so I didn't think anything of it. Just yelled back 'Okay, be careful.' Can you believe that? Be careful." Kevin shook his head. "That was the last time I saw her."

"How much time passed before you realized she wasn't back?"

"Actually, Rusty came scratching at the door at about nine-thirty. I'd already started to worry a little and that just cinched it. She'd left her cell phone at home, so I couldn't call her. I called the police, who wouldn't do anything until it had been twenty-four hours. Never mind it was the biggest snowstorm of the season and anything could have happened to her."

"So nothing happened."

"Said I had to wait twenty-four hours. Some of us started passing out fliers around the neighborhood the next day though." Kevin paused. "Did your sister have a dog?"

"No, she was allergic. We both were. Growing up, all we ever wanted was a dog, but of course the Ps told us to forget it. Then one day, we found a stray in the neighborhood and decided to keep him."

"Uh, oh," Kevin chuckled.

"Yeah, exactly, uh, oh. We hid him in the garage, determined we'd show them we could have a dog. Well, within a half hour, we'd both puffed up to twice our size and had to be rushed to the emergency room. No more pets after that."

Kevin smiled. "Sounds like you two were a handful."

"Yeah. We were good kids for the most part though. Never got into any real trouble."

Sondra cleared her throat. "How long were you married?"

"About a year, but we'd been together about three years. What about you? How did your sister meet her husband?"

All of Sondra's lightheartedness disappeared as she thought of Phillip. She wrinkled her nose. "He filled a prescription for her. They got engaged four months after meeting, got hitched six months after that and were married six months."

"Man." He was quiet for a moment. "Carol was terrible with taking care of her teeth. She had two root canals that year, so we had a lot of Vicodin around the house for a few weeks." He grew silent again. "They were only married six months?"

"That's it."

Sondra blinked; Kevin's words were registering. "Maybe Carol and Tracy had the same dentist?" she said, a hopeful note in her voice.

"Carol and I had the same dentist, over on sixty-third. South Side."

"Shit. I bet Tracy saw some guy downtown. And Phillip worked at a pharmacy downtown…?"

Kevin shook his head. "Like I said, we got everything South. About the only thing Carol did downtown was work."

Sondra shook her head, the threads refusing to connect. "Damn."

"So what happened to your sister?"

"God. That's anyone's guess. All I can say for sure is that she disappeared after she went jogging. And then…"

"And then my wife's body was identified as your sister."

"Right."

"And your brother-in-law IDed the body?"

"Yeah."

Kevin leaned back against the chair, confusion clouding his handsome features. "I mean, I know they looked alike, but how… how could he…?"

Sondra closed her eyes and shook her head. "The only thing I've been able to figure is that in his grief he thought it was Tracy."

"That just doesn't make sense to me." He cocked his head and looked at her. "How could he do that?"

Sondra looked out the window at the cavalcade of people rushing down the sidewalk. "I wish I knew."

"Did you and your brother-in-law get along?"

Sondra scrunched up her face for a moment before she let it fall back into place. "At first no, then yes and now…"

"Where is he?"

"I have no idea."

"So, what about you?"

"What about me?"

"Are you married, single?"

"Choice C, divorced."

"Ah."

"Gary was my professor at NYU Film School—Film Appreciation. We had this just... *crazy* attraction to each other the whole time I was in his class. I was always making up some reason to be in his office during his office hours. Literally as soon as he turned in my final grades, it was done."

"Hot for teacher, huh?"

"That's an understatement. Anyway, we had this torrid affair and then one night after too many tequila shots and not enough common sense, we eloped. Actually, for a couple of years, it was really good." Sondra drifted back to those days when Gary was the best thing about her. "It really was a beautiful, wonderful time, but... well, there were a lot of reasons it didn't work. I think part of it was I grew up—Gary has fifteen years on me. I was still finding myself and all of that. So, after seven years of marriage, we closed that door. Of course, that's when my career really took off. Hell, I even thanked him when I won my Oscar."

"Well, at least you got something out of it."

"Yeah. I still love him though. Always will."

"No kids?"

Sondra snorted. "Oh, no. I'm not exactly the maternal type. Tracy? That was a different story. She was kind of princess-y, but she would have made an incredible mother. God. I hate talking about her in the past tense."

Kevin hunched over his coffee, stroking the top of the lid with his forefinger. "It was months before I would stop talking about Carol in the present tense. The first time I referred to her in the past tense, I almost cried, it hurt so much."

"So over this past year that she was missing, what have you been doing?"

"At first, it was intense. Posting a lot of fliers, a lot of just kind of amateur searching, you know? Knocking on doors asking if anyone had seen her. We got a little news coverage, but not much. It was hard."

"That was actually one of the things that led me on this journey. I was reading a story about this girl from California that had gone missing after she went jogging—like Tracy. And it made national news. Like crazy national news."

"She was white, huh?"

"You got it."

"That's sad."

"I mean, Tracy's station gave hers some play and there were a few items in the local papers, but for the most part, nothing."

"Whatever happened to the girl in California?"

"Remains were found about three weeks later."

"Man."

"I'm sorry, you were telling me about the search."

"Right. Well, anyway, we kept up with that for a while, held some candlelight vigils. After a while though, people began to lose hope, the momentum kind of died down."

"I guess that's to be expected."

"Yeah. I guess. Every once in a while, we'd bug the police, or I'd put up a new round of fliers. Just to feel like I was doing something."

"How are you holding up now that you know she's gone?"

"Relieved. Confused. Sad. Determined to find out what happened to her."

"How has your family taken all of this?"

"We've hired an attorney to find out what our rights are against the police, and we're mobilizing our church and others in our community to put pressure on them to solve the case."

"Well, hopefully between me pestering them and all the support you've got, this won't fall through the cracks and we'll get some justice... for both of them."

"Do you think... Tracy's still alive?"

Sondra shook her head slightly as the question that had been swirling in her head for so long was now finally in front of her. "The rational part of me says no, of course not. The hopeful side of me says... maybe. Regardless, I have to find out what happened to her."

Just then, Kevin's cell phone jingled. "Excuse me, this could be important."

While Sondra waited for Kevin to get off the phone, she thought about her sister's true fate. Would it be as bad as or worse than what had happened to Carol Henderson? She shuddered.

Kevin hung up his phone and gave Sondra an apologetic look.

"That was my job. I've got to go and take care of some things."

Sondra gave him a sympathetic smile. "I understand." She shot her hand out as he started to gather up his things. "Thank you, Kevin, for taking the time out to meet with me."

Kevin shook Sondra's hand. "I just wish it had been for a different reason."

Sondra gave him a small smile. "Me too."

"Well, call me before you leave for New York. Maybe we can have dinner."

Sondra smiled and nodded. "Sure. I'd like that."

Kevin returned the smile and slung his bag on a diagonal across his body. "Sounds good. Talk to you soon."

Sondra gave a small wave of her fingers as she watched him walk out of the shop.

# FORTY-NINE

Paula perched on the edge of the couch, anxious as she waited for Phillip to inspect her work. He'd said if it was found to be satisfactory, she could go across the street to Cindy Cross' house for the once-promised cup of coffee.

"Everything appears to be in order," he said. "You may go. But only for twenty minutes."

"Okay," she nodded, trying to keep the happiness from slipping through her lips.

"Well, I'm ready," he said.

"Oh, right," Paula said as she hopped off the couch. She helped him with his coat, kissed him goodbye and scampered into the bedroom once he was gone. She would wear the blue dress. That seemed to complement her skin tone. After changing into the dress and smoothing down her bun, Paula made the short trip across the street. For summer, it was a chilly morning and the breeze cut into her like a knife. She took a tentative step onto Cindy's stoop.

"It's okay," she whispered to herself. "It will only be twenty minutes, then you will go home and do your work."

Paula took a deep breath and brought a shaky finger to the doorbell, wincing as she pressed it. She waited. Nothing. Paula looked to her right. The silver car was in the driveway, so she must be home. Paula tried again. She rang the doorbell once more and waited.

"She's not here," Paula said aloud, a tinge of disappointment in her voice. With a final sad glance at the door, Paula turned to make the trip back to her house when the door swung open.

"Paula?" Cindy said.

"Oh, hello. I didn't think you were home," Paula said as she turned back to face Cindy.

"I had the blow-dryer on," Cindy said as the frosty morning air whispered through her hair. "Did you need something? More Sweet'N Low?"

"Oh, no, no, I just... well, you had mentioned having coffee sometime and I was wondering if you might like to have some this morning," Paula stammered.

Cindy shoved her hands inside the pockets of her blue terrycloth robe and leaned against the doorjamb. "Yeah, sure. Come on in."

With a grateful, gushing smile, Paula all but skipped inside and found herself facing the stylish, but toy-strewn living room.

"Excuse the mess," Cindy said as though she could read Paula's mind. "My kids were watching TV in here this morning before my husband took them to school. It's amazing the damage kids can do during the space of a thirty minute cartoon." Cindy gestured toward the kitchen as she began to bound up the stairs.

"Let me throw some clothes on. Just have a seat at the table, and I'll be right down."

Paula pulled out the oak chair from the table and sat down, perching on the edge. The Cross kitchen was so different from her own white-washed one. Cheerful yellow curtains decorated with diminutive blue flowers framed the kitchen window, which looked across the street to Paula's house. Two blue and purple plastic bowls were stacked haphazardly next to the kitchen sink, which was adorned with sponges, a half-full bottle of orange dishwashing liquid and a coffee mug with a yellow smiley face on the side. The stainless steel refrigerator was plastered with Crayola masterpieces, assorted colorful magnets, and pizza coupons. The table where Paula sat had a napkin holder crammed full of baby blue napkins and two yellow plastic placemats, each with a tiny buzzing bumblebee, beneath wet Cheerios and sticky fruit juice.

"Okay," Cindy said as she breezed in, now wearing a pair of jeans and form-fitting red t-shirt. "I don't drink decaf, so all I've got is regular. Is that cool with you?"

Paula nodded and smiled. "Oh, yes, regular is fine."

Cindy smiled as she went to pull out the coffee packets. "Good. Oh, and I use sugar and real full-fat milk. None of that creamer or Sweet'N Low crap." Paula winced and Cindy clucked her tongue. "Sorry."

"Your kitchen," Paula said, "it's different."

Cindy turned around from filling the coffee machine and looked at Paula. "Um…thanks. We like it. Still settling in though, you know. As you know we moved in a few weeks ago."

"Yes, you mentioned that."

"What about you? How long have you lived here?"

"About three years."

"Where were you before?"

Paula felt her breath quicken. Phillip had been right. This was a bad idea. "The other side of town," she said, remembering what Phillip had always trained her to say if pressed for details. "My husband got another job and this neighborhood was closer."

Cindy put milk, sugar and spoons on the table before she slid into the chair opposite Paula. "That's funny. That's why we moved over here. Must be something in the water. Any brothers or sisters?"

"No. I'm an only child. So is my husband."

"Oh, I always wanted to be an only child. I have an older sister. We're three years apart. What about your folks? Are they still here?"

"Both my parents are dead."

"Oh. I'm sorry to hear that."

"Yes."

Cindy wrinkled her nose. So, how long have you been married?"

"About two years. We were high school sweethearts."

Cindy's eyes widened. "Oh. Why did you wait so long to get married? I mean, if you don't mind me asking."

"He moved away and got married. She died."

"Hmmm. Wow," Cindy said. The coffee maker emitted a muffled beeping to indicate the coffee was done brewing. Cindy stood up and went to retrieve two mugs from the cabinet.

"You have children," Paula said rather than asked.

Cindy nodded as she poured Vanilla French Roast into the oversized mugs and brought them to the table. "Sure do. Are you and your husband planning to have children one day?"

"I can't have children. Besides, we don't want any."

"Oh," Cindy said as she dumped another heap of sugar into her coffee.

"How old are your children?"

"Jake is six and my daughter, Tracy, is four."

Paula almost dropped the carton of milk she had picked up. "What?"

Cindy narrowed her eyes. "Is something wrong?"

Paula felt her mouth go dry as she tried to regain her composure. "Tracy was the name of Phillip's first wife. I don't like talking about her."

Cindy stirred her coffee, the metal spoon clanking against the sides of the mug. "Okay, we won't," she said as she pulled the spoon out and blew into the toffee-colored liquid to cool it off.

Paula stared down into her coffee, her breath coming in short, heavy puffs. She was longing for the comfort of her pasty kitchen.

"Can I get you something?" Cindy asked. "An aspirin, anything?"

Paula shook her head before she snapped it up. "No. Phillip is the only one who gives me medication of any kind."

"Okay."

"I have to go. I told Phillip I would only spend twenty minutes over here. I have to clean the windows today. Thank you for your time." Paula scraped the chair backwards across the linoleum tiles, her feet getting tangled up with the legs as she did so. She managed to disengage from the chair and darted for the door.

Cindy watched her for a moment before she scooted her own chair back and rose to follow Paula, who already had the front door open.

"Paula, is something wrong? You can tell me what it is."

"No. No. I've already said too much."

Before Cindy could say anything else, Paula had zipped across the street to her own house, entered and shut the door.

# FIFTY

Phillip smoothed down the glued-on mustache and adjusted the edge of the wool ski cap covering the tips of his ears. Keegan was waiting for him by the back entrance, his foot stuck between the wall and the door.

"What the hell took you so long? You were supposed to be here twenty minutes ago. And what's with the fake mustache?" Keegan leaned in. "Who are you hiding from?"

"We're not here to talk about me."

Keegan rolled his eyes and opened the door for Phillip. "Fine. Let's go."

The two men scurried down the bright hallway in silence. Keegan unlocked his office door and Phillip took the chair in front of his desk.

"How's she doing?"

Keegan flipped open a metal chart. "Well, she sleeps twenty hours a day."

"That's the idea. You've been giving her the medication?"

"Yes, everyday," Keegan said, exasperated.

"What else? Is she asking questions when she's awake?"

"Yes. I'm telling her what you told me to say."

Phillip leaned back in his chair and smiled. "That's good to hear. I can't thank you enough, doc."

"Please. I don't want your gratitude. I want to know when the hell this will be over with."

"When you need to know, you'll know."

Keegan rubbed his eyes. "Dealing with you gives new meaning to 'The Longest Winter'."

"All right, enough with this chit-chat. I'm ready to see her."

Keegan stared at Phillip for a moment and shook his head. "You know, it's too bad you didn't stay a psychology major."

"Why?"

Keegan slammed the chart closed. "Because you're real good with the mind fuck."

# FIFTY-ONE

Sondra stubbed out her cigarette on the sidewalk as she waited for Kevin outside Wishbone in the West Loop. Kevin had said it was a favorite of his. She smiled and waved to him as he ambled over to meet her.

"Hi. Been waiting long?"

"Just long enough for a smoke. I'm glad I called for a reservation. This is a pretty hopping place."

He opened the door and ushered Sondra inside. "This is nothing. You should see it on weekends when they do brunch. It's crazy."

"Well, I'm excited to try it."

"I'm glad you called. I kind of needed to get out of the house."

"Well, I'm kind of looking forward to a few minutes where I'm not thinking about Tracy or Phillip or any of it, so I called you for a selfish reason."

Kevin laughed as the hostess seated them. "Well, go ahead and use me. So nothing new, huh?"

"Nada. How has your family been dealing with this?"

"Not good. Like we were talking about the other day, it just brings everything up all over again. Carol's mom has really had a hard time, of course."

"You know what? Let's change the subject."

Kevin smiled and nodded. "Of course."

They busied themselves looking over the menu and slurping down sweet tea. After the waitress took their order, Kevin hunched over the table and looked at Sondra.

"So, I don't think I asked, but are you from Chicago?"

"No, we grew up in California—Stanford. Our mom was on the German Olympic team for swimming and my dad is a professor of cultural studies at Stanford. Written a lot books. Gordon Ellis?"

Kevin's eyes nearly popped out of his head. "Gordon Ellis is your dad?"

"Yeah."

Kevin leaned back in his chair, floored. "Man, I've probably read *Hip Hop State of Mind* a hundred times. More."

Sondra smiled. "Yeah. That one's my personal favorite. I could probably snag an autographed copy for you."

"Wow, that would... wow. Thank you."

"Sure."

"And your mom went to the Olympics?"

"Bronze in sixty, silver in sixty-four."

"So, how did they meet?"

Sondra shifted in her seat. "Well, Daddy is from Alabama and he went to Emory for undergrad and got the opportunity to study abroad in Paris one summer—French Cinema. Mommy was in Paris visiting her sister and they were each sitting at a café one afternoon drinking coffee. Their eyes met and as the saying goes, they've been together ever since."

"Wow. That's beautiful."

"Yeah. Good model. Even if Tracy and I had trouble following it."

"I'm still trying to get over your family... You do documentaries, your mom did the Olympic thing, your dad does his thing and Tracy was a news producer?" Kevin let out a low whistle. "I'm trippin'."

Sondra shrugged. "Oh. Yeah. I don't know. I guess we just all kind of did what we wanted and turned out to be pretty successful at it." Sondra gestured toward Kevin. "What about you? What do you do?"

"Nothing nearly as cool as your family. I'm a social worker for the Chicago Public School system."

Sondra nodded, impressed. "Tough line of work. Very admirable. You've got to have nerves of steel for that one I'd imagine."

Kevin rubbed the back of his neck. "Yeah, that, or oatmeal for brains."

Sondra laughed. "Oh, come on. It can't be that bad."

"You know, I love the work—I do, but man, there are days when it takes all I have to get out of bed."

"If you didn't have to work, what would you do?"

Kevin thought about for a moment. "Pitch a tent on a beach in the Bahamas and sell tacky souvenirs."

Sondra grinned. "Sounds nice."

"Yeah. Pipe dream." Kevin plunked his chin down in one hand and studied Sondra.

"Was it hard growing up bi-racial?" he asked.

Sondra didn't flinch; she was so used to the question after all these years. "Um, you know sometimes, yeah. Like I said, daddy's family is from the deep, deep South and never understood why he married some Amazon German woman. Mimi's family always referred to my father as the 'Negro' who gave her 'Negro babies.' And you know here's my white mother carting her brown babies all over Stanford. People always thought she was our babysitter. But, you know what? I wouldn't change a thing."

"Oh, yeah?"

"Absolutely. I'm proud of who I am and who my parents are. They loved, and still love, each other tremendously and Tracy and I really benefited from that. They exposed us equally to both sides of our culture and I think we came out okay."

"Carol's mom is black and her dad was white. She never knew her father and she was always really messed up about being mixed. It took her a long time to feel comfortable about herself."

"How did you two meet?"

He chuckled. "She was my bank teller."

"Cute, very cute."

"Yeah, that's when she was working out South before she got promoted and moved to the downtown branch. Anyway, I finally had to ask her out, because I almost went broke since I was going to the bank everyday to withdraw money just so I could see her."

Sondra laughed. "I'm glad she said yes."

"Me too."

The waitress came over with their dinner—Louisiana Chicken Salad for Sondra, brisket for Kevin. In between devouring their food, they discussed everything from their childhoods to favorite movies to New York versus Chicago.

"When are you heading home?" Kevin asked as they sipped after-dinner coffee.

"I think tomorrow night. There's really nothing left for me to do here, so I might as well head home."

Kevin nodded his head as he absorbed this. "That's too bad. I've really enjoyed getting to know you."

Sondra looked at Kevin, catching the twinge in his voice. "Kevin... it would be too weird. Your wife, my sister..."

He smiled. "Oh, I know. I know. I guess I just feel some kind of bond to you, considering."

"Me too. But friends?" Sondra held up her pinky.

"Friends," Kevin said as he hooked his little finger through hers.

After Kevin insisted on picking up the tab, the two stepped out into the humid Chicago night.

"Can I give you a lift back to your hotel? It's kind of hard to get cabs around here."

Sondra smiled. "You know, I think I'll walk? It's such a nice night and I just need to be alone with my thoughts."

Kevin hung his head for a moment before looking Sondra squarely in the eye. "The last time I let a woman go out at night, she never came back."

Sondra released the breath she didn't know she'd been holding and smiled. "Okay," she whispered. "Thanks."

# FIFTY-TWO

Cindy Cross stood in her kitchen staring out her yellow and blue curtain-framed window watching Paula's house. It was late, but the light was still on. She wondered what was going on over there. She felt her husband slip a hand around her size two waist and nestle against her neck.

"The kids are asleep and the kitchen and living room are clean. What do you say we go upstairs and get dirty?"

Cindy laughed as Chris began to nibble on her ear and his hand flicked across her nipple. "Mmmm, that sounds good," she said as she reached back and ran her fingers through his thick golden hair. He turned her around and they began to kiss each other hungrily in the middle of their kitchen. They pulled back and Cindy rested her head on her husband's chest, her eyes focused in the direction of Paula's house.

"Still thinking about this morning?" Chris asked.

Cindy let out a deep sigh. "Yeah. In some ways, she reminds me of my mother."

"What, crazy you mean?"

Cindy tried to suppress her knowing giggle. "Stop it. No, you know how socially awkward my mother is."

"True."

"On the other hand, I can't decide if she's a battered wife or what the deal is. It's like she's both afraid of her husband and worships him at the same time. Isn't that usually how it is with domestic abuse victims?"

"You already tried the cops and unless you actually see something—"

"I know, I know. They can't do anything."

"Maybe you should go over there tomorrow. See if you can get her to open up to you."

Cindy snorted. "In one morning?"

"Sometimes, if you ask even the most tightly wound people the right question they'll tell you everything."

Cindy pulled her head back, looked at Chris and smiled. "You're right. She probably wants help and doesn't know how to ask. I'll go over first thing. Now—" Cindy gave Chris a knowing look. "I've got something for you in the bedroom."

"Now you're talkin'. Last one to bed has to beg."

Cindy let out a yelp and with a giggle, started to run upstairs, her husband hot on her tail.

# FIFTY-THREE

He'd taken Tracy to visit his mother once. It was right after they'd gotten engaged, and Phillip was eager for his mother to meet the woman he'd fallen in love with. The Alzheimer's had hijacked many of Betty Pearson's brain cells, though on occasion, glimpses of his beloved mother would shine through.

When Betty laid eyes on Tracy, she lit up like Times Square. Phillip could see it in her eyes; she never imagined her plain, awkward son would have such a beautiful girl on his arm. She fawned all over Tracy's filmy pink print blouse and simple black skirt. She wanted to rub the silky ends of Tracy's "good hair" beneath her fingers and couldn't get over how smooth and clear her complexion was. As was her nature, Tracy was so sweet to Betty, answering each of his mother's prying questions with grace and humor and even complimenting her on the spring green dress she wore. Betty had been delighted with the purple cashmere wrap Tracy had presented to her for her birthday, her eyes filling with tears as Tracy folded the soft material around her frail shoulders. She bragged she'd be the envy of Sunny Shores.

It was true that Betty had passed not too long after Tracy had died—that wasn't bullshit. So what if he'd fudged the dates a little bit? Nobody would know any different. Much as he'd done for his wife, he chose cremation for Betty and scattered her ashes in Lake Michigan, the same spot where his father rested in peace.

Even if she hadn't died, he knew he still would have hidden behind his mother to carry out his delicate mission. Her mind was so far gone, she barely recognized Phillip. She never would have been able to give any details about how often he visited or what her health was like. Not that he expected anyone to come snooping around.

He'd covered his tracks pretty well.

# FIFTY-FOUR

The doorbell pealed, startling Paula out of her sleep. She had crawled back into bed after Phillip left for work, her head about to split open. Lately, she felt sick all the time, but didn't dare tell Phillip. The doorbell tolled once again and Paula staggered to the door to answer it.

"Hi, Paula," Cindy said.

Paula clutched the collar of her pink housedress around her neck. "What do you want?"

Cindy licked her lips. "Listen, Paula, I don't know what happened yesterday, but I just wanted you to know that if you need a friend... I can be one for you."

Paula shook her head, anguish filling the crevices of her face. "I can't. I can't."

Cindy exhaled and lowered her voice. "Does Phillip... hit... you?"

Paula clasped her dress even tighter around her. "No. No! Please, I can't talk to you now. You have to go." Paula went to shut the door but Cindy blocked it with her hand.

"Paula, whatever it is, I can help. Really."

"It's not your concern, now please, leave."

With a final determined shove, Paula closed and latched the door. Breathing heavily, Paula ran her hand over her forehead and tried to get hold of herself.

# FIFTY-FIVE

It had been so easy to fill the Swiss cheese of her brain. Between the drugs and the programming he and Keegan were administering, it was almost like taking candy from a baby.

Every time he went to visit, Keegan would huff and puff and demand to know when this would be over, that he was running too many risks by having her there. Phillip would have to remind him of the risks by *not* having her there. That usually shut him up.

Whenever they spent time together, she was so full of questions. "Who am I?" "What happened?" "Where am I?"

He had stroked her hair and answered her questions in rich, melodious tones. "Your name is Paula."

"Where am I?"

"In the hospital."

"Why am I in the hospital?"

"You've been sick."

"Why? What's wrong with me?"

"You... tried to kill yourself... you drove your car into a tree."

"What? Oh... God... why would I do that?"

"You were upset, because of something you did."

"What did I do?"

"Well... you killed someone."

"That, that, that's not true."

"I'm sorry, but it is."

"Who?"

"My wife. You killed my wife. Tracy. You were in love with me and you wanted her out of the way."

"Oh… no… no, I couldn't have done something like that."

He nodded. "I'm afraid you did," he said matter-of-factly. "But don't worry about anything. I'll take care of everything."

She swallowed. "You will?"

"Oh, yes. I won't let the police take you away. You're not well. I understand that. You were just so in love with me, you couldn't help what you did."

She would look back at him, tears glistening in her eyes. "What are you going to do?" she whispered.

"Don't you worry about a thing. But you have to do exactly as Dr. Keegan and I say, Paula. Otherwise, the police will come and then I won't be able to protect you."

"What do I have to do?"

"Shh, shh. All in good time. Just know that I'll make it possible for you to live a normal life with me."

"Why? Why would you want to help me if I killed your wife?"

Phillip smiled. "Because I care about you. I realized the lengths you would go to for me. I couldn't let you go to jail. You would have gone to jail for the rest of your life for what you did to Tracy. They probably would have given you the death penalty."

"What did I do to her?"

"Stalked her. Told her she had to give me up. When she wouldn't do it, you smashed her face with a rock."

She would cover her face with her hands, horrified. "I could never do anything like that. Ever."

"But you did, Paula. You did."

"What did you do with her body?"

"Don't worry yourself about all that. I took care of everything."

"But, I—"

"So, you owe me your life. Which is why, in turn, you must dedicate your life to me."

"What do you want me do to?"

He smiled. "All in good time. Remember, though… you must do everything I ask. No questions, no complaints. Do you understand?"

She nodded, the slow realization that her life was in his hands beginning to dawn on her. "I... I understand. I'll do whatever you tell me. I promise."

"Good. For now, though, you must rest. You have so much ahead of you and you'll need your strength."

Paula gave him a feeble nod.

# FIFTY-SIX

"Hello, Cindy."

"Oh, my God, Paula, are you okay? You look like you've been crying."

Paula smoothed her hair back. "I'm fine. I was wondering if I might borrow some milk. It's Thursday and today is when I bake Phillip chocolate cake. He used the last of the milk in the coffee this morning. And if I stop and go to the store, my entire day will be off, and I just have a ton of laundry and cleaning to do."

Cindy was puzzled by Paula's calm, eerie demeanor, which was so different from the other day. "Paula… is there anything else you need?"

Paula tilted her head. "I don't know what you mean."

"Well, it's just that the other day, you seemed so upset and I was wondering if you'd like to talk about it."

"Cindy, you should really mind your own business."

"Like I told you the other day, I can help you. If you need to get away from your husband—"

"I'm perfectly fine." She paused. "The milk?"

Cindy sighed, defeated. "Fine. Come in."

Paula closed the door behind her and followed Cindy to the kitchen. Cindy went to open the refrigerator when she stopped. "Oh. Damn," she said as she smacked her forehead. She leaned over to open a drawer. "I forgot to take the ADP," she said as she pulled out a small blue plastic pouch. Paula watched in silence as Cindy popped a tiny white pill out of the foil casing. Her face lit up as she realized what it was.

"Oh!" she said, excited. "We take the same vitamins."

Cindy held her coffee mug in mid-air. "Vitamin?"

Paula nodded. "Yes. Vitamins. Phillip gives me the same kind each morning. I guess they must not be working as well since I've been feeling a little run down lately."

Cindy lowered her coffee and birth control pill on the counter, never taking her eyes off Paula. "Paula," she whispered. "Those are birth control pills. They keep you from getting pregnant—ADP. Anti-daddy pill?"

Paula shook her head, a smile creeping onto her face. "Nooo, they're vitamins. My husband is a pharmacist. I think he would know the difference between vitamins and those, those *things* you're talking about." She sniffed. "Maybe you need a new pharmacist."

Cindy fought to keep from crying as she realized Paula really had no idea what she was talking about. She tried again. "Paula," she said as she placed her hands on her neighbor's shoulders. "Those tiny little pills are birth control. Birth control. They are not vitamins."

Paula's gaze drifted from the counter to Cindy's pleading stare. She shook her head slowly at first, then more rapidly as what Cindy was saying started to set in. "No. No, that's not right. I can't have children. I'm unable to have children. Why would he give me a pill to keep me from having children if I can't?"

"Paula," Cindy whispered in an earnest and deliberate tone. "Maybe he told you that and gives you the birth control pills so that it will be true."

Paula slapped Cindy's hands off her shoulders. "You stop that. Stop it! Phillip loves me and he would never lie to me."

"Paula, please calm down—"

"He, he… he saved my life! He loves me."

Cindy could see Paula was whipping herself into a frenzy. "Okay, Paula, maybe I was wrong—"

Paula pointed a trembling finger in Cindy's face. "That's right. You are wrong. And a liar. You stay away from me!"

Enraged, Paula threw open the front door of Cindy's house and sprinted across the street to her own home.

"Paula, wait!" Cindy called out as she ran to catch up with her.

Paula spun around, shooting daggers at Cindy. "You stay away from me. You're evil. Don't you ever come near me again."

Cindy tried to grasp Paula's flailing hands with her own. "Paula, I'm sorry, I didn't mean to upset you. Why don't you come back and we'll have a cup of coffee, talk about this."

Cindy tried to put an arm around Paula's shoulders and steer her back across the street. Grunting, Paula shoved Cindy, who went flying and stumbled, just barely recovering before she landed in the street.

"Stay away from me," Paula said before she turned and ran home.

# FIFTY-SEVEN

"How long do you think before he finds Phillip?"

Sondra sipped her coffee and shrugged. "Depends on if he's drunk or not. He tends to work better smashed from what I've been told."

Sondra and Cicely were having lunch before Sondra left for the airport to head back to New York.

"Sounds like you've found the right guy for the job. And the police haven't tracked him down?"

"Not that I know of. Well, I should say I called the detective on the case and she said they were still trying to find him. Honestly? I don't think they care."

"Oh, trust me, they care. Especially when it gets out."

"I appreciate you keeping this quiet. I know you can't forever, but, I just—"

Cicely broke in. "One of the investigative reporters at the station got a whiff of what's going on."

Sondra looked up at the ceiling and let out a rumbling sigh. "What happened?"

Cicely gulped her iced tea. "He came sniffing around my desk last night. Said he'd heard some whispers about Tracy's disappearance while hanging around a diner that the cops frequent. I played dumb, but he's asking a lot of questions and it won't be long before he starts piecing things together and this whole thing blows wide open."

Sondra started to nibble on her forefinger, breaking the all-too-familiar seal, salty blood seeping into her mouth. "Fuck," she mumbled. "Phillip could see it and he could run and then we'll never find him. Or I'll find him and he'll change his story. Whatever the hell it is."

"I'm so sorry. Sorry about all of this."

Sondra smiled, clasped Cicely's hand and gave it a squeeze. "I appreciate everything you've done for me." She leaned back and sighed. "I guess all I do now is wait for the shit to hit the fan."

# FIFTY-EIGHT

Paula slammed the door shut behind her as Cindy's dreadful words replayed themselves in her ears.

"It's not true. It's not true. It's not true." Paula dropped to the floor and rolled into a ball in the corner of her living room, repeating the phrase to herself over and over again. She was drenched in sweat and her heart thumped against her chest like a metronome on high.

Phillip loved her. He'd kept her from going to jail. He'd taken care of her. He was always honest with her. Hadn't he told her she shouldn't trust other people because the world was full of liars? Paula wiped her hand across her face, a trail of snot spreading across her cheek. She would just never talk to that horrible Cindy Cross woman again. She should have listened to Phillip when he told her it wasn't a good idea to allow others into her world. Yes. She should focus solely on her wifely duties and on her husband. Feeling better now that she was refocused, Paula pulled herself up and went to sort some laundry.

# FIFTY-NINE

When the shit hit the fan, no one could escape the splatter. Cicely had called Sondra that morning to let her know that Rick Jones, investigative reporter for Channel Four, was running with the story about Carol and Tracy on that night's ten P.M. news. Carol's family had hired an attorney who would be speaking on their behalf in the piece and confirming they would be bringing suit against the police department. The jungle drums said they'd been in contact with the rabble-rousing community activist, Joe Johnson. Cicely warned her it wouldn't be long before the national media picked up the thread and the whole thing would become a powder keg. Sondra thanked Cicely and determined she would lay low for a while and hope Nicky found Phillip first.

It was dusk and she had drawn all of her drapes, shrouding her apartment in darkness. She'd been chain-smoking for hours as she rambled aimlessly from room to room, the low hum of the TV droning in the background. Sondra had just stubbed out what was probably her millionth cigarette of the day and was about to light up another when her cell phone rang.

"This better not be fucking CNN," she mumbled as she looked at the caller ID. The number was blocked and she was about to let it keep ringing when it occurred to her it might be Nicky.

"Hello?" she said.

"Yooooo. What's up?"

Sondra wanted to kiss herself for answering the phone. "Nicky." Sondra swallowed then took a deep breath. "So? What'd you find out?"

"He's going by the name of Pierce now. Phillip Pierce. Married to a lady named Paula."

"Are you sure it's him?"

"Oh, yeah. It was a little tricky, but I am fo' sho', baby."

"Where is he?"

"Livin' in St. Louis. He works for a clinic as a pharmacist. Wife stays home. No kids. Shitload of cash in the bank."

"Do you have an address? A phone number?"

"You know it, baby. You got a pen?"

Sondra fumbled in the darkened apartment in search of a pen and paper. "Okay, shoot."

Nicky gave Sondra all of Phillip's information, including his un-listed phone number, work and home addresses and work schedule.

"Goddamn, you are good," Sondra said, shaking her head.

"You know how I do."

"Next time you're in New York, let me buy you a drink."

"Yeah, man, I would be down. I'll hit you when I'm in town. Bring G, too."

"Oh, the stories that would come out of that night. Listen, Nicky, I gotta go, but definitely, call me when you're in town."

"You got it baby. Tell G I can't wait 'til Caaaabo!"

The phone went dead and Sondra could only laugh at Nicky. She looked down at the piece of paper in her hand, feeling triumphant. She'd come this far; she just had to go a little further.

Sondra shook herself back to the business at hand. "All right, flight to St. Louis," she said as she pulled up the American Airlines website on her laptop. Her phone rang again and groaning, she answered with-out looking to see who it was.

"Yeah?" she said, annoyed.

"Sondra? It's Kevin. Henderson."

"Oh, hi. I'm sorry. You caught me at a weird time. I'm on my way to St. Louis."

"St. Louis?"

Sondra put the phone on speaker so she could tap out flight infor-mation. "My ex-husband, Gary, is, strangely enough, friends with a bounty hunter. Nicky. Anyway, I asked Nicky to find Phillip and he did and I'm on my way there now."

"Wow. It's really him? I mean, he couldn't have made a mistake?"

"Nicky doesn't make mistakes."

"I want to be there."

"What?"

"I want to know why he did this, why—"

"No, no way. This is between me and him."

"I'm in this too. I can meet you in St. Louis, probably make it there before you."

Sondra snorted. "Considering I'll likely be going out of LaGuardia, you're probably right."

"I'll book the flight now. I could even drive down."

"Kevin, I'm sorry, but you're just going to have to stay out of this."

"I'm just as involved as you are. More."

Sondra kneaded the skin of her forehead like it was pizza dough before she looked up and shook her head. "I'm sorry, Kevin. I have to do this alone."

Before he could say another word, Sondra hung up.

# SIXTY

"Bottoms up."

Paula looked at Phillip standing in front of her, brandishing her daily dose of vitamins. She smiled and opened her mouth so that Phillip could place the tiny blue pill and the larger blue one into her tongue. She took a huge swallow of orange juice.

"What's for lunch today?" he asked as she handed him his large lunch bag.

"Oh, dear, you're so funny. The same as every Friday: tuna on whole wheat, tomato soup in a thermos, cheese and crackers and a slice of chocolate cake."

"Well, I just wanted to make sure you didn't forget. You've been quite forgetful lately."

"Oh, don't be silly. I'm fine, dear." She put her arms around him. "Have a good day, dear." Phillip walked out the door and she waited until she heard his car pull out of the driveway. She peeked out the front window to make sure he was gone before she walked into the kitchen and turned on the faucet. She swirled the tip of her tongue behind her bottom teeth and produced the two pills Phillip had given her. She spit them out into her hand and looked at the melting mass of blue in her palm. She put her hand under the faucet until the water carried the powder blue gunk down the drain. She flipped on the garbage disposal as an extra precaution. Clearing her throat, Paula went to grab her yellow mop bucket and fill it up with disinfectant.

# SIXTY-ONE

She was so friendly.

A real chatterbox. But not that it annoyed you, but rather made you want to listen. Drew you in. And always with a smile on her face. Always so full of questions: "Hi, how are you today?" or "How's everything going?" "what's new in your world?" And so eager to talk about herself.

So forthcoming.

That's how he knew about the dog. She'd shown him pictures of her trusty chocolate lab, bragged about how nice and friendly he was, that even people who didn't like dogs loved Rusty.

It took him a little over an hour to get out to Hyde Park. All day, the snow had come down in a steady cascade and the roads were a muddle of salt, ice, and slush. He drove behind a salt truck, which helped. Finally, he pulled up in front of her townhouse and waited. She had mentioned in one conversation what time she usually walked the dog. He looked at his watch. Should be any minute now. If not, he would have to come back tomorrow and he didn't want to have to do that since his in-laws were scheduled to fly in then and who knew what the weather was going to do. When he saw her door open and her silhouette appear just behind her dog, he'd gotten so excited, he accidentally beeped his horn.

Fumbling to open his car door, he put his boot into the mush below, careful to ease his way out. It was quiet, snow the only force capable of silencing the city. He watched her slip and slide over the icy sidewalk as she tried to keep her dog from darting away from her in his glee at being outside. Shoving his hands in his pockets, he whistled softly as he approached her.

"Carol?"

She whipped around and even in the dim glow of the streetlights and blowing snow, he could see a glimmer of fear in her eyes. "Do I know you?"

He laughed. "It's me, Phillip. Your pharmacist."

Her internal guards slithered away the instant she realized it was a friendly face in front of her. "Oh, my goodness, I didn't realize it was you. How did you know it was me?"

He bent down and began to scratch behind Rusty's ears, who moaned in appreciation. "You know, I've heard so much about this guy, I feel like I know him already." He straightened up and looked at her.

"I recognized your coat. It's very distinctive," he said, gesturing to the sky blue and black houndstooth coat she wore.

She tightened her grip on Rusty's leash. He sensed her apprehension. "Oh. I didn't realize you lived around here."

He smiled. "I don't."

Carol looked back toward the house. He knew she was wondering if anyone would come to her aid if she screamed. "So what are you doing out on a night like this?"

"Looking for you."

Carol took a step backward, tugging on the cracked, red leather leash as she did. "Listen, I have to go. Have a good night," she said, her voice rupturing. She tried to yank the dog back in the direction of the house, but Phillip grabbed the leash and held it.

"Where are you going?"

She licked her lips. "My husband will be looking for me. We really need to go."

He shook his head and smiled. "No, Carol, I don't think so."

In one fell swoop, Phillip lunged at Carol, who yelped as he grabbed her by the waist with one hand and clamped his other across her mouth. Rusty sat on his hind legs, his head cocked to the side, just staring at them. Phillip looked over at Rusty.

"If you scream, I'll kill your dog."

Her cries gurgled in her throat.

Phillip dragged Carol in the direction of his car. "I don't want your money and I'm not going to rape you. We have to take a little trip."

She shook her head.

Phillip had unlocked the door with his remote and pulled Carol over to the driver's side. "Slide over to the passenger side." She hesitated.

"That's a really long leash. Just long enough to strangle a friendly, unsuspecting dog."

Her eyes pleaded with him. "Please. Please. Don't. I'm begging you."

"Then move over."

Whimpering, she did as she was told, and Phillip got behind the wheel.

"Put your hands in front of you."

"If I do what you say, will you let me go?"

"I said, put your hands in front of you."

She hesitated a moment before she complied and placed her hands in front of her. He ripped a piece of duct tape from a roll stuffed in the pocket of his coat and cut it with the blade of his Army knife before he jerked it around her delicate wrists. He followed suit with another piece that he slapped over her mouth. Satisfied, he started the car and let it warm up for a few minutes.

"Get down," he said. "On the floor. Get down."

Tears streaming down her face, she looked out the window at Rusty once more, who hadn't moved, before she struggled to crouch down into the tiny space between the seat and the dash. They drove in silence. The roads were still like an Icee and he had to stay focused in order not to crash. He was surprised she hadn't put up more of a struggle. He decided she was one of those submissive types, figuring if she just did what she was told, he would let her go unharmed. Muffled sobs floated up from where she was wedged, and for a moment he felt bad. He never wanted any of this. But he had to do it. He loved Tracy. If he could just take her away from all those distractions. It had to be done.

This was the only way.

He caught another salt truck on the way back North, which made the trip to Belmont Harbor easier. He eased his car into the marina parking lot and turned it off. He closed his eyes and took a few deep breaths. Quickly, he opened the driver's side door and ran to the passenger side. He wrenched her out of the car and brought her around to the trunk, keeping his arm fastened around her waist. He used his remote to pop open the trunk and reached in to grab the small black duffel bag lodged in one dark corner. She was still crying and all he could think was how he would be glad when this was over. Clutching her arm with one hand, he dragged her to the snack shack that sold ice cream and hot dogs in the summer, but now stood boarded up and empty. He shoved her against the side of the building facing the lake. He pulled his Swiss Army knife back out of his coat pocket and flicked it open. The blade glistened, cutting a swath of light against the fluffy bits of white snow swirling around them.

"A Swiss Army knife may be small, but it can do a lot of damage. Especially if I jam it into your carotid artery," he whispered as he trailed it along her exposed neck. "Do you understand what I'm telling you?" Her head jerked up and down like one of those bobble-head dolls people were fond of putting on their dashboards.

Phillip licked his lips. "Good. Now, I'm going to cut the tape and open this bag. When I do, I want you to get undressed and put on the clothes that are in this bag. Don't scream and don't try to run, because I will catch you. Do you understand?"

She closed her eyes and as tears squeezed from beneath the lids, she nodded once more.

"Okay. Go." He pressed the knife to her throat while he watched.

With wobbly hands, Carol stripped her own clothes off. He could see the goose bumps pop up on her quivering flesh as the blowing snow pelted her bare skin. She was still in her bra and panties when she went to reach for the duffel bag. He stopped her.

"Underwear, too," he said.

She shook her head.

He squeezed the tip of the knife against her. "Yes."

Her body shuddering with quiet sobs, she held one hand in front of her breasts and reached the other around the back to unhook her bra. Keeping the same hand in front of her, she awkwardly removed her white bikini briefs and let them drop to the frozen ground.

"There's a bra and panties in the bag. Put them on."

Trembling, she yanked on the black bra and panty set. There was a running outfit of spandex pants and long-sleeved polyester top, thick white cotton socks and running shoes in the duffel bag. Finally, she changed into a bright green windbreaker and stood in front of Phillip, terrified of what was next.

"Give me all your jewelry," he said, holding out his hand.

His eyes followed the bright red tips of her fingers, as she slid her engagement and wedding rings off her finger. She fumbled as she tried to remove the flimsy gold chain that looped through a small cross around her neck, before he got impatient and ripped it off. He fished Tracy's wedding ring set and gloves out of his coat pocket and handed them to Carol.

"Put these on."

She dutifully slipped another woman's platinum band and engagement ring on her finger and her gloves over her hands. Pleased that it was almost over, Phillip seized her arm and began to wrench her in the direction of the massive boulders that lay kitty-corner to the green Indian statue just to the south of Belmont Harbor. He tore the duct tape from her mouth. Her breath escaped her lips in terse puffs as she swallowed the frigid air in gigantic gulps.

"Oh, God, what are you going to do to me?"

"Don't worry, it will be over soon."

"Please, please, I'm begging you, please, please don't do whatever you're thinking." The panic in her voice was palpable, and again he felt a momentary twinge. He brushed it off and concentrated on what had to be done.

"It's too late for that. I'm really sorry. But I have to do this."

She yelped as he grabbed her shoulders and shoved her into the firmly packed snow atop the pointy boulders. She cried as he dropped to his knees to straddle her, positioning them so the rocks wouldn't dig into them. A river of snot ran out of her nose and even in the dark, he could see her eyes were bloodshot from all the crying. She writhed and twisted as she tried to get away. Phillip calmly picked up a hefty rock and held it aloft over his head. Her eyes widened as she realized what he was about to do.

"Please, please! I don't want to die! I just got married! I don't want to die! Please, please don't kill me! Oh, God, please! Please don't do this! Please!"

"I'm sorry," he whispered.

With a quiet grunt, he smashed the rock across her face. The sound of the rock crushing the delicate bones of her face, splintering the sturdiness of her skull and silencing her desperate pleadings was deafening. Her screams gave way first to a choked gurgling before lapsing into a dull buzz. Her body thrashed beneath him before it finally shuddered into stillness. Her face was now nothing more than a jiggly bowl of strawberry and grape jelly. One eyeball had escaped the socket and hung to the side. Blood gushed out and seeped into the brilliant whiteness like a snow cone pumped full of sticky sweet syrup. Panting, he struggled to his feet. Running his gloved hand across his own face, he took deep, jagged breaths.

It was done.

He looked around. It was supposed to snow through the night, so it was likely she wouldn't be found until the end of the week, when a major thaw was expected. Sniffing, he looked down at her one last time, before stepping over her body. He stuffed her clothes into the duffel bag and zipped it shut. On his way back to the car, he tossed the wallet over his shoulder onto the ground, the plastic vinyl inside flap blowing open to reveal the beaming smile on Tracy Ellis' driver's license picture.

# SIXTY-TWO

Paula shut her eyes against the splatters of vomit on the glossy white tiles. She'd been hunched over the toilet for the better part of two hours and now lay in the fetal position on the bathroom floor, her cheek pressed against her fluffy white bath rug. She clutched her stomach, as though she could halt the nausea through mere touch.

She never got sick—well once, she'd had a cold. A bad one. Phillip had been furious, accusing her of getting sick on purpose so she could get out of taking care of him—of breaking her promise. She had been so tired and had just wanted to lie in bed and sleep. He made her keep up with her duties for the two weeks she sick, all through the hacking, chills and tightness in her chest. He'd even forced her to sleep on the floor, complaining that her constant coughing shook the bed and interrupted his sleep. Finally, he'd given her something—some pills of some sort—and her symptoms began to subside.

The only good thing about those two weeks had been no sex.

As she lay on the floor quivering, Paula realized why she must be so sick.

Her vitamins.

She'd stopped taking them a few days earlier. And now this. She started to sob. Why did she think she could go against Phillip? He knew what was best for her; he knew what she needed. She never should have stopped taking them.

She would resume taking them tomorrow. She'd never tell him what she'd done.

Except how was she going to get through this now?

If Phillip came home and saw that she hadn't cleaned the house and there was no dinner… Paula whimpered, trying to decide what was worse; vomiting until her throat was raw or facing Phillip's wrath.

The thought was enough to motivate Paula to flatten her palm against the floor and struggle to get upright. Paula groaned, as she felt the surge again. She stuck her head in the toilet just in time.

# SIXTY-THREE

Phillip had paced outside the hospital, as excited as a ten-year-old hopped up on twenty candy bars. Today was the day. They would be starting their new life together.

House hunting had been fun. He'd spent hours hunched over a map of the U.S., trying to decide the best place for them to settle down. He'd never really liked Chicago. Too cold, too urban. Too many distractions. He wasn't interested in Detroit. Too dirty. Too depressed. He had no interest in going back. He'd finally settled on St. Louis, attracted to the hybrid of city and suburban sensibilities. Money wasn't an issue. Between the sale of his and Tracy's house, her various assets and life insurance policy, not to mention he'd made a good living as a pharmacist—they would be comfortable.

The little house on Red Rose Lane had been perfect. It was a quiet neighborhood full of young families, families who would be far too busy shuttling their brood to swim practice and horseback riding lessons to worry about what he and Paula were doing. The Pavilion had sealed the deal—he didn't want her driving, thus having too much freedom. On the other hand, he wasn't about to spend his time carting her all over town on errands. He'd paid cash for the house that day, not wanting to waste any more time. He would have to move quickly on everything else—new IDs, Social Security numbers; a whole new life.

Getting to this point hadn't been easy. Not that he had expected it to be. First, he had to get through the funeral. And then his in-laws—always offering to stay and help or have him come out to California. The endless phone calls from her friends, co-workers, neighbors. It was excruciating, because timing was everything and he had been anxious to get going.

After a few weeks, he'd started dropping hints to people that his mother wasn't well. After about a month and a half, he let people know his mother had taken a turn for the worse and he would have to take care of her and wasn't sure how long he'd be gone. That's when he'd gone house hunting. After another month or so had passed, he returned to Chicago to break the news that he would have to move back to Detroit to take care of his mother full-time. People nodded, seeming to understand, wondering how much grief one man could be expected to bear in such a short amount of time.

And now, here they were.

He'd been connecting the dots for her, and he would continue to do so. It would be much easier now that they would be together all the time. He relished having her all to himself. No meddling friends, no job—no nothing. Just them, together.

Forever.

Keegan slammed the back door open and motioned for Phillip to follow him to his office. As usual, the two men stormed down the hallway without a word. Keegan opened the door and Phillip glided in, bursting with glee.

"So, is she ready?"

"Yeah, Phillip, she's ready. And so am I—ready to be fucking done with all of this."

Phillip dropped down into a chair. "I've got to hand it to you, Keegan. I didn't think you had it in you. I thought for sure you'd screw this up."

"Yeah, well, an ax hanging over your head is a great motivator." He paused and looked at Phillip. "But I guess you knew that when you dragged me into this, didn't you?"

Phillip shrugged. "All I did was call in a favor."

Keegan snorted and pulled out her file. "As far as I'm concerned, you and I are even. Forget my name, forget my number, forget I exist."

Phillip chuckled. "I hope *you* return that favor."

Keegan flipped on his shredder and fed the individual file pages into the machine's eager teeth. "No problem."

"Well, I'm ready, so let's go get her. I've got a long drive ahead of me."

"I feel sorry for her. Being stuck with you, spending the rest of her life under your thumb."

"She needs me. I can take care of her better than anybody else."

"You keep telling yourself that." Keegan shook his head and stood. "Let's get this over with."

The two men headed down the hall to the padded rooms. Keegan unlocked hers and as usual she was sitting quietly on the bed staring straight ahead. She jumped up when she saw Phillip and rushed into his arms.

"Oh, dear. I've been waiting for you. I've missed you so much. When was the last time you were here?"

Phillip squeezed her a moment before pulling back to look at her. "Don't worry about that now. I've got a surprise for you, Paula. We're leaving today. We're going to start our new life."

Paula clamped her hands over her mouth, her shoulders hunched together with delight. "Really? Oh! I can't wait."

Phillip smiled. "Me neither."

# SIXTY-FOUR

Phillip opened the door to the house on Red Rose Lane and stepped inside. She waited awkwardly out on the front steps.

"This is where we'll live?" she asked.

"Yes, Paula. This is our home. This is where you will spend your days. Come. Let me show you around."

She tiptoed inside, soaking in her surroundings as Phillip took her on a tour of the house, explaining what each room was for. Everything was plain and white just like the hospital. He could see the fear seizing her, as she thought about what this new place meant. She clutched the collar of her dress and Phillip walked over to her and took her hand.

"Paula," he said as he slipped a thin gold band on her ring finger. "We're married now. And that means you will do everything I say."

"But what if I can't do it?"

"Paula, I don't understand. You were so happy earlier when I told you about our new home. What's wrong?"

Paula rubbed her forehead and looked around. "I don't know if I can do it. What if I can't be a good wife to you, like Tracy—?"

Phillip walked over and placed a hand on her shoulder. "Shhh, shhh. You will, Paula. You will. I know in time you'll prove that you're worthy of my love. That everything we *both* did was worth it."

She chewed the bottom of her lip and looked around at the sparsely furnished house. "I just don't want to disappoint you. *Especially* because of everything you've done for me."

Phillip rubbed both her shoulders now. "Just do what we talked about, and you'll be fine. It is very important, Paula, that you do everything I've told you. You take care of me and our home, and you don't tell anyone about your past. We don't want to tip anyone off about you. Then I'll never be able to help you."

Paula nodded. "Okay," she whispered.

He cocked his head to the side. "Paula…"

She smoothed back her hair with one hand, fiddling for a moment with the severe bun at the nape of her neck. "What I meant to say was, yes, dear."

Phillip smiled. "There. That's better. Now. I'm very tired after the long drive. It's time for you to make dinner. I took the liberty of having the realtor pick up groceries. The recipe cards are in the kitchen." He took off his jacket and settled into the beige recliner in the living room. "You'd better get started."

She swallowed and clasped her hands together. "Yes, dear," she said before she scurried to the kitchen.

# SIXTY-FIVE

When Sondra finally turned her phone back on, Kevin had left her three frantic messages, two begging her to tell him where she was going and a third saying he was contacting the police. Sondra briefly considered calling him, but decided to take her chances and wing it to St. Louis. She called Cicely in the cab on her way to the airport to tell her what was going on. Cicely tried to talk her out of it, telling her to let the police handle it. Sondra pretended like the call dropped and hung up. She wouldn't let it go. She couldn't.

Her flight was delayed while they waited for a vicious summer storm to pass. Sondra's colossal lust for a cigarette almost drove her to light up in the bathroom. It wasn't worth it, of course, so instead, she chewed on the ice from the countless cups of ginger ale she'd sucked down while they waited. Drumming her fingers against the armrest, Sondra hoped it wouldn't be too much longer before they could leave. The shivers were back and Sondra knew if she didn't get to Phillip now, she might not ever find out what happened to Tracy.

# SIXTY-SIX

The nausea passed and Paula felt well enough to begin washing the windows inside and out. Except her head was pounding and she had to stop several times. Everything felt wobbly, slippery. But she would fix that. She just had to get through today and she would start taking her vitamins again tomorrow.

"I'll be fine," she whispered to herself as she soaped one window, the creamy white streaks soothing her. "Phillip knows best. I'll never go against him again."

Paula ventured a smile to herself before a stab of pain seared across her temples and she dropped her jumbo yellow sponge on the floor.

"Oh my God," she said as she doubled over, clutching the corner of the counter. It came again and this time she fell to the floor, the sting too great.

"Oh, no," she whispered. She looked up and her kitchen became a blob of white. She held her hand to her head. Another wave of nausea rose up and she barely had time to stand up before the vomit came flying out of her mouth and sprayed the side of the sink.

She stood over the sink, heaving and crying. This was too much for her to handle on her own. She needed Phillip. Except it was early afternoon. He wouldn't be home for hours.

She couldn't wait that long. She'd have to call him, beg him for help.

Except she didn't know how to use a phone. Phillip had never taught her how. And besides, he kept it locked up in his office. She didn't even know where he worked. She grunted and tried to drag herself to the bathroom when there was another jab to the inside of her head. She keeled over and rolled onto her back, trembling. She stayed there, staring at the ceiling and fighting to catch her breath.

She stayed there a few more moments, coming back to her senses. She couldn't let Phillip know what was going on.

# SIXTY-SEVEN

It had been bliss.

Coming home to her every day. To a hot meal. To her grateful love and devotion. He often had to pinch himself over how lucky he was.

And smart.

He was so happy. She was so obedient, doing everything he told her without question, without rebellion. He was finally in total control. It was empowering. Energizing.

The only black mark was when he'd have to pull her back in line. Sometimes she forgot. He'd wonder if he should adjust her dosage, but always decided against it. Give her too little, she'd start to remember; give her too much, she'd be catatonic. He'd just have to supplement the chemistry with his words and actions. What was it they'd called it in the handful of psychology classes he'd taken? Positive reinforcement. It usually worked and everything would settle back down to normal.

He would do whatever it took to keep his perfect world perfect.

# SIXTY-EIGHT

Don Keegan shook his head as he watched the Channel Four news and the exposé of the Tracy Ellis/Carol Henderson debacle. He knew Phillip Pearson was a sick fuck, but he had no idea just how deep it ran.

Don would forever rue the day he got mixed up with that guy.

Years ago, he'd been a high-flying psychiatrist with a thriving private practice, a Lincoln Park mansion, a Porsche in the garage and a bevy of hot blondes for each arm.

He also had a raging drug addiction, courtesy of a back injury from slipping on pool tiles during a vacation in the Caymans. Physical therapy wasn't cutting it and surgery made him skittish—hence why he wasn't a surgeon. He started with Vicodin, moved on to Percocet, before falling prey to Fentanyl. He became desperate in his attempts to secure drugs, going so far as to falsify prescriptions using aliases, multiple addresses and skipping around to different pharmacies in the suburbs and city. He stuck to large pharmacies, where no one was likely to remember his face.

Except he'd tripped up and gone to Phillip's pharmacy twice in one week.

Phillip threatened to turn him in and a terrified Keegan had begged him to keep quiet, swore that he'd get help if Phillip kept his secret. Phillip agreed, but promised he'd be calling on him for a favor one day. A desperate Keegan agreed to the terms before he checked himself into rehab the next day.

Rehab had been a grueling exercise that alternated between humiliation and torture. By the time he was done, his life was in shambles.

He'd been away from his practice too long, resulting in lost patients, lost income, and lost reputation. Patients who'd caught a whiff of his troubles started to sue, claiming a hopped-up shrink was unfit to provide competent medical care. The lawsuits had grown to impressive levels, and time he could have spent rebuilding his practice was lost to long sessions with his attorneys trying to settle the damn things. The Lincoln Park mansion fell into foreclosure and the Porsche was repossessed. He'd barely escaped homelessness by convincing one of his old bedmates to let him bunk on her couch for a few months.

Once he'd made the last settlement, a med school buddy was able to get him a position on staff at a mental hospital in Berwyn of all places. He hated the suburbs. And the work was everything he vowed he'd never do. It made him long for the days of listening to Gold Coast socialites drone on about their prick lawyer husbands putting them on a shopping allowance and their lovers' demands for more spending money.

He knew he wouldn't do it forever. Still, it had gotten him back into treating patients and allowed him to begin rebuilding. He'd even managed to get back into Lincoln Park, even if it was a one bedroom apartment. It was a start.

The jungle drums had told Phillip where Don had landed and on that cold January night three years ago, he'd made good on his promise to cash in his favor.

It wasn't until Don saw the photographs of Tracy Ellis and Carol Henderson splashed across the front page of the newspaper that he'd put two and two together.

Sick fuck, indeed.

Don picked up his cell phone from the small glass coffee table in front of him. He twirled it in his hand, his eyes still trained on the TV, which had now moved on to weather. It would be sunny, a high of eighty-five.

Maybe he could make it rain on Phillip tomorrow.

Don punched up the Channel Four website on his phone in search of the station's phone number.

# SIXTY-NINE

It was late afternoon before Paula's nausea subsided. Fortunately, dinner that evening was easy—spaghetti with meat sauce, garlic bread and salad. She'd forced herself to be as upbeat as ever for Phillip that evening, even though she felt like dropping to the kitchen floor and staying there all night. She held her breath as her hands squished into the raw beef she would use for the sauce, struggling not to let the smells or cold, wormy texture dislodge her stomach. She managed to stumble through the torture with a smile on her face, not daring to show Phillip her pain.

It worked, since Phillip had commented how she seemed to be improving in her duties. He'd even kissed her on the forehead and congratulated her on a job well done. Paula had breathed a sigh of relief that she'd passed inspection. She couldn't take a night in the closet. She was just too worn out. That night, she clutched her pillow against her stomach, feeling comforted as she drifted off to sleep.

# SEVENTY

"You seem rather chipper this morning."

Paula smiled as she placed a cup of coffee in front of Phillip.

"Oh, I am. It looks like it's going to be a beautiful day outside."

Phillip looked over Paula's shoulder to the kitchen window behind her. "Yes, I guess it is going to be a nice day today."

"I think I might shampoo the carpets today. It will be good to do while the roast for tonight's dinner is cooking."

"Well, you know what I always say. Efficiency is the hallmark of a well run home."

Paula placed a stack of steaming pancakes on the table. "Oh, thank you dear. I'm so glad you're happy."

Phillip nodded as he waited for Paula to butter the pancakes before drenching them in maple syrup. She ducked back into the kitchen for a plate of turkey sausage links and patted Phillip on the shoulder. "Eat well, dear."

Phillip smiled and bit into a link. "I intend to."

Paula busied herself finishing Phillip's lunch of ham and cheese on wheat, a chocolate chip cookie, and a baggie of six carrot sticks. The trauma of yesterday had passed and she couldn't remember when she'd felt so good.

If ever.

Phillip cleared his throat and Paula whirled around as if she was floating on air, the brown paper bag with Phillip's lunch in hand. She handed him the bag and picked up the dishes in one fell swoop. She ran to the closet to extract Phillip's blue blazer. She turned around to find him holding a glass of water and her vitamins.

"Open wide, Paula."

She stopped and hesitated a moment, debating whether or not to tell him she no longer needed the vitamins. She thought better of it. He wouldn't like it. Better to let him go on thinking they were still necessary. For now at least. She plastered on a smile.

"Thank you, dear," she said as she opened her mouth and took a hearty gulp of water.

Phillip nodded and set the glass on the coffee table before he let Paula slip his jacket on for him.

"Have a good day, dear," Paula said.

"You, too," Phillip said as he gave her a peck on the cheek. "I look forward to seeing what you do with the carpets."

Paula chuckled and gave him a wave. She waited until he was out of the driveway before she spit the pills into her palm. She rinsed them down into the garbage disposal and washed her hands before filling a glass with water and gargling to wash the bitterness away.

She glanced up at the clock on the stove. She should take the meat out to defrost for dinner. She didn't want to get behind schedule.

# SEVENTY-ONE

It was almost 11 P.M. before the flight finally left JFK. The flights Sondra had taken across the globe while doing her documentaries couldn't compare with this two hour, nine minute flight, which was turning into the longest of her life. The flight attendants got tired of giving her cups of ice; they finally plunked a plastic bag of it on her tray table. Her fingers were so demolished, at one point she sat on them. But then she couldn't help herself and was gnawing on them again as they began their final descent. She found the last rental car available in St. Louis, and when she finally dropped into the hotel bed, she didn't know whether to sleep or stay awake.

She compromised and settled on a few hours of sleep. She was up at seven and was now sitting in her rental car in front of the clinic where Phillip worked. If things had gone how she originally planned, she would have been able to go to his house last night. So it goes. She checked her watch again. It was eight-thirty and the hours posted on the door said they opened at nine. She took another sip of coffee and sighed. A burgundy Mazda pulled into the parking lot and she sat up, peering closely to see if it might be him. A few minutes passed before the door swung open and a petite black woman dressed in a multicolored pharmacy smock and green scrub pants got out. Sondra blinked several times.

"Oh, my God. That's his wife. That's Paula." She remembered what Phillip's letter had said. "I thought he said she was a housewife," Sondra muttered. Shaking her head, Sondra flung the car door open and ran over to the woman who was getting something out of the trunk.

"Excuse me. Excuse me," Sondra called out as she reached the woman.

"Yes?"

Sondra held out her hand. "Hi," she said, slightly out of breath. "I'm Sondra Ellis. Phillip's sister-in-law. Well, I guess, former sister-in-law. He still works here, right?"

The woman eyed Sondra, skeptical. "Yes, he works here," she said. "He should be here any minute."

"Oh. Oh, good! I'm actually glad we had a chance to talk before he got here. Forgive me if I sound rude, but I thought he said you stayed home?"

The woman placed her hand on her hip and stared Sondra down. "I'm sorry, but what do you want?"

"Oh, gosh, Paula, I'm sorry to—"

The woman cut her off. "Paula? Wait, did you just call me Paula?"

Sondra frowned. "Yeah?"

"I'm not Paula. That's his wife. I'm Maxine. I just work for Phillip."

Sondra saw the words tumble out of the woman's mouth, but wasn't quite able to catch them. "Excuse me?"

The woman rolled her eyes. "*Paula* is his wife. Phillip and I just work together."

"Oh, my... God, wait, wait a minute." Sondra groped inside her bag for the picture. "Phillip sent this picture of the two of you to my mother and said you were married." Sondra held the picture in front of Maxine, an anxious look on her face. Maxine took the picture and looked at it a moment before she handed it back to Sondra.

"Yeah, that's me. It was taken at our Christmas party last year. Are you sure that's what he said?"

Sondra looked back down at the picture clamped between her trembling fingers. "I don't understand. I know he said—" She glanced back up to see an irritated Maxine gazing at her. Sondra gave up, knowing if she tried to explain this whole mess, the woman wouldn't believe it anyway.

"You know, I'm mistaken. He never said that." Sondra dropped the picture back into her bag. "Look, I would appreciate it if you didn't say anything to him about this. I want to surprise him… kind of a family thing. Please? Don't say anything?"

The woman set a hard stare on Sondra for a few seconds before she rolled her eyes and nodded. "Yeah, fine, whatever. I gotta get to work." She pulled a duffel bag out of the trunk, slammed it shut and went to step around Sondra.

"Oh, um, just one more thing." Sondra opened up the crumpled piece of paper that she had shoved into the pocket of her jeans before she left New York. "Can you tell me how to get to Red Rose Lane?"

Maxine rolled her eyes again. "Yeah, just go out to Miller Road here, make a right, take that about three miles until you see a sign for The Crossings, where you will make a left. Then make another left at Red Rose Lane. Can't miss it."

"Thanks so much," she said as she turned back toward the rental car. Sondra slid into the front seat, replaying her encounter with Maxine.

She heard her phone jangle from inside her purse. She dropped her hand inside until her fingers closed around it. It was Cecily.

"Hi Cecily, I can't talk right now."

"Sondra, listen, it's important."

"If you're gonna tell me to go to the police—"

"We got a call from a guy who knows Phillip. A doctor."

"What kind of a doctor?"

A psychiatrist. Sondra, listen, I need to let you know what he told us."

Sondra gripped the steering wheel. "What?"

Cicely sighed. "According to this guy Keegan—"

Sondra's phone went dead. She groaned and looked at the battery and realized she'd forgotten to charge the phone.

"Damn," she muttered and threw the phone onto the passenger seat. She'd have to call Cicely when she got back to the hotel. She sighed again, wondering what to do about Phillip. She checked her watch and bit her bottom lip. Paula. She'd visit with Paula. Maybe she could glean some insight about Phillip. Sondra wrinkled her nose as she started the car. Paula could be the key to all of this.

Paula.

Why would Phillip try to pass another woman off as his wife?

Paula.

What didn't he want them to know?

Paula.

Carol.

Maxine.

Tracy.

Paula.

Carol.

Tracy.

Tracy.

"Fuck!" Sondra pounded the steering wheel. "Fuck!"

Tracy had been alive all along.

"That son of a bitch. He lied and lied. To all of us. He killed Carol and said it was Tracy, he said Maxine was Paula and… ugh… dammit." Sondra slammed her foot on the accelerator, racing to get to her sister. Too late, she realized she had skidded through a red light as she saw the blur of lights and heard the sickening crunch of metal right before she passed out.

# SEVENTY-TWO

Paula stepped back to admire her work. The white tufts of carpet gleamed and the scent of water lilies from the shampoo mixed with the roast cooking in the oven. She smiled as she hauled the steamer back into the laundry room and started humming. She stopped. She'd never done that before. She shook her head and smiled, elated as she realized she didn't need the vitamins anymore. She wanted to wait a few days before she told Phillip. She knew he only did what he thought was right. She just didn't need them anymore. Surely, he would be happy to know all his good work had enabled her to feel better than she ever had.

She still didn't believe that Cindy Cross woman that one of her vitamins was to keep her from getting pregnant. Paula shook her head. Like *she* had a medical degree. Paula pulled out her roast to baste it before shoving it back into the oven. She went to the pantry to pull down her ingredients for the peach cobbler they would have for dessert that night. The buzzer on the dryer sounded and Paula loaded her laundry basket with Phillip's shirts and khakis. She tiptoed across the still-damp carpet to the bedroom and turned the basket over on the bed. She went to grab a handful of hangers out of the closet and frowned as she looked at the plastic hanger in her hand. Had she always used plastic? Didn't she use wooden hangers once? Paula looked over at her side of the closet and had another flash as she looked at the array of house-dresses. She blinked as an image of a long white coat with black piping flashed across her mind. Paula shook her head to wipe away the image.

"Silly," she mumbled as she quickly hung up Phillip's clothes. She'd iron everything later. Paula headed back to the kitchen to start work on her peach cobbler.

# SEVENTY-THREE

Sondra moaned as her eyes drifted open. It felt like someone had thrown a pile of bricks on top of her head. She could hear a faint beeping in the background. She was lying in a bed, and wherever she was, it was dark. She went to put her hand to her forehead and realized an IV was snaking out of the vein in her arm.

"Holy shit," she mumbled as she looked around. The hospital. She was in a hospital. The accident came rushing back to her. She'd run a red light and didn't have time to swerve before a black SUV came screeching towards her.

"Oh, my God," she said as she felt pain jolt through her. The door creaked open, bringing a flood of fluorescent light. A tall redheaded nurse came into the room, a bright smile on her face.

"I'm glad to see you're awake. You've been out all day."

Sondra ran her tongue across her parched lips. "Where am I?"

The nurse checked the machines and wrote some things on a chart. "You're at Memorial General Hospital. The ambulance brought you in. You're pretty banged up. Nasty concussion," she chirped in her Midwestern twang. "We have to keep you overnight."

"Oh, no, no." Sondra shook her head as she struggled to sit up and ran smack into the brick wall in front of her. She sank back against the flat concrete pillows. "I can't stay, I have to get to my sister—"

"Ms. Ellis, I'm gonna need you to lie down. You're really hurt."

Sondra shook her head and once again licked her dry, cracked lips. "Tracy. Have to get to Tracy."

"Does she live here? We found a number for a Gary Tate in New York in your wallet for an emergency contact number. He's on his way."

Sondra swallowed, her mouth crammed with paste. "Jesus, I wish you hadn't done that." She blinked several times, trying to get oriented. "I told you, I can't stay. I have to go."

"Ms. Ellis, you aren't going anywhere. You are seriously hurt. Now, lie down and the doctor will be in shortly to see you."

The nurse turned to leave the room and Sondra waited until she was gone before she slowly pushed the fraying blue blanket away from her body. She moaned and waited a moment before trying to move again. Every part of her screamed out in pain, but she didn't care. Her eyes darted around the room looking for her clothes. She spotted them folded up in a plastic bag on a wooden chair with an orange pleather cushion. Sucking in her breath, she eased out of bed and stood up. She swayed back against the bed, panting. Taking a few deep breaths, she again attempted to stand up. The IV stand pulled against her as she tried to edge over to the chair.

"Well, that will slow me down," she said under her breath as she looked at it. Impulsively, she jerked it out and blood squirted out of her arm and splattered across the white tile floor.

"Shit," she muttered as she locked her palm across the gusher. She waited a few moments, her breath heavy, before she chanced taking her hand away. The blood spewed out again, so she raised her hand over her head, cursing the entire time. She managed to pull on her jeans and sweatshirt, wincing in agony with each movement. She didn't have time to think about that now. She picked up her purse and slid her feet into her black ballet flats. She tiptoed over to the door, partly so no one would hear her and partly because her body was throbbing and that was about all she could do. She eased the door open and looked into the hallway. She squinted against the fluorescent lights bouncing off the pink and yellow floor tiles. There was one person at the nurse's station whose back was to her. She glanced to her right, saw a red exit sign, and race-walked for it, the rubber of her shoes hissing across the shiny floor. She backed into the door and grimaced, as she had to expend more effort than usual to get it open. Her breath coming in terse spurts, she stood at the top of the stairwell, wondering how many flights it was.

"At least it's not up," she said as she grabbed the railing and began to inch her way down. She stopped several times to sit and catch her breath as trails of blood ran out of her arm, soaking the sleeve of her sweatshirt. Finally, she reached the lobby and wanted to kiss God when through the open automatic doors, she saw a cab pull up to the curb and let someone out. Limping now, she stumbled toward it and fell inside.

"You all right?" the cabbie asked. "You don't look so good."

Sondra pulled her purse onto her lap, fumbling for Phillip's address. "I need you to take me to this address," she said as she waved the piece of paper in front of his face. "And keep the meter running when we get there." She leaned her head back against the seat. "I have a feeling you'll be bringing me back here."

He glanced at the paper before looking back at Sondra. "You sure you oughta be leaving? You look terrible."

Sondra closed her eyes. "I'll double the meter if you leave now."

"You're the boss," he said as he put the cab in gear.

With considerable effort, Sondra rolled the window down and let the muggy late afternoon air wash across her face. The warm wind made her drowsy and she had to blink several times to keep herself awake.

The cab turned down a residential street and slowed to a stop in front of a small white house. The driver twisted around to look at her.

"Here we are. You need some help getting out?"

Sondra stared at the house, sadness, fear, and disgust welling up inside of her. She shook her head and struggled to push the door open. "No, but stay here."

Sondra grunted as the struggled to get out of the cab. She stumbled up the front walk and rang the doorbell.

# SEVENTY-FOUR

Business had been brisk that day. Lots of prescriptions to fill, ordering to be done. He liked days like this. He looked at his watch. It was four, almost time to go home. Phillip rolled his neck around a few times before he turned his attention back to the paperwork in front of him. Out of the corner of his eye, he saw two of the nurses from the clinic engaged in an animated discussion in the corner. He shifted his weight and focused once again on the claims he was processing. He didn't bother himself with the rampant gossip many of the women who worked there used to fuel their own miserable lives. Maxine, his second-in-command, walked up to him, brandishing a thick sheaf of papers.

"I just finished the inventory. I need you to check it over."

Phillip's head jerked over in Maxine's direction. "What?"

Maxine rolled her eyes. "The inventory. I'm done."

Phillip relaxed. "That will be all, Maxine. Thank you."

"Sure. Oh. How was your family thing?"

"What family thing?"

"Oops. I wasn't supposed to say anything."

"Maxine, what *are* you talking about?"

She sighed. "That woman who came by this morning. Said she was your sister-in-law and wanted to talk to you."

Phillip felt his blood go cold. "Maxine, you're not making any sense. I don't have a sister-in-law."

"Well, it was this crazy-looking woman with all this hair," Maxine said as she waved her hands in the air near her head.

The realization started to sink in. It couldn't be anybody but Sondra.

"I think she said her name was… Sondra. You don't know her?"

Phillip's heart slammed against his chest. "No, uh, no. It must have been a mistake." He wiped his suddenly damp hands across his pants and adjusted his glasses.

She shook her head. "It was weird. You know for some reason, she thought I was Paula. She had that picture we took at that Christmas party." Maxine cocked her head to one side. "Why would she think that? Come to think of it, how'd she get that picture?"

Phillip cleared his throat. "I'm sure I don't know. Listen Maxine, I just remembered an errand I have to run." He yanked off his pharmacy smock. "I won't be back today. I'll see you tomorrow," he rasped, backing towards the front door.

"Uh, sure. Have a good night."

Phillip gave her a faint smile and rushed out to his car. This couldn't be happening, not after all his hard work.

He wouldn't let it.

# SEVENTY-FIVE

Paula heard the doorbell and groaned. She was in the middle of peeling her potatoes and had picked up a nice little rhythm. The roast was out of the oven and resting under a sheath of foil on the stove, the peach cobbler nestled beside it in its glass baking dish. She hoped it wasn't that Cindy Cross woman. She was in no mood to deal with her today. Besides, stopping for even a moment would put her woefully behind. The doorbell rang again and Paula rolled her eyes and wiped her hands on her apron as she went to answer it. Paula frowned at the mangy looking black woman with long, black hair, a bloody sweatshirt and sloppy jeans. Paula recoiled as the woman gasped.

"I'm sorry, but I don't give money to homeless people." Paula went to close the door, but the woman blocked it with her foot.

"Tracy... oh my God, Tracy." The woman started to cry.

Paula sprang back, panicked. "My name isn't Tracy," she said, her voice trembling. "It's Paula. Paula Pierce."

"Oh, no, Tracy, no. Tracy, listen to me—"

"Stop it. Stop calling me that. I told you, my name is Paula. Now go! Leave, or I'll have to get the police—"

The woman slapped her hand against the door and pushed it open. She slammed it shut behind her before she slumped against it. "Good. Call the police, FBI, whoever. Whatever we have to do to get you out of here."

Paula backed away, terrified. "Please. Leave my house. Now."

The woman grabbed for Paula, who winced and tried to twist away. "My God," the woman said, as she looked her up and down. "What the hell has he done to you?"

Paula threw her shoulders back. "What are you talking about? Who are you?"

"Tracy, please. Please. Look at me. It's me, your sister. Sondra."

"I don't have a sister. I'm an only child," she said through clenched teeth.

Sondra bent over. "Jesus, I need to sit down."

"Phillip will be home soon. He expects to have his dinner when he gets here. Now get out of here. Go. Now."

Sondra struggled to get upright. "Tracy... you and I grew up in California. Mommy won medals in the Olympics and daddy is a professor. I'm three years older—"

"My family is all dead. Phillip is the only family I have."

"You went to college at UC Santa Barbara and majored in sociology. Your senior year, you met some joker named Amhad with shit for brains who thought he was a singer. Mommy and daddy gave you a graduation gift of ten thousand dollars. You and this loser moved to North Carolina so he could mooch off you while he pretended to be in some band. When the money ran out, so did he and the only job you could get was as a researcher at the TV station in town. You liked it so much, you decided to make a career out of it and you started off as a writer before you worked your way up to producer. And you were good. You were so good and you worked in Santa Fe, then Phoenix and Philadelphia before you moved to Chicago. And that's where you met Phillip—he filled your prescription for Vicodin after you had some cavities filled—and four months later he proposed and six months later, you got married and six months after that you disappeared and they said you were dead, and we've missed you so much and now..." Sondra was hyperventilating because she was talking so fast. "But you're alive," she cried. "You're here and you're real."

Paula jammed her hands over her ears. "That's not true. None of that is true."

Sondra grabbed Tracy's arm with her good hand. "Tracy, please—!"

"Tracy's dead and I killed her. She's dead! I wanted Phillip, and she was married to him and I killed her to get her out of the way. She's dead. She's gone and I did it. Now get out!"

"Oh, my God. Baby, you didn't kill anyone. He lied to you. You're Tracy. Please. Let me prove it."

Paula shook her head, tears spilling out of her eyes.

The door flew open and Phillip burst through it, his breath coming in jagged bursts.

# SEVENTY-SIX

"Get away from my wife!" he yelled as he went to pull Sondra away from Paula. Sondra tried to throw herself in front of Paula.

"What the hell did you do to her, you son of a bitch?" Phillip ignored Sondra and looked at Paula calmly.

"Dear, whatever she has told you, don't believe it. She wants to take you away, for what you did."

Sondra turned and looked at Paula's tear-stained face. "Baby girl, whatever he told you, it's a lie, I swear. Don't believe him."

Phillip looked at Paula. "Have I ever lied to you, dear?" he asked.

Paula looked back and forth between the man who had protected her and kept her safe and the grimy, bloody creature calling her by the name of the woman she had murdered.

"Of course I don't believe her, dear," Paula said. "I know how much you love me."

Phillip gave Sondra a smug look. "You heard my wife. She doesn't believe these lies you're spewing."

"How long were you planning this, huh? When you first met? After the wedding? When?"

"I have no idea what you're talking about, Sondra." He looked over at Paula, who stood uncomfortably in between the two.

"You see, Paula," Phillip said, "this is Tracy's sister. She's very upset about her sister's death. And she just wants to confuse you, to make you pay for what you did."

"I know what you did, Phillip."

Phillip looked at Sondra, a malicious grin on his face. "Really? Because I didn't do anything."

"You almost got away with it, didn't you?"

"Sondra, you don't look well. Whatever happened to you, you should really see a doctor."

"Identifying Carol as Tracy, playing the role of the grieving husband for the TV cameras. How'd you find Carol, anyway? Were you stalking her?"

"Sondra, really. Do you hear yourself?"

"Then you made my sister think she was someone else, that you were her savior. But you and I know the truth, don't we, Phillip? That Tracy was leaving you—"

Paula looked at Phillip, confused. "Tracy was leaving you? I don't understand—"

"She was filing for divorce. She wanted you out of her life forever."

"Dear, she's trying to confuse you," Phillip said to Paula. "Don't listen to this nonsense."

"And then you sent that letter to my mother. Just had to rub it in her face that you'd stolen her daughter. You smug, fucking bastard."

"Sondra, I know you're upset. I can give you something—"

"Oh, like you've been giving my sister?" She nodded at Paula. "You've been drugging her, haven't you? Pretty easy for a pharmacist to get his hands on all kinds of drugs. And what about this? A housedress? Tracy would never dress like this."

Beads of sweat popped up all over Phillip's forehead like blisters. "Paula likes to dress simply," he said, his voice quivering.

Never taking her eyes off Phillip, Sondra rooted around in her bag, searching for the photo album. "Tracy, I told you I could prove who you are." She pulled out the purple photo album she had been carrying around all this time.

Phillip's face registered panic as he recognized the small book. He ran to snatch it from Sondra, who eluded his grasp. "She's trying to trick you, Paula," he said as he lunged for Sondra. "Don't look at it."

"Why doesn't he want you to see it? If it's not a big deal, why is he trying so hard to keep it from you?"

Paula bit her bottom lip, unsure of what to do. "I'd like to see it," she finally said.

Phillip looked at her, stunned. "I really don't think it's a good idea, dear. It will just upset you, make you relive that terrible time all over again."

"Look at it, Tracy. Look at it!"

With trembling fingers, Paula took the book from Sondra's hands, but before she could open it, Phillip whipped out a pistol he had tucked into the back of his pants and grabbed Paula by the neck. Sondra screamed as he pointed the gun at Paula's head. Paula gasped and squirmed as she realized what was happening.

"I will blow her fucking brains out."

Sondra licked her lips and held her hands out in front of her. "Don't do it," she said. "This all has to stop now."

Phillip shook his head. "I can't do that." He began to back toward the door, tugging his wife with him. Keeping one hand fastened around Paula, he opened the door and pulled Paula through it.

"What are you doing?" Sondra whispered and started to run after them.

Phillip waved the gun at Sondra. "Stay back," he ordered.

Sondra stopped short as she watched him dig into his pocket for his car keys. The cab driver, who had been waiting, got out of his cab and started walking toward Phillip.

"What's going on here?" he asked.

Phillip snapped around, aimed the gun at the driver's head and squeezed the trigger, depositing a single bullet into the guy's brain. He dropped into a heap on the driveway, blood gushing from the crater in his forehead. Sondra screamed, briefly paralyzed both by what she had just seen and by the realization that Tracy was slipping through her fingers. Again. Doors across the normally quiet Red Rose Lane flew open like falling dominoes. Other neighbors poked their heads through their drapes and blinds to see what the commotion was.

As Phillip shoved Paula into the open door of the taxi, Sondra summoned what little strength she had and lunged for him. He pushed her down and she landed with a thud on the concrete. He leaned down until he was inches from her face.

"I'm going to kill her for real this time," he said, spraying her with spit. "You should have just left us alone."

Sondra clawed at Phillip's arm, trying to keep him from getting into the cab. "No, no, take me, kill me instead, let her live," she pleaded, hardly able to breathe.

Phillip placed the gun against Sondra's cheek, caressing the delicate bone. "As tempting as that is, I can't do that." He jumped up and ran backwards toward the taxi, never pointing the gun anywhere but at Sondra. He started up the cab and screeched into the street. Sondra struggled to get off the ground and ran after the car, crying and screaming.

"Phillip you, son of a bitch," she sobbed before she had to stop her pursuit, a stitch gnawing at her right side. She stood in the middle of the street, helpless and crying as the brake lights disappeared from her view.

# SEVENTY-SEVEN

"Do you see what I do for you, Paula?" Phillip ranted as they wound their way down a long ribbon of highway. "I continue to protect you from everyone. Do you even *appreciate* what I've done for you?"

"You're going to kill me, aren't you?" she sobbed.

"Yes, Paula, I am. I have no choice."

"Oh, please, please, don't, don't—"

"We'd just have to keep running and running and this is the only way to protect you. Because you know what she's done, don't you? She's called the police and they will come and take you away. That's why we had to leave." He shook his head and stared at the lights bouncing off the highway in front of him. "And that's why I have to take you away for good now. I can't let you spend your life in jail."

"But can't we just go somewhere else? Somewhere where no one will find us?"

"And where would that be, Paula? The FBI will be looking for you. The CIA. Everyone! And they don't rest, Paula, until they find the person they're hunting." He clenched his jaw. "Don't worry. It will be over by morning."

"Oh, please, I'll do anything, I just—" Paula rocked back and forth in her seat and smothered her face in her hands. "I don't want to die. I'm afraid to die."

"Well, Paula, you should have thought of that before you cracked open Tracy's face," he said as he punched the armrest repeatedly to emphasize his point.

"But I loved you."

He licked his lips and stared over at her. "Yes, you did. You did what you had to do." He flicked his eyes back to the road in front of him. "Just like I'm going to do what I have to do."

# SEVENTY-EIGHT

"Oh, God," Sondra cried, clutching her abdomen. By now, Red Rose Lane was flooded with stunned onlookers, clucking over their eerie neighbors, who had just disappeared in a bloody haze. Someone ran to assist the cab driver, while others swarmed over to Sondra, grabbing at her with a barrage of questions and concerns. Sondra heard none of it, her eyes still seeing the retreating brake lights of the cab carrying her sister away to certain death.

"My God, are you okay?" a short brown-haired man asked Sondra as he took in her bloodstained clothes. "Did you get shot?"

"Call, call the police, the police," she said, not hearing what the man was saying to her, not seeing him in front of her. She tripped over her shoes as she tried to wrench away from the endless voices and limbs crowding her.

"We need to get you to a hospital."

"Phone, police," Sondra muttered, frantic, babbling now. "Call the police. He's going to kill her; he'll really do it this time."

"Ma'am, the whole neighborhood heard that gunshot, so the police oughta be here any minute."

On cue, the squeal of sirens blasted down the street and three squad cars and one ambulance came to a dead stop in front of the little white house on Red Rose Lane. The ensuing minutes were like a merry-go-round spinning off its axis. Sondra was bombarded with questions from the police, prodded by paramedics and given bewildered, sympathetic glances by fluttering neighbors. The police sealed off the driveway while Sondra, refusing medical assistance, had taken refuge in the house.

The police interviewed neighbors about the odd couple who had lived on Red Rose Lane. Meanwhile, Sondra wandered throughout the house, soaking in the macabre scenes from the life Phillip had forced her sister to live along the way. The pristine and plain living room. The spare white box of a kitchen with its perfectly lined shelves of color-coordinated, alphabetized cans and boxed goods. The roast and cobbler still snug on the stove, the partly peeled potatoes starting to turn brown. The blank space over the bathroom sinks where a mirror should have been; the closets filled with frumpy, oversized housedresses and row after row of sensible flats and dresser drawers stuffed with every variation of flannel nightgowns possible.

Sondra found herself in Phillip's office, the locked door of which the police had busted open. The office was the only room in the whole house with any personality, which considering how sparse it was, wasn't saying much. There was a laptop on a bare wooden desk with a yellow legal pad next to it. A cup of pens and pencils rested on one corner and a phone and a page-a-day calendar sat opposite it. A three-shelf bookcase housed hulking volumes on anatomy, drugs, and psychology. There were two pictures on the walls; one of which Sondra guessed was Phillip's mother, and the other of Tracy when she was still Tracy. Sondra made her way back into the living room and dropped onto the couch. She wished she could go to sleep, wake up and find the whole thing had been a nightmare and that Tracy had never gotten mixed up with Phillip. A phone began to trill. It was Phillip's cell phone, which Sondra realized must have dropped out of his pocket during their scuffle. Everyone stopped what they were doing to stare at it. Sondra looked down at the caller ID and her heart sank.

# SEVENTY-NINE

Phillip exited the highway and pulled into the parking lot of a non-descript motel.

"Stay here," he said before he got out to check them in. Paula gave him a meek nod and sat alone in the car, kneading her hands. She closed her eyes, the blood rushing in her ears. She heard her door open and felt Phillip's fingers dig into her flesh as he jerked her out of the car. Looking over his shoulder, he jammed the keycard into the silver slot on the door and pushed her inside. He ran his hands along the wall until he found the light switch and the room was bathed in harsh fluorescent light.

"I saw a burger place a few miles back. I'll go get us something to eat. You sit on the bed and don't make a move, not a single twitch until I get back. Do you understand?"

"Yes, dear," Paula said, her voice soft. With a curt nod of his head, Phillip was gone, the door thundering closed behind him.

Sitting alone in the dark, Paula could hear her heart pounding in her ears. She was terrified to move, certain if she did, Phillip would come exploding back through the door, the police behind him with handcuffs dangling from their hands, ready to clamp them around her delicate wrists.

But now, she was going to die for what she had done. Wouldn't it be better to go to jail? She fastened her hands around each elbow and squeezed her eyes shut, trying not to think about the morning.

She felt her bladder press against her, begging to be emptied. She jiggled her foot, Phillip's warning pinging around in her head. Unable to hold it in, she scurried in the direction of the bathroom, plunking herself down on the toilet in the dark. She flushed and turned to wash her hands when she caught a glimpse of her outline in the mirror. Impulsively, she reached for the light switch. She blinked several times as she stared at the foreign image in front of her. She placed her fingertips against the smooth expanse of glass and trailed her finger along the round edges of her reflection. She couldn't remember the last time she'd looked at herself in the mirror. She didn't know what to think. Her face was swollen from all the crying and her lips were withered like a prune. She turned off the light and realizing she was thirsty, picked up the glass on the counter and filled it with tap water. She drained it in three gulps.

Paula Pierce put the glass down on the counter and looked up.

And that's when Tracy Ellis remembered who she was.

# EIGHTY

"All right people, check your rundown because the top of the show has just been turned upside down," Tracy yelled out to no one in particular and to everyone in particular. "We're going with a live shot from the Loop where a fire has just broken out in a high-rise. Bryan and a crew are on their way over there now. We're bumping our Wrigleyville dead bodies live shot to the second story and moving our abandoned comatose drug baby up to third—desk just told me he died. Stories four, five and six will stay the same."

Tracy's fingers were flying across the keyboard faster than the words on the screen could keep up. She looked at the clock on her computer. The ten started in a little over an hour and she still had a ton of script changes to make. Tracy furrowed her brow and leaned closer to the screen, almost willing the changes to appear magically. The phone on her desk rang and a glance at the caller ID convinced her not to answer it. She kept typing and the ringing stopped. Then one of the desk assistants beeped her.

"I'm busy, Frank," Tracy said over the din of the newsroom to the desk, never taking her eyes off the screen. "Take a message or throw it into voicemail."

"It's your husband. Said it's important."

Tracy rolled her eyes and shook her head. "A hangnail is an emergency with him," she muttered as she reluctantly let her fingers leave the keyboard to pick up the phone.

"Phillip, I don't have time to talk to right now. The newscast starts in an hour and I've got a lot to do before then."

"I don't feel good about how we left things this morning."

"Phillip, please. Not now."

"But, Tracy, I just can't concentrate on anything until I know that we're okay. We're okay, aren't we?" His voice took on that pleading whininess that was like nails on a chalkboard to her ears.

"Phillip, have a good convention. I'll see you next week."

Tracy slammed the phone down and resumed her marathon tap-tapping across her keyboard. She groaned when the phone rang again and she saw Phillip's cell phone number flash across the panel.

She snatched up the phone. "Quit fucking calling me," she said under her breath. "This is the fourth time in the last hour, now stop it."

"But, I miss you. I miss us. I just want things to be the way they used to be."

Tracy molded the creases of her forehead, wishing she could put the phone under her car and roll over it. Anything so he would just leave her alone.

"If you call me one more time, just once, by the time you get back on Wednesday, I will have thrown all your stuff out. Got it?"

"Tracy, please…"

"I am dead fucking serious. Goodbye."

She smashed the phone back in its cradle, took a deep breath and closed her eyes.

"Bad news?"

Tracy looked up to see Cicely standing in front of her sipping one of her ever-present Diet Cokes through a straw.

Tracy forced a smile. "I'm fine. Just some stupid PR hack who keeps calling me to pitch something. Don't they teach them in PR school not to call an hour before a newscast?"

Cicely cocked her head. "Pretty late to be calling, even for a flack."

"Oh, it was from the West Coast. You know how flaky Californians are." Tracy winked at Cicely to cover her agitation and looked back at the screen. "Did you see the top of the show changed?"

Cicely nodded and took a sip of her Coke. "I did, but you haven't said who is taking what yet."

Tracy scrunched her face as she took another look at the rundown. "Yeah, I keep getting interrupted," she mumbled. "Check back in a few minutes, it'll be done."

"Thanks, sweetie. See you in a bit."

Tracy spent the next twenty minutes polishing her show before she declared it done. She printed out a copy of the rundown and script, scooped up her bottle of water and joined the other producers in the control room. Tracy watched Cicely and her co-anchor Ken Allen on the monitors as they rehearsed to themselves, calling out words in a story and making scribbles or notations in the margins of their scripts. During this time, they were always oblivious to the other's presence, concentrating on refining their individual parts. But once that red light came on and the floor manager gave them their cue, they had the cuddly anchor shtick down pat.

As the show progressed, Tracy kept a close eye on the timing and pacing of the stories and made notes, occasionally speaking into the microphone connected to the anchors' earpieces. At ten thirty-five, the closing credits rolled and the anchors bid the audience good night. The newscast post-mortem to discuss what worked and what hadn't ended at a little past eleven and Tracy was happy to be heading home. Phillip would be out of town for a few days and she was looking forward to some time alone without his constant hovering. She had the number of a divorce lawyer and planned to call him so she could file for legal separation.

"Hey, do you wanna go grab a drink?" Cicely asked as she stopped by Tracy's desk.

Tracy picked up her Kate Spade bag and shook her head. "No, I'm gonna go ahead and head home. Get an early start on my mini-vacation."

The two women started to walk in the direction of the closet, where Tracy took out her white wool coat with black piping and shrugged her arms into it.

"Well, a drink is the perfect way to start off a vacation. Get as drunk as you want since you don't have to worry about stumbling in here tomorrow."

Tracy smiled. "I'm doing a spa day tomorrow and I don't think a hangover would go good with that."

"Good point. Doing anything else fun this weekend?" Cicely asked as she buttoned her coat.

"Just relaxing and getting a few little projects done around the house." *Like sweeping my husband out of it.*

"I love my husband and kid, but there are times when it would be nice to come home to an empty house. I'm jealous."

Tracy chuckled as they walked over to the elevator that would carry them to the parking garage. "Yes, I'm looking forward to it."

"When's Phillip back?" Cicely asked as the elevator dinged and the doors slid open.

Tracy grimaced at the mention of her husband's name. She'd been very cagey about what was really going on in her marriage. She wasn't in the mood to hear the chorus of "I told you he was weird."

"Wednesday," she said as the punched the "P" button for parking.

"What's he out of town for again?"

"Some pharmacy thing in Milwaukee."

"Ah." Cicely nodded as the elevator reached the parking level.

"Hey," Tracy said and stopped to look at Cicely. "Let's do something this weekend. Catch a movie or a beer. Or five. You could stay over so you don't have to haul back to the 'burbs. That is if they can spare you at the ranch."

"Are you kidding? Jimmy's been out of town every weekend for a month. He owes me."

Tracy smiled. "Excellent."

"It'll be like a slumber party. Can't wait. Call me."

Tracy smiled again. "Okay. Talk to you then. Have a good show tomorrow."

"We'll try to get along without you."

Tracy snorted. "Don't try too hard. I need the gig. Later, sister."

"Bye."

The two women went in opposite directions to their cars—Cicely to her cream Escalade, Tracy to her black BMW. The teeny-tiny three-inch heels of Tracy's tall black leather boots click-clacked across the cold concrete as she hurried to her car. She hit the button to start her car so it would be somewhat warm by the time she got there.

She took one perfectly French-manicured nail and flipped on Sirius XM, smiling as the sounds of the Black Eyed Peas filled the car and she bopped her head along with the beat. As she backed out of the space, her cell phone started to sing "Let's Stay Together" from the bottom of her purse. It was Phillip's ring. They had danced to that song at their wedding, and vowed to each other that night that no matter what, happy or sad, they would stay together.

"What a difference six months makes," Tracy said aloud as she let the call go to voicemail. She knew the phone would ring four or five more times before she got home. And she would ignore it four or five more times. Better yet... she reached into her purse and brought the phone out. She turned it off and threw it back into her bag. She turned up the music and sang along loudly as the Black Eyed Peas implored her to get it started.

Northbound traffic on Lake Shore Drive was light as she made her way home. This was always her favorite time. She enjoyed seeing the lights of the city winking at her; she sometimes winked back. She hummed to herself as she reached Belmont and thought about lazing in front of the TV eating chocolate chip cookies without anyone to complain about crumbs, or whine about the dish and glass she had yet to load into the dishwasher or that her toothbrush was in the wrong slot in the cup holder. Yes, she was definitely looking forward to her freedom, both over the next few days and after she served Phillip with divorce papers.

Tracy pressed the button to open the door of her garage and ex-pertly guided her car inside. Shutting off the engine, Tracy gathered her purse, opened the door and ran outside. She pressed the remote again to close the door and darted through the alley to her front door. Shiv-ering, she shoved her key into the lock and was grateful for the rush of warm air that washed over her as she stepped inside her house.

Tracy flipped on the light and threw her keys in the silver bowl in the front hallway as she walked toward her bedroom, relishing the vivid colors and textures along the way. Rich red draped the walls of the hallways and kitchen; the deep tan walls of the living room were the perfect backdrop for her plum-colored couch and love seat. Mahogany shelves housed books along with pictures and accessories. Crystal vases filled with fresh flowers made the house smell like a garden. Dimmers on all the lights and lamps in every room contributed to the overall cozy atmosphere. While it was a visually stimulating environment, it didn't overwhelm with silly knickknacks collecting dust or junk just to have junk. She always thought it was weird for people to have stuff in their house just because they thought they should, not because it meant anything to them.

Tracy turned on the bedroom lamp and dropped down onto the pewter-colored duvet that covered her bed, a soft grunt escaping her throat. She unzipped her boots and tugged them from her tired feet. She wiggled her toes beneath her stockings before she pulled her silk chartreuse turtleneck sweater over her long brown hair and tossed it on the bed.

Letting out another quiet groan, Tracy walked in her bra, black skirt and stocking feet to the bathroom to wash her face. She scrubbed the day from her face, feeling refreshed. She brushed her teeth and in an act of rebellion, put her toothbrush in Phillip's slot when she was done. He got so fussy about that stuff. She'd never understood it. It hadn't bothered her that much before they got married, but now, like so many other things, it bugged the shit out of her.

Tracy finished undressing and pulled on a pair of blue polka-dotted pajama bottoms and baby blue tank top before she headed into the living room. She dimmed the overhead lights and scanned the elaborate metal CD shelf until she found what she was looking for. It was a jazz compilation CD Sondra had given her for her birthday years ago and the melancholy riffs spoke to the cloud she was under tonight. She wondered how Sondra was. She hadn't seen her since the wedding and they'd had only sporadic communication since she left. Tracy missed her sister and couldn't wait for her to come home.

She inserted the disk into the stereo and the plaintive wail of a weeping saxophone purred out of the speakers. Her bare feet shuffled over the maple hardwood floors as she padded into the kitchen. Tracy slid a goblet from the wine rack and clamped her hand around the bottle of Riesling in the refrigerator before she carried both into the living room. She settled into the deep welcoming cushions of her couch and poured a glass of wine. Tracy took a long, thoughtful sip before she leaned back with a sad sigh and contemplated the state of her life.

She had run into an old acquaintance at an industry gig about a month ago. Tracy remembered she'd gone through a divorce about a year earlier. She made up a story that she was looking to do a piece about divorce and asked for the name of her attorney to get her started. The woman whipped the guy's card out of her wallet and handed it to Tracy. She'd kept his number tucked away, not sure if she was really ready to pick up the phone and dial those numbers. If nothing else, she wanted to have options.

That is until her cup tipped over a few days later. She and Cicely had spent a Saturday holed up at the station editing a special series to air during sweeps week. When she got home, Phillip had unleashed a tirade against her for valuing her job more than him, for leaving him alone all day—what was he supposed to do without her? He'd badgered her, hurled insults at her before falling to her feet, begging her to never leave him. At that moment, Tracy knew there was no saving the marriage. Phillip was too far gone.

She decided to wait and pull the trigger while he was out of town for his pharmacy conference. That way, when he got back, she'd be ready. She would call Damon Randall tomorrow and see if she could make an appointment for next week. She'd get the locks on the house changed; the house was still in her name and Phillip contributed nothing toward the mortgage and barely anything towards its upkeep, so she doubted that would be a problem. She would have the divorce papers drawn up and urge Phillip to quickly and quietly put their marriage out of its misery.

Tracy had never wanted it to come to this, but he'd left her no choice. She'd tried to reason with him, suggested counseling, tried the patient approach, tried the loving approach. But each and every time, it was the same thing. The clinging and the jealousy. The erratic behavior. One minute, he would opine about how much he loved her and how important she was to him, the next what a bitch she was because she wouldn't spend every minute of the day with him. He had expected after they got married that she would quit her job. She thought he was kidding, but his constant whining made it clear he was serious. He resented the time she spent with friends, tried many times to crack her voicemail code so he could listen to her messages. If she hadn't thought he'd call every single person who left her a voicemail, demanding to know who they were, she would have happily given it to him. She and Jack had had each other's voicemail codes, but Jack wasn't crazy.

God. She hadn't thought about Jack in a while. She always thought they would get married. Her friends all loved him, her parents were crazy about him, his about her. Unfortunately, he didn't want to get married, said he probably never would. So she left. Not too long after that, she'd met Phillip. Maybe that's what most of the attraction had been. She knew Phillip was ready to commit.

Tracy had wondered many times over these past few months how she got here. Had she missed the signs? Had she been so burned by Jack's refusal to get married that she'd blinded herself to Phillip's neuroses?

Maybe.

Or maybe he was just that good at hiding them.

She thought back to the fight they'd had before he left for Milwaukee. She told him to have a good trip and he had replied that she was probably thrilled he'd be gone so she could spend the weekend cruising the clubs for one night stands. She'd just rolled her eyes and told him goodbye, her resolve stronger than ever. He'd sensed her disgust and perhaps her ambivalence and, per his usual, dropped to his knees begging her forgiveness. Nevertheless, the damage was done. It had reaffirmed her decision that she was doing the right thing.

She took a huge gulp of wine. She just didn't know who he was anymore.

Maybe she never had.

# EIGHTY-ONE

Sunlight poked through the sheers of Tracy's bedroom urging her to wake up. She propped one eye open and looked over at the clock on the nightstand. Eight. She stretched across the bed, relishing that she was in it alone. She flung back the sheets and duvet, swung her legs around and placed her feet on the floor. She'd go for a quick jog, hop in the shower and then... make the call. Satisfied, she bounded into the bathroom to empty her bladder and brush her teeth. She hastily threw on some stretch pants and a long-sleeved blue jogging top. As she twisted her hair into a ponytail holder, she wondered where she'd left her chapstick. She found it in the pocket of her green windbreaker and glossed her lips with it. She stopped in the kitchen to drain a glass of orange juice before she grabbed her keys out of the bowl.

She did a few warm-up stretches before she started a slow jog toward Belmont Harbor. It was freezing outside, but Tracy didn't let that deter her. She tried to run at least four times a week, five if she was having a good week.

Not many people were out on the lakefront this frigid morning. This was one of the perks of working from two to eleven. By the time she was out, everyone else was at work, so it was like having the trail to herself. She pumped her arms and relished the crunch of the gravel beneath her feet. She passed the snack shack, now deserted but a welcome friend in the summer months thanks to the abundance of cold drinks it served to the masses that crowded Lake Michigan's sandy beaches. She continued on, whizzing past the green Indian statue as the wind whooshed in her ears.

She was coming up on Diversey Harbor and she looked up to see Chicago's skyline. She would run up to Oak Street Beach, then turn around and run back, about six miles. She was in the zone. Sweat beaded her forehead and her ponytail had become a chocolate blur against the white morning sky as her feet popped against the ground like gunfire. Her nose began to run but she didn't care. She was alive.

And soon... soon she'd be free.

# EIGHTY-TWO

Damon Randall's card was wedged beneath a stack of papers on her desk at work, so she popped in to grab it. She called him from the car on her way to see Trish at Tricocci for her regular six-week wash and trim. He could see her on Monday. She'd have to remember to put that in her date book when she got home. Trish gave her the usual. She'd been growing her bangs out since the wedding and her long brown hair hung straight down her back with a part down the middle, kind of like Cher circa Sonny and Cher. She was thinking in the summer she'd go shoulder-length and maybe get some highlights. Divorce would probably be final by then. An updated look would be in order.

After her facial, massage, manicure and pedicure, Tracy was in a fantastic mood. She looked revitalized, she would see Damon Randall on Monday, Phillip was gone until Wednesday and even then she wouldn't have to see him for very long.

Tracy hummed to herself, looking forward to a quiet night at home, when like one of those shampoo commercials with a wind machine and slow-mo camera work, she saw him.

Jack.

His six-foot-two-inch frame filled out his black leather coat like a shrink-wrapped package, and on cue, Tracy's senses filled with that intoxicating scent of rich leather and Lagerfeld cologne.

He stopped when he saw her, a small smile pulling at his lips, his paper-white teeth in stark, beautiful contrast to his silky chocolate skin. She tried to hide her feeble smile and gave him a little wave.

"T. It's been a while."

She swallowed and tried to force the words out. "Yeah. It has."

He cupped the fist of his right hand into the palm of his left. "So word on the street is you're an old married lady now. Congratulations." He touched her elbow and she trembled. "I'm happy for you."

Tracy forced herself to smile. "Oh, yeah, thank you, thank you," she replied with false sentiment. "What about you?"

"No, no, just keeping busy with work."

"Some things never change."

They both stood on the sidewalk, shivering and looking at each other in uncomfortable silence.

"Do you want to grab a drink?" he asked finally. "Ian's is just up the street."

Tracy pinched her lips together for a moment and looked off to the side. "Sure," she said as she turned back to face him.

They walked south on Michigan Avenue in the direction of one of their old haunts. The longtime, flame-haired waitress, Stacy, would always greet them with a Riesling for Tracy and a Scotch neat for Jack. They would sit huddled in the corner of the small room, nursing their drinks for the better part of an hour before heading home for the night. Tracy was apprehensive now as Jack pushed the revolving door for her and they found themselves standing on the threshold of their past.

"Well, hello you two. Haven't seen you in here for a long time," Stacy said, a smile curling beneath the familiar smear of orange paint across her lips. "How've you been?"

Tracy opened her mouth to spit out another forced gaiety when Jack stepped in. "We're good, Stacy, thank you." Jack said smoothly, as if he sensed Tracy's reluctance for small talk. "We'll have the usual."

Stacy nodded, beaming. "Coming right up," she said as she made the few steps to the bar.

Jack held out a chair for Tracy and helped her into it before settling into the chair across from hers. Tracy cast nervous glances around the bar as she pulled off her leather gloves and placed them on the table in front of her before shrugging out of her coat. She shifted in her chair and cleared her throat several times while Jack continued to sit in silence, hunched over on the table looking at her. Finally, she let her eyes come to rest on his penetrating gaze.

"So," she said. "You're good?"

He nodded before he let his chin drop into the palm of his right hand. "Yeah, yeah. Both places are doing really well, and I'm thinking in a couple of years I might try to do L.A. or New York. But I want to take it slow, you know? Make sure I've got all my stuff together."

Stacy slid Jack and Tracy's drinks in front of them before retreating to the far end of the bar. Tracy let her fingers slip along the stem of her wine glass, afraid of what she knew was coming next. She picked up the glass and took a long gulp, enjoying the warmth as it crawled down her throat and into her stomach.

"That's great," she said placing her glass back on the table. "I mean that you're thinking about expanding into other markets."

He nodded, watching her. "How's Channel Four?"

"Um, good. Still number one in the market, still crazy, but I love it."

He chuckled. "Man. I remember when you first got here, that show was number four behind reruns of *The Golden Girls*. You've come a long way."

"Oh. Yeah," she chuckled. "Thanks."

"I saw Cicely not too long ago. She looks good."

Tracy licked her lips. "Oh, yeah, she mentioned that," Tracy said as she picked up her wine glass for another long swallow.

"So how's married life?"

Tracy almost choked. "Huh?"

Jack gave her a small smile. "You used to always get this way when you had a big project coming up."

Tracy frowned. "Get what way?"

He looked down sheepishly before he met her questioning stare. "Whenever you were about to get into something big—like you had a big story you were researching, or doing something to the house, you would get real quiet, not always talking like you usually do. Distracted." He leaned closer. "So. What are you working on?"

Tracy looked into his brown eyes and longed to tell him that she was miserable and ask him where they had gone wrong. Instead, she flashed him one of her patented bright and shiny smiles. "You're right. Big story... nothing I can really talk about. You understand."

Jack gulped his Scotch and nodded. He circled one long, slender finger around the rim of his glass as he stared down into the watery brown liquid inside. Tracy pursed her lips, watching as he did this. She'd always loved his hands.

"You didn't answer my question," he said, never looking up. "How's married life?"

It was Tracy's turn to look down at her drink in an effort to avoid the topic. Finally, she shrugged. "Fine," she said before she smiled again.

"T...?"

"Yes?"

Jack licked his lips and looked into Tracy's eyes. "Are you happy?" he asked, his voice low and husky.

Tracy squeezed her lips together and fought to keep the tears from slipping out of her eyes.

"No," she finally whispered. Horrified, Tracy fumbled for her gloves on the table and stood up, the legs of her chair refusing to move. The table almost tipped over as she tried to run out of the restaurant before she lost it completely. Jack held out his arm to try to stop her from leaving.

"T, wait!"

Tracy gave her chair a quick shove as it stumbled over the dark carpet.

"Goodbye, Jack," she murmured, the tears hovering just beneath the rims of her eyes.

Jack tried to stand and only succeeded in banging his knee against the table. He grunted and cursed under his breath and twisted around to run after Tracy. He darted into the street and searched in vain for her.

But it was too late.

She was gone.

# EIGHTY-THREE

Tracy ran all the way back to the garage at the Nine Hundred North building to get her car. The tears that streaked her face evaporated as they made contact with the icy surface of her cheeks. She wasn't altogether sure how she made it home, likely by rote, but before she knew it, she was pulling into her garage. She sat in her car crying for a few moments before she took a long, shuddering breath and dabbed at her eyes with the sleeve of her sweater.

She finally opened the car door and got out. She went through the alley and was about to unlock the front door when she remembered she was in such a hurry to come in from the cold last night, she hadn't checked the mail. She flipped the top of the box open and grabbed the envelopes shoved inside. There was a thick manila envelope wedged in such a way that a corner of it had caught on a groove at the bottom of the box, ripping the paper.

She looked at the envelope she'd just torn. The whole front with the address on it had been pulled away so she had to reach in and bring the contents out so she could read them.

At first she frowned.

Then she was confused.

And then she was pissed.

"That fucker," she said as she shook her head, still not believing what she was seeing. She thumbed through the thick report, reading in disbelief. It was a detailed dossier on her comings and goings for the past two months. From what she wore each day, to every time she'd gone out for lunch or dinner or a work event. The summary had concluded that the subject was not having an affair.

"He hired a detective to follow me," she said, stunned. "Mother-fucker," she said as she slammed the report down on the hall table. The silver bowl jumped down and clattered against the hardwood floors. She started to pace the hallway, wondering yet again how she'd gotten into this mess.

"That's what you get for not going to the dentist for fifty years," she said with a bitter laugh. She looked down at the report for a moment before she snatched it back up. She'd take it to Kinko's tomorrow and make a copy to take with her to Damon Randall's office on Monday.

"Well, Phillip," she said as she tucked the report under her arm and went into her office. "You've just made my case for me. Thank you very much."

She opened a desk drawer and tossed it inside. After Kinko's, she'd call the locksmith then pack up his shit. All of her relaxation from earlier in the day had vanished. Seeing Jack, the discovery that her husband had her followed. It was almost too much to handle. Tracy pulled the half-full bottle of Riesling from the fridge and plopped down on the couch, exhausted.

# EIGHTY-FOUR

First, she heard the doorknob being jiggled. She jumped up from her nap on the couch and grabbed the empty wine bottle, ready to smash it over whoever was about to appear. She remembered her phone was in her purse, still sitting next to the hallway table. Phillip's face emerged, a sheepish grin on his face.

"Hi," he said as he dropped his keys into his coat pocket.

Tracy lowered the wine bottle. "What the hell are you doing here? You're not supposed to be back until Wednesday."

He held his hands out in front of him in a pleading motion. "I know, I know, it's just that I kept calling you last night and you didn't answer and I just needed to talk to you."

"So you drove all the way from Milwaukee."

"It's only an hour and a half away. I told you last night, I hated how we left things. I couldn't stop thinking about you, so I got in the car to come home so we could work things out."

Tracy heaved a huge, tired sigh, realizing she was pretty buzzed. "Didn't you tell me you were sitting on a panel tomorrow?"

"I'm skipping it."

"You know, Phillip… there really isn't anything else to say. I think we both know where this is headed."

"No… no…" Fat tears rimmed Phillip's eyes. "Don't say that. Anything but that."

"Phillip, I've tried everything and you just keep on with this… crazy behavior… and I'm done. We're done."

"I'll change, I'll get help, I'll get the therapy. Whatever you want, I'll do it, but please, please don't walk out on me."

"There's something else."

Phillip started to tremble. "Oh... God. There's someone else, isn't there? You're leaving me for another man."

Tracy leaned back against the couch cushions. "Not according to your detective."

Phillip gasped and put his hands over his mouth. "How did you find out?" he whispered through his fingers.

"Your little report came here today. The corner of the envelope got caught in the mailbox, ripped the whole front of it off. Front page, plain as day, 'Surveillance on Tracy Ellis'." Tracy shook her head. "So stupid to have it sent here, Phillip. So stupid. But I have to thank you. It's finally in black and white that you need some help."

Phillip let out a howl and beat his hands against his temples. "They won't let me get personal mail at work," he said, that all-too-familiar whimper creeping into his voice. "I told him to wait, wait until I got back into town and I would pick it up." He banged his palm against the wall. "Damn it," he whispered.

Tracy shook her head, in shock over Phillip's delusions. "Yeah, well, it doesn't matter anyway. I'm filing for divorce."

Phillip stopped his tirade and looked up at Tracy, his face swabbed with fear. "What?"

Tracy stood up and started to pace. "I was going to wait to tell you this, but I've made an appointment with a lawyer first thing Monday."

"No. I won't accept that."

"We both know it's for the best."

"Just give me another chance. I'm begging you," he pled, dissolving into shuddering sobs.

"You can't stay here tonight. There's a Best Western on Diversey. I'm sure they have some vacancies. Or better yet, go back to Milwaukee, finish your conference."

"Tracy, please, I love you. You are my life, my... my reason for living. If you leave me, I won't have anything, no reason to go on."

Tracy looked down at the rug, trying to fight back her tears of pity and guilt. "I'm sorry, Phillip. I'm sorry. If you had just... trusted me, trusted in what we had, things could have been so different."

"They can. We can, I mean, I can. Let's just take some time and regroup and I'll work on things, I'll trust you, I'll be the man you fell in love with. I swear. I swear."

Tracy held out her hand. "Please give me all the keys."

"Tracy, no—"

"Phillip, don't start this bullshit with me. Text me and tell me where you're staying, I'll have a messenger deliver your things."

Phillip lunged for Tracy in an attempt to take her in his arms. Frightened, Tracy ducked away from his grasp. She lost her footing and with a soft "oh," tripped back against the hallway table, hitting the back of her head.

And then there was darkness.

# EIGHTY-FIVE

Tracy Ellis stood now in that tiny bathroom in a motel somewhere in the United States. She looked to her right, turned the bathroom light on again, and looked at herself in the mirror.

"Tracy," she whispered at the woman staring back at her. Numb, she turned and walked into the bedroom and lowered herself onto the edge of the lumpy bed.

She replayed the last three years in her mind. The subtle yet effective brainwashing that Phillip had pulled on her. Dr. Keegan. The hospital. Convincing her she'd committed murder for him. Telling her how much she loved housework, programming her to serve him and locking her in closets if she took a single misstep. Slapping belts across her bottom. Making himself her entire world, shutting her off from everything else. Not letting her drive, or pick out her own clothes, making her... oh, God. Tracy ran a hand over her hair. Dyeing her brown hair black. She dropped her face into her hands. It was like he had a remote control and was using it to dictate her every move, every thought. Every aspect of her life. He had to have everything just so and she wasn't allowed to have an opinion at all. Wasn't allowed to think for herself, do anything but clean, clean, clean and be his twenty-four-hour-a-day slave.

No friends.

No family.

No nothing.

Just him.

Only him.

Which was the way he always wanted it.

She thought about the house on Red Rose Lane: the bleak white walls, the immaculate white carpet, everything so dull. Lifeless

Just like Phillip.

He'd been so threatened by her energy, her love of life. It both attracted him and repelled him. He had fallen in love with it, but was distraught when he realized he couldn't control it.

And so he stole her, made her believe she was dead and remade her into the perfect little woman he'd always wanted.

Feeding her birth control pills to ensure a baby wouldn't take any of her attention away from him.

What else had he been slipping her?

Tracy didn't know whether to cry or to scream or to laugh.

The motel room door flew open and Phillip came in holding two greasy brown bags and a holder of soft drinks.

Tracy looked up at him for a moment before she gave him a sweet smile. "Hello, dear. What took you so long?"

Phillip's eyes narrowed. "There was a long line. Took me longer than I had anticipated." He motioned to the table across the room. "Come now. Let's eat."

"I'm not hungry."

Phillip stood rooted where he was. "I went out of my way to get you food. Now eat."

Tracy placed her hands behind her on the bed and leaned back. "Oh, you're always going out of your way for me, aren't you, dear?"

Phillip licked his lips. "Yes. I've always done a lot for you. You know that."

Tracy seemed to contemplate this. "Like what?" she said.

"Excuse me?"

"You heard me. Like what?"

"Paula, I really don't appreciate this tone you're taking with me. I suppose you are tired and need the rest. Perhaps you should sleep now." He carried the bags of food in the direction of the table.

"Don't you mean Tracy?"

Phillip stopped. "What?" he asked without turning around.

Tracy smiled to herself as she picked up on the tremor of terror in his voice. "Don't you mean... 'Tracy, I don't appreciate this tone you're taking with me'?"

Phillip dropped the fast food bags on the table and turned to face her. "You can't believe the garbage that woman was saying. I told you, she was just trying to confuse you."

"Oh, you mean Sondra?"

"Yes, Sondra is Tracy's sister."

"No. She's my sister."

"Paula, I am losing my patience with you."

Tracy ran her tongue along her teeth and crossed her legs, cupping her hands over one knee. "I wish you would call me by the name my parents gave me... not the one you did."

"What?"

"Tracy."

Phillip swallowed. "No."

"Say it."

"I can't. I won't."

"Tracy."

He shook his head, and Tracy could see the tears pooling along the edges of his eyes. "Please."

"Tracy."

The tears fell out and splashed against his cheek. "Just let me explain," he sobbed.

Tracy stood up and walked over to Phillip. "Explain what? That you, you brainwashed me into believing I was someone else? That I had killed someone?"

"You don't understand—"

"Oh, I understand. You lied to me and kept me good and tight under your thumb." She was circling him now, like a panther stalking its prey. "Just like you always wanted. Me just so... devoted to you, only thinking about you. No friends, no family, nothing, nothing but you, you, you."

"I had to."

"And the clothes, no mirrors, dyeing my hair, all so I would never know what I really looked like, in case I remembered."

"Tracy—"

Tracy stopped and folded her arms across her chest. "Tracy. How many times did you almost slip and call me by my real name?"

"I didn't, I—"

"I mean after all, Tracy was dead, because I killed her." Tracy shook her head in disgust. "You fucking bastard. Because I was so in love with you and had to have you at any and all costs. What was it again? Split her face open with a rock?"

Phillip smashed his hands over his ears. "Stop it."

Tracy pulled at his arms. "And in order to keep me out of jail, you dumped the body and helped me escape. To keep me safe. And just now, telling me that the FBI was coming to get me? The CIA?" She stopped and laughed. "God, you're so much better than I ever gave you credit for."

"You don't understand—"

"What were you giving me? What were you pumping me full of every day to make me forget who I was?"

"All I ever gave you were vitamins, I swear."

Tracy slapped him and he recoiled. She shook her finger in his face. "Don't you lie to me anymore. I know about the birth control pills and I want to know what else you were giving me."

Phillip looked at Tracy, his eyes wide. "Tracy, please. Please, don't do this."

"What else Phillip?"

He crumbled. "It's a drug called Propranolol. It causes memory loss."

Tracy narrowed her eyes at Phillip, struggling to comprehend what he was telling her. "What else have you done to me?" she whispered.

"I loved you. I loved you more than any man could ever love you."

"Oh, that's a good one. Lying to me, controlling me—"

"It was better that way. That's how it should have been all along."

Tracy clicked her tongue and rubbed her eyes. "Oh, God."

Phillip dropped his face in his hands, wild sobs shaking his body. "I just wanted you to love me again." He wiped a hand across his runny nose. "And you did. You... you worshiped me," he said, his voice tinged with hysteria.

"Paula Pierce—" Tracy stopped and shook her head wryly. "Even changed your last name," she shook her head. "Paula Pierce worshipped you. Tracy Ellis is disgusted by you and is leaving."

Tracy turned to walk out the door when Phillip lunged for her, locking himself around her waist. "Please, please don't leave me. I can't live without you. I need you."

Tracy gave him a bitter laugh. "There's the Phillip I know and remember."

"I won't let you go, Tracy. I can't."

Tracy wrenched around, trying to unscrew his hands from her body. "Let go. I'm leaving and you can't stop me this time."

"No," he said as he grabbed her arm.

"Damn it Phillip, let me go, stop it," Tracy panted as she fought to get away from him. She was surprised at how strong he was.

Phillip reached behind him and pulled out the gun.

Tracy stopped struggling as she came face to face with the gaping hole of the pistol.

"I meant what I said. I'll kill you before I let you walk away from me."

Tracy licked her lips and stared at her captor. "You were really ready to splatter my brains all over the highway, weren't you?"

He nodded. "Yes," he whispered. "I would. If I can't live without you, why should you get to live?"

Tracy took a deep breath. "You have to catch me first," she whispered as she kneed him and ran for the door.

# EIGHTY-SIX

She ran straight for the highway. Maybe she could flag someone down, get them to take her to the police. The bottoms of her sensible flats were slick and she skidded across the gravel in the parking lot, landing on her butt. She scrambled up and, limping, started to run again. It had been so long since she had run that, at first, it hurt. Her lungs were greedy for air and she clutched the painful stitch in her side. The hem of the housedress slowed her down some, so she gathered it in her fingers and lifted it until it bunched around her thighs. She pumped her other arm rapidly and soon, her body began to cooperate, remember, that they had done this every day for years, that this routine wasn't so strange.

She flipped her head back to see Phillip staggering after her, the gun clamped in his hand. She looked straight ahead and tried to find the entrance ramp to the freeway, but it was too far. She saw what looked like a forest in front of her and darted into it. Her mother made her join Girl Scouts when she was a kid and she had aced the survival portion. Tracy laughed out loud. It felt so good to have memories again, memories that she could make sense of, that she could identify. She couldn't see Phillip anymore and wasn't sure what had happened to him.

The twigs and grass crunched beneath the soles of her feet and she could hear water. She crouched down as she inched toward it. She ran toward what she realized must be the Mississippi. Her fingers trembling, she yanked the housedress over her head. She grimaced as she looked down at the industrial strength bra and panties Phillip made her wear. Nothing at all like the pretty, flimsy things she used to parade around in. She flung the shoes off and was about to step into the water when she heard Phillip's voice.

"Tracy! Tracy, please, I had no choice. You'd hit your head on that stupid table in the hallway and you wouldn't wake up. I thought you were dead and no one would believe it was an accident."

Tracy stopped, listening to him. She could hear him sobbing, trying to catch his breath.

"I was just going to wait for you to wake up to make you understand that I didn't mean to hurt you. Then you woke up and asked me who you were and where you were."

He started laughing and crying all at the same time. "And in that one moment, I saw a chance, a chance for us to start over. I thought if I nursed you back to health and showed you how much I loved you and how much you meant to me, you wouldn't leave."

"So I carried you out to my car. I left you with Keegan. And then I killed you."

By now she'd hidden behind a tree, alert and listening for the sounds of his feet snapping against the twigs and brush along the ground. She swallowed, waiting for him to finish the story.

"And I fooled all of them. Every single last one of them." He chuckled. "It was lucky, really, the way it all worked out. I had decided to come home. My car was parked in back of the hotel, so the surveillance camera never saw me leave, which was good when the cops checked my alibi. They saw me come in from dinner and leave for the convention hall the next morning." He laughed. "God. Who knew that would work out to my advantage? Sunday night, I called Cicely in a panic saying that I hadn't heard from you and was calling the police. I drove back to Chicago and played the part of the frantic husband searching for his missing wife. Cooperated with the police in the investigation, was cleared from any suspicion right away since so many people saw me at the convention." Phillip laughed again. "No one ever suspected I had you tucked away in Berwyn of all places. And then... Carol."

Tracy blinked and scrunched up her face, remembering something Sondra had said at the house. "Carol?" she mouthed to herself.

"God, she looked just like you. You could have been twins. She used to come into the pharmacy all the time. It was funny though. I wasn't attracted to her. And then you came in that day and I fell in love right then and there. And then I remembered. You were the same height, same skin tone, weight… I knew I had to do it just right so they would think it was you. I forced her to get in the car with me. We drove to Belmont Harbor. I made her put on your clothes—even your underwear—your wedding ring and then, I… got rid of her face."

Tracy choked back silent tears as she waited for him to say what she already knew to be the horrible truth.

"I smashed her face in with a rock. Just enough so it looked like it could be you, but not so much they would have to do any DNA or anything. I tossed your wallet near the body—took out all the cash, but left the license in there. We had a big blizzard that night. She wasn't found until Friday. They called me to make the ID. And I did."

Tracy was suffocating on her tears as it sunk in what he was saying to her. He had killed another woman to cover up that he had kidnapped her.

"Don't you understand that I had to? I couldn't have them looking for a body for God knew how many years. I had to be with you so we could start our new life. I had to let everyone think you were dead. Don't you understand now what I would do for you?" He stopped talking and Tracy strained to hear him. His voice still sounded far away. She blinked her eyes and searched for his silhouette in the darkness.

Tracy looked to her left and saw she was just steps from the river. There had to be a park or campground nearby. It had been ages since she'd been swimming but she thought she could probably make it. Taking a deep breath, she crept toward the water, silent moans of terror and disbelief racing through her body.

Suddenly Phillip let out a tortured howl. "God!" He carried on with his one-sided conversation. "You wouldn't even take my last name."

She looked behind her as she remembered that conversation. She had told him how much it meant to her to keep her name since there weren't any brothers on her father's side of the family.

"Well, what about my name?" Phillip screamed, enraged, as if he too was thinking back on that conversation. "You were my wife. You cared more about everyone else than you ever cared about me!"

Tracy stopped, keeping her ear cocked for him.

"Oh, God, Tracy…" Phillip said, his voice suddenly soft. "That day you came walking into the pharmacy, those little high heels you had on, that pink shirt and that perfume that smelled like the sweetest flowers I've ever known. You were just… you were so beautiful. Never in a million years did I think I had a chance with a woman like you. But I thought, why not? Take a chance—even though I never take any chances. I couldn't believe it when you said you would go out with me. And then when you kept going out with me… I kept waiting for you to leave me. Every day, I lived in fear that you would leave me and it just… it made me crazy."

Tracy sniffed. "If only you had trusted me," she whispered to herself. "We would have had a chance."

"You didn't leave me any choice. You started being so secretive and I knew, I knew I was losing you."

Tracy dipped her toe in the rushing waters of the river in front of her. "Now or never, girl," she muttered as she filled her lungs with a huge swallow of air and jumped in. It was like diving into a huge tub of ice. There was only darkness underwater and she finally had to come up for a few breaths. She poked her head through the surface and looked around. She wasn't sure what direction she was going in, but she began to breaststroke, her arms and legs moving in perfect smooth unison, slicing through like a propeller in the water. That had been her best event. She turned her head to the side for a spare breath and saw Phillip running alongside the bank, waving the gun at her. He must have heard the splash. She stopped and ducked beneath the bobbing waves and began to butterfly underwater so he couldn't see her. She had gone several feet when she thrashed her arms above her head in an effort to make it to the top. Heaving, she smashed her head into the air, gulping, gasping for oxygen. She looked around and didn't see Phillip. She rubbed her eyes and circled around, searching for him.

"Keep going," she said as she submerged herself once again beneath the water. She continued to swim with as much force as she could find, pushing herself to go as far as she could. Finally, neither her lungs nor her limbs would carry her any farther. She would have to chance getting out. She waded to the shore where she collapsed on her back among the rocks and twigs. She placed her hand over her forehead, violent coughs shaking her insides. She shivered in her wet underwear, but her entire body was on fire from the physical torture she'd just put herself through. She opened her eyes and saw Phillip standing over her.

# EIGHTY-SEVEN

"I forgot you were a swimmer," he said.

Tracy tried to make her legs go, to run from him again, but they wouldn't, and she couldn't. She scoured her brain for something, anything. All she could do was stare at him, her body teeming with fear and limp with exhaustion. He was holding the gun with both hands and had aimed it right for her heart.

He crouched down over her and gave her a sad smile. "I love you so much," he said. "I'd do it again, you know," he whispered as he looked down at Tracy, his eyes shimmering with tears. "If I had it to do over again, I wouldn't change a thing. These past two years with you have been magical."

"What are you going to do with my body?"

"Tracy, didn't you hear me? This time we've had together has been wonderful."

"Wonderful for you. I didn't know who I was."

"I did it for us. It was all for us."

"It was for you, Phillip."

"No."

"You killed and lied and drugged and God only knows what else."

"Tracy, why can't you understand?"

"I'll never understand. Never." She paused. "You didn't answer my question. What are you going to do with my body?"

He twisted around. "I guess I'll roll it into the river."

"What are you going to weigh it down with?"

Phillip looked around as if he hadn't thought of this. "I guess I'll figure that out later."

"What about you? You said you couldn't live without me. How are you going to kill yourself?"

He shrugged. "I haven't thought about that either. I only have one bullet. For you." He sighed. "Maybe I'll jump in after you to weigh you down. Then we'll be together forever. Like it always should have been."

The shore was flooded with lights and Phillip clamped his hand over his eyes to shield them.

"Put your hands up, Phillip. We've got you surrounded."

Tracy tilted her head back and, sure enough, saw a swarm of troopers, lights and bullhorns. There must have been an army of guns pointed at Phillip. She closed her eyes in silent, thankful prayer, wondering how they'd found her.

Phillip tapped the hard, cold metal against her chest and Tracy found herself flinching, terrified the gun would accidentally discharge.

"Back off!" he yelled. "This is between me and my wife."

"Phillip, drop the gun, stand up and put your hands in the air."

Phillip pressed the gun closer into her chest until the end of it fell neatly into the groove of her collarbone.

"I'm a better shot than you are, son. I guarantee you won't make it out of this alive unless you drop the gun right now."

Phillip's gaze fluttered down to Tracy and he looked deep into her eyes. "You have no idea how much I hurt," he said, his voice cracking. "I have to stop it now."

"Phillip, please—"

"I just wanted you to love me again," he sobbed. In one swift motion, he shoved the barrel of the gun into his mouth.

"Phillip, oh, God, Phillip—!"

Phillip yanked the trigger and his head exploded like fireworks on the Fourth of July. Tracy choked as he fell forward, blood spattering and running in rivulets down her chest, bits of brain and skull flying backwards and raining down on the tops of her feet and legs like confetti. His body slumped on top of her, pinning her to the ground. She tried to push him off, to run, far, far away. He was too heavy and all she could do was screech in hysterics for someone to help her as she tried in vain to shove away his dead weight. The troopers rushed in and lifted him while simultaneously pulling her from beneath the wreckage that used to be her husband. Someone rushed to throw a blanket around her shoulders, but Tracy barely noticed.

# EIGHTY-EIGHT

*She was underneath the water, thrusting her arms like Ginsu knives as she drove forward. She felt her lungs filling up with water and she struggled to get to the surface before it was too late, before the water filled up her lungs and suffocated her. She popped up and screamed when she saw Phillip flapping around in the water right in front of her, his hand digging into the flesh of her arm. She flailed and tried to push away from him, but he was too strong. He raised his other hand out of the water and she saw the gleam of a small gun in the moonlight. He smiled at her calmly before he pumped a single piece of lead into his brain...*

Tracy jumped up screaming, trying to rip out the IVs attached to her veins. Sondra, who had been dozing in the lone chair in the room, flew to Tracy's bed and punched the on-call button as she tried to calm her sister down.

"Tracy, Tracy, it's okay, he's gone and he's not coming back."

Tracy stopped screaming and gripped Sondra's forearms and looked at her, still hyperventilating. "Oh, God. Is this ever going to stop?"

The doctor came busting in. "Ms. Ellis," he said as he eased Tracy back down onto the bed. "Please, calm down. You need your rest. We need to continue detoxing you; your foot is still infected from that cut you took on the bottom of the Mississippi. Please, settle down." He pulled the pink blanket up to her chest and made a notation on her chart. Sondra stood by the doorway fidgeting before she stalked out into the hallway waiting for the doctor.

"Can't you give her something for the nightmares? She's not sleeping, barely eating."

"Ms. Ellis, your sister has suffered a series of horrible traumas. It will take some time for her to get over that. Now, we gave you the names of some doctors in Chicago for her to see when she gets back there. I highly, highly recommend she make an appointment with one as soon as you get back to town."

Sondra took a deep breath, still frustrated. "Fine, fine. We will."

The doctor looked at her for a moment before giving her a slight nod. "All right. I'll be by to check on her in a bit."

The doctor went bustling down the hall and Sondra stayed outside the door for a moment before she went back in the room.

Tracy was sitting up, staring blankly at the wall opposite the bed.

"Hey, baby girl—you feeling better?"

Tracy turned a sullen gaze at her sister. "I want to jump out of my skin. I can't take this anymore."

Sondra sat on the edge of the bed. "I know, I know. It will get better, I promise. We'll be leaving in a few days, getting you home—you sure you don't want to stay with me in New York? I've got plenty of room."

Tracy leaned her head back against the pillows. "No, no, I just want to get home." She let out a wry chuckle. "Even if it's not *my* home."

"Look, mommy is getting that apartment ready for you right now, and as soon as you're back on your feet, you'll get another house or whatever you want. Besides, would you want to live there, I mean, since you lived there together?"

Tracy sighed and propped her head back up. "I guess you have a point."

"You still want to drive back? We can fly. It'd be a lot quicker."

"I can't deal with being in a confined space right now."

Sondra nodded. "Okay. It's okay. I got us a convertible. Pretty cool, huh? The Ellis sisters on the open road, the wind whipping through their hair?"

"You mean your rat's nest?" Tracy deadpanned.

Sondra looked at her sister for a moment before she burst out laughing. Tracy dissolved into giggles too, each moment getting funnier and funnier.

"Sondra?" Tracy said, her face serious.

Sondra stopped laughing. "Yeah?"

"Thank you. For finding me. For coming to get me."

Sondra's eyes misted over as she tried to keep the tears from escaping. "I just had to know what happened to my baby sister."

"I had dreams about you. About everyone really. And it just scared the shit out of me because I knew who everyone was but I just couldn't make any sense out of it…"

"It's okay. You're safe and you're going to move on from this."

"I hope so."

Just then, the door opened and Cindy Cross made a little knocking motion on it as she peered into the room. "Hi. Are you up for visitors?"

Tracy smiled. "Yeah, gosh, come in, come in."

Sondra stood and fished her electronic cigarette and cell phone out of her purse. "I swear, between this thing, the patch and the gum, I should be able to quit any day now." Sondra twirled the fake cigarette and shifted her weight. "Besides, I promised Gary I'd call him before he heads back to New York."

"Tell Gary thanks again for coming," Tracy said. "And that he better come to Chicago for a visit."

Sondra winked. "No prob. See you in a bit."

Cindy waited until Sondra had left before she sat down on the chair. "So, how are you?"

Tracy ran her fingers through her hair, which hung long and loose across her shoulders. "Ready to get the hell out of here. Haven't reached the point where I can close my eyes and not see his head blowing up in front of me."

Cindy shook her head. "What a monster."

Tracy shrugged again. "Yeah, well, I'm the idiot who married him."

Cindy was silent for a moment. "I wanted to say how sorry I am… that I didn't do something—"

Tracy broke in. "What could you do? I was doped up and brainwashed. You had no idea. *I* didn't have any idea."

Cindy looked down at the pink bedspread. "I knew something wasn't right, though. I thought he was beating you."

"Well, I did get the belt sometimes," Tracy said, fingering the Tiffany necklace now around her neck. "So, yeah, I guess he was."

"Oh. God. How awful."

Tracy closed her eyes and shook her head. "If I did something like forget the Sweet'N Low or not make the bed the way he wanted, out came the belt."

Cindy leaned back in her chair, disturbed. "Well, that explains you flipping out that day," she mused.

Tracy started laughing. "Oh, my God," she gasped, unable to keep the giggles away. "You must have been so freaked out by that."

Cindy gave her a knowing look. "Yeah, I was sure you were a nut job after that."

"Hmmm. Well, he did have me locked up in a mental hospital for a few months."

"I read about that. The medical board wants to strip that doctor of his license to practice."

Tracy shrugged. "I don't blame him. Much. Phillip was blackmailing him. He didn't know what was going on. Not really."

"So, when are you leaving?" Cindy asked.

"Sondra and I are driving back to Chicago in a few days. My parents are going to stay with me for a while. And at some point, I'm going to try and get my job back."

"Your sister said you were in the news business? That's pretty cool."

Tracy smiled as she thought about it. "Yeah. It was. I miss it. I used to dream about it, although I didn't know at the time that's what it was."

Cindy started to speak, but then stopped herself.

"What?" Tracy asked.

"I... well, I was wondering if you would ever come back to St. Louis."

Tracy ran her tongue across her teeth. "Yeah, I don't think so. But I'd love it if you came up to Chi to visit."

Cindy shook her head and smiled. "You don't even sound the same. Like the way you talk, I mean. It's like you were two different people."

Tracy inhaled. "I was."

"Wild. Well, I'd love to come for a visit. Just let me know when."

"Whenever."

The door creaked open and Sondra poked her head into the room. "Hello, ladies," she said as she walked in. "Gary sends his love. And he said when he comes to visit he'll bring a bottle of club soda."

Tracy raised her eyebrows. "Not the usual Dewars?"

"Ah, you remember. That's a good sign." Sondra sat down on the edge of the bed. "We've kind of made a deal. If he'll try sobriety and I can get the nicotine monkey off my back, we're going to try and make a go of it again."

Tracy gave her sister a reassuring smile. "I'm glad to hear that. You guys belong together."

"Yeah. Maybe this time it will work."

Sondra was quiet for a moment. "Jack..." Sondra's voice trailed off and Tracy nodded her understanding.

"I know. One thing at a time." Tracy sighed. "God. Carol. That's what I regret the most."

It was Sondra's turn to look out the window. "Don't worry. Carol will get her justice."

# EIGHTY-NINE

He folded up the newspaper and let out a low whistle. It was quite a story. If he hadn't been personally involved, he would have never believed it.

Phil's plan hadn't been so foolproof after all.

He'd been mildly surprised that day he walked into the pharmacy to pick up that prescription for Carol and Phillip Pearson handed it to him. The two had gone to college together at UIC, had known some of the same people and had hung out together casually. They met for beer and a game of darts to catch up and after many bottles, unloaded on each other over their respective problems. When both men compared pictures, they were shocked at the resemblance of the two women—literally and figuratively.

Phillip was convinced Tracy was cheating on him and was consumed by that fear; Kevin had fallen out of love with Carol long ago, his ardor having cooled to a mild affection. She was nice…sweet, but she just didn't do it for him anymore. Except, a surprise pregnancy had changed his plans to end the relationship. Both families swarmed around them with good cheer and guilt trips—the good Lord didn't look too kindly upon children born out of wedlock. They turned up the pressure to full boil and Kevin found himself knee-deep in wedding preparations to a woman he didn't want to be with. Carol miscarried shortly before the wedding and he thought that would help ease him out of the situation. Unbelievably, that only intensified her insistence they needed each other more than ever to get through such a difficult time.

To make matters worse, Carol's rich doctor daddy, who she never knew, died and left her half a million dollars. Kevin thought she would at least use the money to pay off their debts, put it to some use. Carol said she wanted nothing at all to do with that man and once the estate was settled, was going to give all that money to the church. Here they were, swimming in debt from credit cards and student loans when a lifeline was dropped in their lap and she wanted to throw it all away. It just burned Kevin beyond all reason. He had half-joked with Phillip that if she were dead, he could do whatever the hell he wanted with the money.

He was shocked when, not a month or so later, Phillip called him and asked if he really wanted Carol gone, because if he did, he had a plan that would give them both what they wanted. Tracy had amnesia, he was going to get her out of town, but he couldn't have her missing. Then the plan wouldn't work. What if he killed Carol and passed her off as Tracy? They looked enough alike that in death, you wouldn't really be able to tell the difference and they both knew missing black women didn't get much media attention. Kevin would get Carol's money, Phillip would have Tracy all to himself—they both came out winners.

Kevin had tossed and turned for two nights, wrestling with what to do. Carol questioned him about what was wrong, but he brushed it off as work troubles. He remembered staring at her over a bowl of oatmeal that last morning, thinking about how he'd never be free. She'd never give him a divorce; she considered it a sin. She'd make him stay shackled to her for life.

He just couldn't do it.

He called Phillip from a payphone later than morning and said to do it.

Phillip gave Tracy's phone to Kevin and told him to be in the area of their house on the North Side at certain times over the weekend, so when the police checked the phone records—and they would—her cell phone signal would ping off the right towers. Phillip warned him to only answer the phone for him; Tracy had people calling her all the time. They couldn't risk him accidentally talking to someone he shouldn't and blowing the whole thing to hell. Phillip took the phone back from Kevin Sunday night and slipped it into Tracy's purse, so no one would ever be the wiser.

For his part, Kevin told Phillip he would make sure Carol was the one to take the dog out that night and that he would be on the phone with his brother; Phillip had to be there at that time. Kevin didn't want to know how it was done, he just wanted it done.

Sure enough, Carol was misidentified as Tracy, Kevin got the money and played out the charade of grieving husband for the prying eyes around him.

It had worked like a charm.

Phillip's big mistake—among many—had been that letter. His smugness convinced him to get in touch with Mimi Ellis. Almost like he couldn't resist shoving her face in the fact that her daughter was alive and well while they all grieved. He had a mailbox store in Michigan forward his mail, so in case anyone ever came looking for him, that's what they would find.

But then, Sondra started putting everything together. And then the media got involved, which just blew everything to hell. He tried to call Phillip and warn him to get out of dodge before the cops caught up to him. He'd tried calling him on his cell phone using a disposable cell phone, but no luck getting a hold of the guy.

Kevin shrugged now. Oh, well. It was done. The guy had blown his brains out, Tracy was reunited with her family and all was well that ended well.

What Kevin didn't know was that the night he called Phillip, Sondra Ellis had seen that Chicago phone number on the caller ID.

What Kevin didn't know was that Sondra Ellis had called Detective Marion Wallace to say she thought it was a little strange that Phillip was getting calls from Chicago, a place he hadn't lived in three years and had virtually no ties to, so she should probably check it out.

What Kevin didn't know is that even though Detective Wallace hadn't been able to track down that disposable cell phone number, she had pulled Carol's financials and discovered that, indeed Carol was a regular customer at Phillip's pharmacy all those years ago. She'd also researched enrollment records from UIC and discovered that indeed, Phillip and Kevin were in the same class at the same time.

What Kevin didn't know was that Detective Wallace had checked Phillip's iPhone, which had dropped out of his pocket when he kidnapped Tracy and discovered a simple calendar entry from three years ago with his address and the time Carol would be out walking the dog.

What Kevin didn't know was that the police were pulling up in front of his house to arrest him for conspiracy to commit murder.

Kevin looked up as the doorbell rang, wondering who it was.

~ ~ ~

# ACKNOWLEDGMENTS

Big ups to my sister, Kathryn, for her comments and for giving me her seal of approval—I know you don't hand it out often. Glad I made the cut.

To Dr. Elizabeth Loftus for her insights.

To Stephanie Lott for her copyediting assistance.

To Karyl Paige for giving the book the shine it needed.

To Torrie Cooney for designing such a beautiful cover and then giving me *another* beautiful cover. Mostly, thank you for "getting me."

Big thank you to my "author crush," Joy Fielding, for the great advice, awesome class and reading material.

# Spring 2005...

The day Kelly Ross killed her husband, she went to the nail salon for a fill and a pedicure, then met her girlfriend, Sheila, at Tavern on Rush for lunch. Afterward, she and Sheila meandered around Oak Street for a few hours, shopping its exclusive boutiques and enjoying the eighty-degree spring day. Kelly thought that when she got home she'd sit outside on her balcony and wade through the stack of magazines that had been piling up on her coffee table over the past few days. Later the two friends said their goodbyes and promised to meet midweek for drinks. As she enjoyed the balmy Saturday afternoon breezes rolling off Lake Michigan, Kelly swung two shopping bags alongside her as she walked the few blocks home to her condo in the Gold Coast, the tony Chicago neighborhood that glittered with mansions and luxury high-rises and was one of the most desirable addresses in the city.

She didn't recognize the doorman who opened the door for her—must have been one of the temporary guys they paraded in and out on weekends. She checked the mail before taking the elevator up to the fifty-third floor. Bills, bills, bills. Wasn't that a Destiny's Child song from a few years back?

Kelly let out a contented sigh as she opened her door and set the mail and keys down on the occasional table immediately to the right of the entrance. She reached into her purse for her cell phone to see if she'd missed any calls. Seeing that she hadn't, Kelly put her phone down on the table next to her keys and gripping her shopping bags, meandered through the spacious living room toward the bedroom. She began to whistle, something she usually did when she was in a good mood. Her husband Mark hated it. Of course, he hummed, so she figured that made them even. Speaking of…Kelly checked her watch. Three-fifteen. He'd gone to the office after she left for the salon and said he'd be back around five. She'd call him in a few minutes to see if he wanted to meet somewhere for dinner, preferably al fresco.

She reached into her bag, wanting to try on her purchases one more time before hanging them in the closet. When she hit the doorway, she did a double take. Mark had made the bed. He usually left that chore to her or their twice-weekly cleaning lady.

"Huh. That's weird," Kelly mumbled, shaking her head. "Must have left the toilet seat up." Whenever Mark did something unexpected around the house, she knew it was usually because he'd done something stupid somewhere else in the house. Like load and run the dishwasher after leaving an empty milk carton in the refrigerator. She walked over to the bed and took a peek, running her hand down the smooth expanse of the sumptuous beige silk duvet: plumped pillows and fresh sheets with the spritz of lavender linen water he knew she liked. She was impressed. Kelly turned and saw that last week's swirled ivory sheets hadn't quite made it into the hamper. She chuckled to herself as she walked over to pick up the ball of sheets lying on the floor. Sometimes he was such a man.

Kelly snatched up the pile and felt something cool land on her foot. She frowned and looked down, her eyes wide, her heart racing. Shaking, she dropped the sheets and knelt to the floor for a closer look.

A condom.

They'd made love that morning, but hadn't used condoms since they got married three years ago and she'd gone on the pill.

A condom.

"That son of a bitch," she said, hot tears stinging her eyes. Wiping the snot starting to run out of her nose with the back of her hand, Kelly fumbled toward the bathroom for a tissue. She looked at herself in the mirror. What the hell was he thinking? She'd been a goddamned supermodel for chrissakes. You didn't cheat on goddamned supermodels! Regular Pilates classes and jogging a few days a week, coupled with good genes, kept her 5'9 frame trim and toned. With her hazel eyes, long, light brown hair, full pink lips, and champagne complexion, people sometimes mistook her for Vanessa Williams. She was a great wife.

Wasn't he always telling her what a wonderful wife she was? How lucky he was?

Unable to look at herself any longer, Kelly turned to leave and her eye fell on the wedding photo sitting on Mark's nightstand. Slowly, she walked over and picked it up. Mark, a handsome and successful partner with one of the city's most prestigious law firms, single-handedly building its booming sports practice; she, one of those ubiquitous 90s supermodels who'd left the business and launched a thriving cosmetics company. Their wedding had gotten major press, including a short article in "People," the New York tabloids, "Jet," all the Chicago columns, and every gossip site on the Internet. A fresh wave of rage tore through her veins. She hurled the glass-framed photo in the direction in the bathroom mirror. Both the frame and the mirror shattered as they collided with each other. For some reason, that made Kelly cry even more.

She was heaving now, tears spilling out of her eyes like water gushing from a faucet. She felt sick. How could he do this? How? Didn't they have the perfect marriage? Didn't Mark's friends marvel at how he'd landed her? Didn't her friends look at her with a twinge of jealousy whenever Mark sent her flowers for no reason or bought her a beautiful, touching gift commemorating some anniversary or just because?

Of course. It was guilt. She'd always assumed it was because he was such a loving, thoughtful, and wonderful husband. Bitter laughter escaped her lips. Well, now she knew he was a lying sack of shit. Kelly started to sink down on the bed before she bolted upright, as though she'd sat on a hot stove. He'd brought his tramp here to their bed.

Kelly began to pace. What should she do? Pack up her things and leave? No, screw that. She'd found this place and made it into a showplace for friends, family… Mark's clients. He could leave. She'd get a quickie divorce. She didn't need or want anything from him. Simple and painless.

She looked at her watch. It was now three twenty-five; Mark would be home at five. Didn't matter. He wouldn't be staying long.

Kelly stalked over to his closet, yanked it open, and pulled down one of his suitcases. In a blind rage, she jerked shirts, pants, and suits off their hangers and launched them into the suitcase. His carefully assembled shelves of clothing and shoes were dismantled in seconds as Kelly continued to toss Mark's belongings into their new home. She filled the suitcases until no more were left and then dragged everything out into the living room. As she turned to walk back to the bedroom, she saw pictures. There were pictures of them everywhere—vacations, parties, family gatherings. Kelly marched into the kitchen, grabbed a trash bag from underneath the sink, and began to throw every picture she saw of the two of them into it.

She went back into the bathroom. Tiny shards of glass were scattered across the ceramic tile floor and marble countertop where she'd smashed their wedding photo. She grabbed a towel from the rack next to the door and picked up the frame from where it had fallen on the floor. She placed it in the trash bag, and began to make a mental list of every gift Mark had ever given her. Mostly jewelry, some books, lingerie, a music box she'd spotted in a shop in Madrid a few years back—things like that. Kelly grabbed whatever she could think of and into the trash bag it went.

By the time she was through, there were five huge garbage bags full of memories stacked next to Mark's suitcases. She looked at her watch. Four-thirty. What would she say to him? She hadn't gotten that far yet. The need to get him out of the house had superseded any confrontations they were going to have. Kelly was standing in the middle of the bedroom when she saw it.

The condom.

In the middle of everything else, she'd forgotten the condom. She walked over and bent down. Thank God for long acrylic nails. Wincing, she picked up the slimy piece of rubber and held it out in front of her as she scurried into the living room and dropped it on top of the pile of suitcases and trash bags. Let him take it with him when he left. Kelly stood there staring at everything, feeling numb. She was restless, ready to fight, yet still in shock over what had happened. She wrung her hands as though they were wet dishtowels and let out a deep breath. She needed a drink to calm her nerves.

With an agitated gait, she went to the kitchen and pulled open the refrigerator door. There was still a half bottle of Shiraz they'd had with the dinner she'd made for him last night. He'd raved about it—roast chicken, garlic green beans, whipped potatoes, an apple tart for dessert. How could she have known that would be their last meal together? Kelly clamped her hand around the bottle and shut the door. She placed it on the counter and stood for a moment with her eyes closed, her hand wrapped around the slippery coolness of the wine bottle. She opened her eyes, methodically took down a wine glass, and poured herself a drink. She took a hearty gulp, welcoming the familiar warmth as it filled her insides. She put the glass down and stared unseeing at the butcher-block table in the middle of the room, her eyes filling with tears once more.

# ABOUT THE AUTHOR

**BIANCA SLOANE** is the author of the suspense novels, *Killing Me Softly* (previously published as *Live and Let Die*), chosen as "Thriller of the Month" (May 2013) by e-thriller.com and a "2013 Top Read" by OOSA Online Book Club and *Sweet Little Lies*. When she's not writing, she's watching Bravo TV, Investigation Discovery, reading or cooking. Sloane resides in Chicago.

For playlists, reading guides and to sign up for her author newsletter, visit her website at www.biancasloane.com.

37367461R00175

Made in the USA
Charleston, SC
06 January 2015